WOLF'S OBSESSION

MAFIA MONSTER SERIES

ATLAS ROSE

BE THE FIRST TO KNOW OF A NEW RELEASE!
Click here to signup for my newsletter.
Like my Facebook Page
Join my Facebook Group

1

CARINA

If you want to change...you have to invite chaos.

Chaos.

The word surfaced, sending a flare across the center of my chest, burning and singeing, trembling with the kind of hunger that brought me undone. Dark. *Malevolent.* Hunger. Seeping from the Unseelie ward carved into my chest.

Mojin's words resounded in my head as I tore out of the FBI office and stabbed a number on my cell...*the only number that mattered.*

"Hey, Chase!" one of the agents roared as I left a flurry of scattered files behind. *"Chase, what the hell is going on?"*

I left him behind, left my office behind...my gun, my badge, and my life. None of that mattered now. Not the battle inside me, or my betrayal of the Vampires. *Only my Wolves mattered now...and right now, one of them was in danger.*

"Answer the damn phone, Phantom!" I barked as the line on the other end rang and rang...*and rang.*

That burn in my chest deepened as I thumbed the button for the elevator and tapped my foot, lifting my gaze to the lights that moved slower than daylight. I tore my gaze right, to the closed stairwell door. With a grunt, I lunged, lowering my phone as I grabbed the handle and yanked.

I could still hear the agent calling me even as the door to the stairwell banged shut. But I was already leaping, gripping the railing, hauling myself down two and three stairs at a time.

The phone's screen faded under the movement as I hit Phantom's number once more. It rang…resounding in my head.

It's all my fault.

All my goddamn fault.

I shoved those words aside and scrambled down the next flight of stairs. Hard breaths consumed the sound as the phone rang and rang.

"Come on…*Phantom, please,*" I begged as the CCTV image from the file on my desk came to life again inside my head.

The image had been grainy. Nothing more than a black and white blur, taken from a night shot outside the safehouse I'd been confined to. The one Harlan had taken me to that night I'd been taken from my pack. Back when I'd had to pretend I was still one of them. One of the good guys. One of the *squad.*

But I wasn't. Not anymore.

I was part of a pack. Part of a *family.* Phantom, Church, Vitold, and Arran. They were more than my Wolves to me, more than lovers. They were the tethers that kept me from unravelling. The binding of my fucking *Chaos.* The *only* ones I'd die for…*and betray for.*

I'd fought the darkness for them and battled this Unseelie curse in my chest, and in the darkness of the night, I'd left that safehouse behind. But it wasn't just the FBI hunting us. It was *the Wolf.*

The midnight beast had come for me that night I'd been lured by Murphy to the farmhouse where he'd waited for me, waited with hate and hunger. He wasn't the only one. The midnight Wolf had been there…and when Murphy's body was found hours later, burned and left on Phantom's doorstep, it had triggered a hunt no one had expected.

So we ran.

It felt like I was still running, still desperate to get to them, ready to do whatever it took to stand beside my Wolves once more. I'd run forever with them, and stand and fight, as well. I'd do whatever it took…

Yes, that ache whispered in my head. That *sickening* voice that both took from me and gave, leaving me with nothing like I'd hoped for. I lifted my gaze, catching the *First Floor* sign above the exit light on the doorway and lurched through the door, coming out into the foyer.

My trembling fingers fought to enter Arran's number as I rushed through the metal detector and past the night guard, who just rose from his seat. "Please, Arran…*just answer.*"

But the number didn't even ring, it just went straight to voicemail. Panic crammed into every cell inside me, shooting sharp pains across my chest as I stumbled through the glass double doors at the entrance to the FBI building.

The streets were empty, the night closer to morning than it was to dusk. Tears threatened my eyes as I started forward, the echo of my boots picking up pace as my strides quickened. I scrolled my contacts until I stopped on the last entry. *Vitold.* "Please…please." My words were nothing more than a gasping croak as I ran.

Headlights slashed the darkness, blinding me as a car rounded up ahead…*fast.* Tires howled, the squeals piercing the night, punching my pulse into the stratosphere before the car skidded sideways and came to a stop in front of me.

Under the white smoke of the rubber, the passenger's door was thrown open. "Carina, get in."

I jerked my gaze toward the growl, finding a handsome face half hidden by shadows. "Church?"

"Phantom sent me. *Get in.*"

I scurried forward, throwing myself through the open door, my words a panicked rush. "You have to take me to him...*now*, Church...*NOW!*"

He just sat there, stunned for a second, a deep scowl carving a line down the middle of his forehead. "That's the plan."

But the way he spoke...the way he just sat there. *He didn't know.* "He's in danger—"

"Tell me something I don't know," he muttered, cutting me off. "And he's not the only one."

Desperation howled inside my head, tearing me apart from the inside out with teeth and claws, vicious claws belonging to a midnight Wolf, as I lunged across the car and grasped his shirt, my face close to his. "The Wolf that's after us isn't Finis."

The faint hint of a smirk died on Church's face. There was that scowl again...that deep-seated flare of worry. His voice turned stony as he gave me his full attention. "What are you talking about?"

I wasn't sure...wasn't sure about *any* of this. But I knew intuition when I felt it, and Chaos whispered in my soul...*hurry*. "Take me across the river, Church. Take me to Phantom as fast as you can. I think...I think he's in trouble."

He didn't need to be told twice as that fear finally registering. I let his shirt go, leaned back enough to grab the door and yank it close. "Hurry," I pleaded as he shoved the sleek, powerful car into gear and punched the accelerator, spinning the rear of the car around before driving us forward.

*Please...please...please...*I pressed Phantom's number once more, lifting it to my ear as we sped through Crown City's abandoned streets.

I wasn't sure...

About any of it.

But what I did know was that deadly stare of the Wolf as it looked straight into the camera. It didn't care that we saw it, didn't care at all. An animal like that who'd finally stepped out of hiding was only after one thing...*and that was blood.*

2

PHANTOM

"Marian?" I mumbled, her name like a punch to my chest.

I swept my gaze over the shining midnight coat, unable to meet those yellow eyes. The same yellow eyes of our mother. The ones I couldn't look into then when she was dying, just as I couldn't look into them now.

The deep snarl reverberated around the study. White fangs shimmered, growing as she stood there illuminated by the hallway lights of the private quarters of the Hunting Ground. The place I called home.

She took a step, slowly, carefully. *Swaying.* My gaze dropped to the swell of her belly before I froze. That snarl from her only grew louder, tearing my gaze from her middle to watch as she eased her weight onto her haunches and lunged.

That *feral* sound only grew louder, until it consumed the room. Time seemed to slow, the deep thud in my chest like the painful ticking of a bomb as I slowly rose from the chair, flinching as it hit the floor with a *bang!* She was on me in an instant, through the doorway and slamming into me.

Fangs sank into my arm, tearing through flesh and sinew

with blinding pain. I bit back a howl, swallowing it down, and grabbed her neck. I slid my hand to her jaw and shoved, driving her body upwards until both of us fell to the floor. *Don't hurt her. Don't fucking hurt her.*

My fingers sank into her coat, finding the hard ridges of bone underneath. Jesus, she was thin…*so fucking thin!*

"Marian!" I roared, meeting those eyes now, seeing the blinding rage. "Marian, *it's me! It's Phantom!*"

But as I stared into her eyes, I saw the truth.

This beast was no longer my sister.

Not my sweet, innocent sister. *No, this beast was broken.* Shattered somehow, reduced to nothing more than emotion, fueled by the kind of sickness that rendered a Wolf incapable of anything but slaughter…of others, and then of itself.

I pushed, kicking the chair out of the way, and rolled, driving her off me with a hard shove. But she was back on me in an instant, hitting harder than her bony frame should have been able to. Terror filled me, terror for her…*and the baby she carried.*

"Stop this…*please stop this! It's me…it's your brother. It's Phantom.*"

My plea only incensed her rage, driving her to bite once more. Her fangs sank into my side as I twisted, wrestling her mouth away. Agony followed as her fangs tore free. All I saw was hate, and rage…and under all that, the permeating scent of Alpha filled my nose.

Terror filled me as that bitter, sting settled deep. This wasn't right…*cannot be right.* Headlights splashed through the window of the study as the sound of squealing tires howled. Marian pulled away, climbing to her feet with a shake of her head, then stepped backwards.

"Wait." I pushed the floor, shoving myself upwards as she wrenched her head toward the thunder of footsteps heading this way.

Her hackles rose, bristling as she backed away.

I knew the moment I lost her, the split second that shift in her eyes took over.

Black lips parted before she stilled in the middle of the hallway, her white fangs now coated with blood. *My blood.*

"I can help you," I pleaded.

But it was too late...inside her head she was already gone, it was just that her body needed to catch up. She whipped her gaze from me and leaped, tearing from my sight in an instant. I shoved forward, driving myself through the doorway as the *thud...thud...thud...* of her paws echoed in the hall.

A cry of alarm followed. Shouts and screams, both Church's and Carina's, before the piercing sound of shattering glass followed. I stumbled toward the sound, the shock wearing off, leave me trembling...and desperate for answers.

I shoved through the open door of the club and came face to face with Church. The brother just stood there, his fist curled, desperation and fear abating in his eyes.

"What the fuck was that?" he bellowed, racing after me as I covered the distance and climbed the stairs.

"Phantom." Carina's wide, shell-shocked gaze tore from me to the blur of black running into the darkness.

Glass crunched under my boots as she took a step toward me. But I couldn't look at her...not yet. I lowered my gaze to the smear of blood on a shard of glass. The sight was a fist to my gut. I slowly crouched, knowing that hunting her would only make her fight harder to get away from me.

But there was still blood on the ground outside my nightclub.

My sister's blood.

"Who is she?" Carina asked.

I flinched at the question and dragged in a breath. My fingers skimmed the jagged edge as memories fought to surface.

"She?" Church repeated.

"Yes..." I finally spoke, and rose to my feet, my gaze drifting to the quiet street. "She."

Church's car was sideways, the doors thrown open, engine still running. Plumes of white smoke drifted from the exhaust, disappearing into the night sky.

"Phantom." Carina called quietly.

I turned away as she lifted her hand toward me and it fucking killed me to do it, to shut her out. And I wanted to shut her out. Her and her betraying...*scheming...Chaos*-controlled ways. But fuck me if I didn't still want her, too.

Two battlegrounds waited...with the dead left behind.

Hate her.

Forgive her.

No matter what Elithien and Mojin said, I still couldn't do either. I was stuck at an impasse. A wide, gaping chasm of darkness, and I was teetering on the edge as it crumbled all around me.

"Please...let me explain," she pleaded as I stepped through the smashed front door to the Hunting Ground and went back inside.

"There's no need," I answered, although I doubted she heard me.

I knew why she'd betrayed the Vampires, knew better than she probably knew herself. I knew it like a rag down my fucking throat, shoved deep on the business end of a fist.

That didn't mean I had to fucking like it.

What the fuck was it with the women in my life? One would burn down every relationship I'd created over a lifetime just to keep me...and the other one just wanted me dead. I shook my head as I strode back through the club and made my way to the study once more.

But no matter how hard I tried to shove the image of my sister from my mind, there was one part of the puzzle I couldn't forget. *Her stomach...*

The room was still permeated with Alpha as I stepped inside and bent, righting the chair.

Dangerous, my beast snarled inside. "No shit," I answered. "Just like everything else in my life."

My phone vibrated on my desk. I looked past the insurance paperwork of the clubs and glanced at the caller ID. *Pathfinder.* I snatched up the phone. "Yes?"

"We found them."

Relief swept through me before the cold plunge of fear. "Alive?"

"For now. We're closing in, should have them before daylight."

I turned my gaze to the window and the darkness outside as footsteps sounded in the hallway...careful footsteps, *light footsteps.* "Call me as soon as you have them...and Path."

"Yeah?"

"The doctor...make sure she's alright."

"Will do," he acknowledged before ending the call.

A shadow clung to the doorway, spilling darkness into the study. "Did they find them?"

I closed my eyes at the sound of her voice, fighting that rising burn. *Christ, the woman affected me.* My skin shivered, my cock twitched. Just the sound of her fucking voice had me hard.

It's more than sex for her, more than a need. Mojin's words rang in my head. *You're hers and no matter who or what threatens either one of you, expect her to come out all fucking guns blazing—Unseelie style.*

I knew what it was to fight for the one you loved.

Knew all too fucking well.

But to betray, just like that? With no call...no word of warning...just walk out of here after bonding with Church, then hand over the Vampires on a silver platter? That was a whole new level of deceit. That was fucking brutal.

"Phantom, please."

I turned at the sound of her anguish, my eyes lowering to the spill of shadows on the floor. She flinched at the movement as I took a step toward her. Her breath caught, her pulse sped. I was aware of this woman, more aware than I was comfortable with, more aware than should be safe.

"Phantom, I'm s—"

I closed the door to the study in her face, cutting off her words.

*I'm sorry...*I didn't want to hear it.

Not yet.

Not until I could think.

Not until I could look at her without feeling the burn of treachery.

The Vampires would want blood...*and for me to pick a goddamn side.* Elithien was waiting. They were *all* waiting. I yanked out the chair and sat down at my desk, but unlike before, the paperwork didn't numb me. Instead, my thoughts were pulled out of my body...just like my damn heart, as the soft thud of Carina's footsteps faded down the hallway.

The flick of a TV came on moments later...then the bass of Church's voice. Muffled words not intended for me to hear.

He was trying to console her, trying to explain the unexplainable. Trying to...*fuck,* I didn't know what he was trying to do. I didn't know what *I* was trying to do. Survive, maybe? That was all that was left for us at this time...just fucking surviving.

I shoved back from the desk, hating the sight of the fucking paperwork. All I could see were those fucking yellow eyes. Eyes that looked at me with betrayal.

Marian.

Carina.

Seemed like that was the goddamn theme lately. So what the fuck was I going to do now?

3

———

CARINA

"Give him time," Church murmured. "He's hurting. We're all hurting. What happened…with the Vampires, that's going to take a while to come to terms with."

"I did it *for* him."

The words spilled from my lips, and even as they left me, I knew they were a lie. I'd done it, not just for him…but for myself, too. I closed my eyes. *How could I have been so fucking stupid!*

"No, you did it for yourself, Carina. You did it because you didn't trust us…because you didn't trust *him.*"

The room swayed. Of all the fucking times for the Chaos inside me to leave me faltering, the bitch chose *now*? I was caught in the lie, one I hadn't been in control of, one that had taken over me, used me…*then discarded me.* "Oh Jesus, Church. What the fuck have I done?"

He didn't answer. That hurt the most.

Silence isn't golden. Silence is death by a thousand cuts, each one leaving their mark. Each one cutting a little deeper and deeper until you're bleeding and there's no hope to stem the

12

blood. This was what it felt like, to stand there, see yourself bleeding, and know it's useless to try to stop it.

I took a step backwards until my boots smacked the sofa, and I glanced toward the door.

"Don't do it," Church cautioned. There was an edge to his voice, a warning tone. "You run from this and you'll be running forever. He won't chase you again."

Won't?

I met his eyes, and froze. My throat clogged, my heart pounded. Church knew Phantom better than anyone.

"Who won't chase you again?" Vitold questioned as he stepped through the doorway and into view.

My heart sped at the sight of him. His bright eyes were dull, his mouth twisted in a wince as he strode closer. But as soon as he saw me, he smiled, leaving agony behind for love.

"Vitold." I stumbled toward him. He looked beaten…moving slowly and with a limp, but still he held out his arms as I neared, wrapping me in them.

"Christ, I've missed you," he murmured against my hair.

He set me back a bit, his hands sliding down my shoulders, then down my arms until my fingers entwined with his. I closed my eyes and inhaled his scent, thick and musky. The scent of fur and hunger and…*freedom.* An ache cut across my chest, choking my words. "I've missed you too, Wolf."

He pulled away a little, his perfect lips still curved into a smile, his thick Russian accent even bolder now. "What have you gotten yourself into this time, *moya lyubov'?*"

I shook my head and slipped my hands from his, my heart heavy, my mind racing. "Something I need to get myself out of."

"And how do you intend to do that?"

I flinched at the coldness of Phantom's tone. Vitold stepped to the side as he took one look at Phantom and the hole in the wall beside his head. "Well, you look like shit."

One critical scan and the Alpha muttered, "You don't look so good yourself, pissant."

That ache in my chest moved deeper, claws wrapped around my heart and clenched tight. There was a shrug from Vitold before he answered, "I'm healing...slowly."

The attack at the park taken too much out of him. There'd been too many injuries, too many broken bones and torn muscles...too many bite wounds, some still red and raised on his arms. He'd come to my rescue that night, fought off Wolves twice his size. Still the FBI had hunted him, driven him through the darkness and forced him to run, and it was all because of me...

No, because of her...*the Wolf who was just here.*

"Why the fuck does it smell like Finis in this place?" Vitold snarled, eyeing Phantom.

"I was about to ask the same thing."

My heart fluttered at the sound of Arran's voice. The cocky bartender didn't look so cocky right now. There was usually a smile plastered on his face, his eyes were always twinkling, with a swagger in his step. But there was no swagger now. He just stepped inside and cautiously glanced along the hallway toward the study before his gaze went straight to me. "Trouble, it's been a while."

I crossed the living room and took two steps before leaping into his arms.

He caught me like I was nothing, gripping my waist and lifting until my legs wrapped around his waist.

"Hey there." He held me against him with one hand and smoothed my hair with a stroke of his other. I dropped my head, pressing my forehead to his chest. I hadn't realized how much I'd missed them, how much I'd craved them. *How much I wanted to be here with them...until now.*

"Want to fill us in on what happened here?" Vitold asked.

I lifted my gaze, seeking the comfort of Arran's. He stared

into my soul, his black pupils expanding as though he mapped the world by my face alone.

"Nothing happened here," Phantom answered.

"Nothing, my ass," Church refuted as he stepped out of the kitchen and faced his Alpha. "Are you going to tell them, or will I?"

Tension grew all around me, standing the hairs on my arms.

"Careful there, second," Phantom warned.

Fear rippled through me with the tone. Phantom had changed in the days we'd been apart. Maybe he'd always been like this…maybe I'd just never seen it? But I was seeing it now.

"You going to threaten to banish me, as well, Phantom?" Church turned toward the Alpha. "Or are you going to tell the truth this time…and explain why your sister was here?"

My body stilled, my legs released, leaving me to slide from Arran's body until my boots hit the floor.

"What the fuck?" Arran whispered behind me.

"Sister?" Vitold whispered, and cut a glance from Church to Phantom.

Anger seethed in the living room, cold, savage anger. The kind that sent chills along my spine. "Sister?" The word was a breath across my lips.

The image of that black beast surfaced inside my head.

My mouth went dry.

Cold chills raced through me as I took a slow step forward, drawn by something deeper than fear. *Sister? That…*thing *was his sister?*

"Are you sure?" Vitold muttered, earning a cutting glare from Phantom as a low warning snarl echoed from the hollow of the Alpha's chest.

We *all* stared, until I voiced the only question there was. "What does she want?"

There was a wince in the Alpha's stare as he met my gaze,

then looked away. "If I knew that, I wouldn't be standing here, would I?"

"We need to find her," Arran started.

"No."

Arran took a step forward. "No?"

"No." Phantom repeated. "We *don't* find her."

"No." That cold settled deep into my bones. "We don't have to, do we? She'll find us."

That made the Alpha flinch and in that one movement, I knew exactly what he was thinking. We were being hunted by a vicious, savage enemy. One who seemed to know everything about us while we were in the dark about them. Questions swirled around inside my head. But only one lingered in the darkness…and it was the Chaos inside me that reached out and snatched that question from my mind, holding onto it.

Why indeed, Chaos urged. *What possible reason could she have to hate the Alpha so much as to go after his pack…and his mate?*

"She must've said something?" Church moved to the fridge, yanking the door open and staring into the white glare. But the Wolf never made a move to reach for anything. He just stood there, just…*waited.*

We *all* waited, hooked on every damn word the Alpha said. The only problem was…*he wasn't saying anything.* Heat ravaged my chest, stealing my breath, drawing me from the tension in the room. Memories drifted to the surface. That night at the farmhouse. The night Murphy'd attacked me…then the brutal way Murphy's body had been found, throat ripped out, claws had savaged his chest, tearing it open. Rage fueled an act like that. The kind of rage that was bottomless. The kind of rage that severed the bonds of family, pitting Wolf against Wolf.

Phantom flicked his gaze to mine, then turned, making his way back along the hall until the *bang* of the study door resounded, leaving us standing there with nothing but the stunned silence. The refrigerator door closed before Church strode back out of the kitchen and glanced at Vitold. "We need security, get the rest of the pack here for a meeting. The last thing we need is for her to slip through again…"

"Or for one of us to kill her," Vitold added.

My breath caught. I hadn't thought of that. Kill her…kill Phantom's sister. I glanced along the hallway to where the study door sat closed. He was almost feral now…imagine if anything happened to her? I tried to shove the image from my head. But the darkness waited, unleashing the kind of image that broke a man. His sister dead, mutilated just like Murphy had been.

He'd never forgive himself.

He'd never forgive us.

"That can't happen." I shook my head.

"We *won't* let that happen," Vitold added with a growl.

He turned, grabbed the phone from his pocket, and walked away, limping. I heard him on the phone, snarling commands to someone.

"Now we just have to figure out how to keep the FBI off our backs." Arran shook his head and strode past me, heading to the kitchen.

There was thoughtful silence for a second, long enough for him to yank open the refrigerate and yank out steaks and eggs.

"I don't think we're going to have a problem with that," Church muttered under his breath and glanced my way. "Are we, Carina?"

Heat scorched my cheeks as Arran turned from the open refrigerator and met my gaze. The door closed with a soft *thud.* "Why?"

I met Arran's gaze and felt the room shift as he focused on me. "What am I missing here?" he inquired.

I swallowed hard, listening as Vitold ended the call and strode back toward us. He took one look at Arran, then me, the scowl on his face deepening. "What's going on?"

"Carina was just about to explain why we don't have to hide

from the FBI anymore," Church answered, casting me a sideways glance.

Arran and Vitold scowled. But they didn't say anything, just watched me.

"Carina," Church urged. "They'll find out either way."

"Find out what?" Arran frowned, and reached for me.

I shook my head, stilling his movement, and met their focus. "I made a deal with Harlan. I thought it was the only way out. I thought it'd help." My shoulders sank and I stared at the floor, the weight of it all too damn heavy. "I betrayed Ruth and the Vampires."

Silence consumed the space, until a low groan slipped from Arran. "Oh fuck, Carina."

But Vitold never made a sound and he didn't move. He just stood there in cold silence. Tension rippled through me until I lifted my gaze, meeting his. But there was no bitter disappointment in his eyes, no stunned displeasure at all. There was just *nothing*. Cold. Stony. One nod of his head sent a shudder through me, and Chaos smiled.

He understood her. Understood that cruel, heartless darkness, for it was the same darkness that moved through him. Like called to like. I licked my lips and took a step closer. "Don't you have something to say, Vitold?"

In my head, I was back in those guest quarters at the Vampire's decadent mansion before this all went to hell. I was with my Wolves, kissing, touching, Vitold's fingers deep inside me. *That's it, Carina, .ride my hand...*

"You did what you had to do," he answered, his accent thicker, his brown eyes darker.

Hunger bloomed between us.

"You put the pack first." He came closer, then lifted his hand and caressed my cheek. "Which is exactly what a mate does."

"If we're on our own, sure," Arran grumbled. "But here, we

need allies, and the strongest allies we have are the Vampires and the Fae."

I swallowed hard, unable to take my eyes from Vitold as he held my gaze.

"Phantom…" I whispered.

One nod from Vitold told me all I needed to know. It didn't matter what the pack wanted, didn't matter what the pack thought. They lived and breathed by one man alone—*the Alpha.*

I could be cast from the pack. The ties that bound us would be severed forever and left floating on the wind. Strong enough to choke me, all because of one stupid mistake.

"You have to go to him." Vitold urged. "He's the only one who can decide where we go from here."

"If he doesn't?" The words slipped free before I realized. "If he decides…"

Arran shook his head and lowered his gaze to the floor, but Vitold didn't flinch and never looked away. My protector just held my gaze, and in his eyes, I saw a flicker of desperation. One strong enough to defy orders…but as a ripple of excitement tore through me, doubt and sorrow followed, moving in like a storm, clouding Vitold's love.

Maybe he'd leave the pack for me.

But we'd be running forever.

Outcasts.

Agony moved through me, chilling me to the bone. I glanced at Arran, and Church. There was no one or the other here. It was the entire pack or nothing at all.

Nothing at all…

Vitold lowered his hand as the words hit home. Dread moved through me as I pulled away from his touch. I met Arran's gaze, then Church's. There was no getting around this, no amount of pleading and screaming would change what I'd done. I lived and breathed by one man's sword. I glanced along the hallway…

He was the only man who mattered in this moment.

The *one* man who'd started it all.

The one who'd carried me from that warehouse and plunged me into his world.

Phantom.

I took a step away from the others and turned toward the hallway. My damn mouth was dry, fear nothing more than a beast inside my chest. One that breathed fire, shifting under my skin.

He will forgive you, Chaos urged. *He'll take you into his arms and back into his bed. After all, the Alpha—*

"Shut the fuck up," I snarled. "Don't you think you've done enough here?"

Chaos quietened for a second, and that was all I needed. I reached into the darkness of my mind and slowly went toward the study. I clawed for some kind of divider, some wall that would separate us. I wanted to chain her, to muffle her. To *smother her.* But there was no wall between us, no chains or gag to quiet the voice inside my head.

There was just her…malevolent and malicious. I wished I'd never stepped foot in that warehouse, wished I'd never met that Unseelie. If only there'd been another way to find my way to the Wolves. But there hadn't been…

Only this…*only her.*

Pain flared through my chest with the thought as I lifted my gaze to the closed study door and stopped outside. It was quiet inside. Too quiet. There was no muffled conversation, no shuffling of papers. I stared at the doorway, my senses boring a hole right through the wood to see into the room. He was in there, that I knew.

Hate rippled through the air, seeping out of the cracks of the doorway to reach me where I stood. I lifted my hand, my damn fingers trembling as I reached for the seething ripple. One word from him and I was as good as gone, cast aside by the Alpha of the pack. One word from him and no one could help me.

Helpless…

The emotion was a lump in my throat. I swallowed hard, but that wad remained. My fists clenched by my side, the kick of anger burned that weaker part of my nature. I forced myself to move and lifted my hand. One hard knock and I reached for the door handle without waiting.

If I waited for Phantom to see me, I'd be waiting a while.

Time to force the issue.

I shoved the door open, finding him standing at the far end of the study, staring through the high window into the night. I entered, closing the door behind me. Still he didn't turn, didn't even acknowledge I was there.

I waited, glancing at the desk, finding the strewn paperwork illuminated by the overturned desk lamp. The room was a mess. Fallen paperwork littered the floor, an overturned chair was shoved to the side. The urge to straighten the room wasn't lost on me. But it wasn't just the room that was a damn mess…was it?

"Phantom." I said.

Silence filled the room. There was no turn of his head, No heavy fall of his shoulders. No…*anything.* That lump in the back of my throat moved lower, growing heavy as I swallowed once more.

"Look, I know I fucked up." I winced. "And there's nothing I can do to take it back. I know you don't want my excuses, but when it comes to you, I'll *always* put you first…and the rest of the world can just go to Hell."

He didn't say a word, didn't turn, just stood there like a fucking statue.

"I don't know how this world works. I'm not made for alliances and goddamn politics and power plays. But I know you're mine and I'm yours—even if you don't want me."

The screams inside my head begged him to turn around, to give me *something*. Hate. Anger. *Anything*. Just not this empty silence, this cruel fucking rejection.

"So, we're done." The words detonated inside me like a goddamn grenade. I fought the need to sway from the impact. *Swallow. Breathe. You're alive. You're alive.*

I waited for him to lift his head, waited for him to turn and drive home the last nail in my coffin. *Just fucking do it already.* I waited until I couldn't wait any longer, then turned away, my hand reaching for the handle once more. "For what it's worth, I'm sorry about your sister."

"Where the fuck do you think you're going?"

"I'm leaving," I answered.

"The fuck you are."

I turned, finding him facing me as fear and anger unleashed. "You don't want me here, that's plain to see. Yet I can't leave?"

"Got that right." His lips curled as he spoke, baring his teeth.

So this was what it felt like to feel his wrath. The mighty *Phantom*. The mighty fucking Alpha. "I'm not going to play your games."

One brow rose. "Oh, you're not? I thought you were all for playing games, Carina?"

"What the fuck is that supposed to mean?"

He closed the distance between us in an instant. Jesus, he was fast. I didn't see him move, not even a fucking twitch. He towered over me, forcing me backwards. I glanced at the doorway and a growl reverberated in the back of his throat, savage and chilling.

My pulse thundered as sweat broke out across my skin.

"Try it," he dared, that silver shine glinting in his eyes. "See how far you get."

He wouldn't hurt me...wouldn't...

"I'm leaving, Phantom," I whispered, my voice shaking. "I can't stay here, not like this."

He barred my way with one massive arm, bracing his hands on either side of my head, daring me to run with that bestial stare. We'd been here before…mere hours ago. Look how that'd turned out.

"You run and I'll drag you back. You go *anywhere,* and I'll drag you back."

"Drag me back?" I flinched at the words and shook my head. "No, you won't. Church said you—"

"Church *doesn't* speak for me, female. You'd do well to remember that."

"So, you'll drag me back just so you can hate me?" I jerked my gaze to his, anger burning in my chest, along with lust. "So you can look at me like you're looking at me now? So you'll hate me even more. Say it…tell me the truth."

"I fucking hate you enough now."

My world stopped with those words.

Heart stuttered. Stomach dropped. Savagery sparked in those eyes. He swallowed the room in that moment, all dark rage and poisonous hate. Muscles rippled along his shoulders, his hands curled by his side. He'd been pushed too far, bordering on the shift from man to beast.

"But that doesn't mean I'm letting you go," he added. "You *belong* to me, Carina."

"I. Belong. To. You?"

His lips curled with a chilling sneer. "Bingo."

4

CARINA

Bingo?

B Fuck him. *Fuck* him and his goddamn vindictiveness. I opened my mouth to say that as he stared at me. *Daring me to say a word.* He was so…so goddamn *Alpha.*

Alpha asshole, more like it.

All fucking muscles and power. All fucking ruthless *beast,* just standing there towering over me.

"You have something to say, Carina?" the bastard stabbed, one brow rising.

He took a step closer, the heat of his body radiating all around me. In an instant, he was all around me, smothering me with the scent of danger and desire, molten, seductive. Jesus, this wasn't fair. I became blindingly aware of him, how he moved, slow, lazy.

"Do you have something you want to say to me?" he repeated, his voice deepened, moving through me like thunder.

My pulse sped as a chill raced across my skin. Even the Chaos inside me writhed at the deep bass of his murmur.

I hated how he affected me like this, hated how he could make me feel like I was being torn apart and stitched back together. I hated how he made me want him, even now as I stood here, my fate in the pack still unknown. I licked my lips, my breath catching as he lifted his hand and braced it on the doorframe alongside my head, boxing me in.

"You don't want me," I protested.

"You're right," he answered. "I don't."

But even as the words left those perfect fucking lips, I knew it was a lie. He lowered his gaze to the base of my throat, and there it lingered. Muscles clenched as I swallowed. He stared at the movement as though he envisioned his hands there, clenching, squeezing. Heat bloomed through me with the thought. I pushed backwards, flattening my spine against the door.

He said he didn't want me. I lowered my gaze to the hard rise of his chest, then to his stomach and the bulge between his thighs. *But his body said otherwise.*

I clenched my jaw, biting down hard to stop from smiling. He wanted to play this game, wanted me to grovel...*to beg*...he wanted me here and yet he didn't want me at all.

Meet rock.

And hard place.

Two could play at this. I could be just as fucking stubborn, just as cruel. Just as fucking *Alpha* as he was. He lifted his gaze to mine, finding that ruthlessness burning deep inside me. There was a twitch in the corner of his eye, a second where he might've said something to end the game, until his cell phone rang amidst the mess on his desk.

He moved in a blur, tearing away from me to snatch it out from under a pile of papers.

"I'm here." He stilled, then slowly turned his head until our gazes connected. "Yes, she's right here. We'll be there soon."

A band tightened around my chest as he hung up the call and lowered his hand.

"We'll be where, Phantom?"

But the sonofabitch never answered, just let that beast move through his gaze once more as he reached out, opened the door, and left. *He goddamn left.* Rage simmered deep inside me, mingling and burning with the Chaos.

I spun, listening to his heavy footfalls echoing down the hall. "Go *where, Phantom?!*"

Murmured voices before a barked, "Make sure she turns up. If she runs…*shackle her and drag her there if need be, kicking and screaming."*

Shackle her? Kicking and screaming?

I ground my teeth and pushed off, following the sound, but before I could get there, the connecting door to the club opened and closed. Then he was gone. *Just like that.*

I wrenched my gaze to the others, who just stood there, staring at me wide-eyed and trying not to look like they wanted to run. "And where the fuck are you supposed to drag me to?"

Church looked away.

Arran just swallowed…*hard.*

But it was Vitold who held my stare and who answered. "The Vampires', my warrior. We're to take you to see the Vampires."

The Vampires? The room seemed to sway. "No…*no no no.*"

One nod of his head and Vitold told me all I needed to hear. Fear raced through me. To face Phantom was bad enough, but to face the ones I'd betrayed. I closed my eyes. And Ruth, of course. How could I forget Ruth Costello?

A tremor cut though me. This was what it was like to be part of the pack, always pushed to the brink of apprehension.

"We do not back down." Vitold took a step closer, and brushed his hand along my arm. "We stand strong and face our enemy, no matter what."

"Even if that enemy has good excuse to end you?"

He held my gaze. Strength waited in there. Strength tempered by pain…and battles. He's fought for me, and almost died. I straightened my spine as the Chaos inside me moved to the surface. Silver sparkled in his eyes. His Wolf was there, hovering under the surface, ready to do what needed to be done.

"Okay," I murmured, then exhaled hard and gave a slow nod. "I can do this. I *will* do this."

Vitold nodded very slightly as I lifted my head. I needed his strength more than anything right now, more than I needed anything else. Arran just stared at the floor, shaking his head as he went to the connecting door to the bar. Church reached into his pocket and yanked out his keys.

I followed Vitold, leaving the living quarters of the Hunting Ground behind, and made my way through the darkened club before climbing the stairs to the busted door. Glass crunched under my boots as the cool night air hit me. I lifted my gaze to the full moon in the sky, and stopped walking.

"Carina?" Church called.

I hadn't noticed the moon before, the way it seemed even brighter tonight, its silver glow washing over everything… washing over me. I closed my eyes feeling, that pull, that *clarity*.

"Carina, we have to go," Arran urged beside me.

"I know." I opened my eyes and found Church beside the open door of his sleek sports car.

The vehicle was still sideways in the street, the doors still open. I wondered why the engine wasn't still running. Adrenaline spiked inside me at the sight. It was only minutes ago I'd lunged out that open door…mere minutes, and yet my world had changed dramatically.

The woman who'd charged forward had been confident, even in her delusions. But this woman…this woman didn't know where her loyalties lay. I couldn't leave, and yet to stay here…felt like fucking torture.

I exhaled hard and pushed off the curb, stepped down and squeezed into the back seat of Church's car. Arran followed me, leaving Vitold to take the passenger's seat. Seconds felt like hours as Church climbed in, started the car, and pulled out into the quiet street once more.

I pressed my spine into the plush leather, my mind drifting back to that night at the warehouse, when Phantom had put me in the back seat of his Camaro and bitched about the leather seats being new. A tremor cut through me. The Alpha consumed me, demanded more from me...pushed me harder than I'd ever been pushed before.

Something was cracking inside me, some kind of shell I'd carried all these years, a shell I'd built out of hate and revenge. One that had made me feel safe. But that shell was falling apart now. Every word from the Alpha, every look, made the cracks just that little bit wider. I wrapped my arms around my middle. The only thing was, I didn't know what waited underneath.

Soft, pliable...like molten lava spilling out between the cracks, I was losing myself. *Unbecoming* the woman I'd made.

To become something stronger, Chaos whispered in the back of my mind.

But I turned away from her, ignoring that voice. It whispered lies and delusions. Lies that had brought me here, hurtling through the night to meet a brood of pissed off Vampires...and Ruth Costello.

Church handled the car, turning on a dime, only to punch the accelerator and spear us into the darkness. The headlights carved through the dark, splashing against the trees as we turned off the main road, heading to somewhere I'd never been before. A pale blanket of fog seemed to rise out of nowhere. I leaned closer to the window, watching it rise like an incoming tide.

"Um, Church," I murmured as the fog rose along the side of the car and then the window.

"It's alright," Vitold answered. "The Vampires don't like guests."

"No shit." I watched the fog sweep over the car until we were blanketed in the damn thing, and shifted in my seat. I didn't like this, didn't it at all. Not the damn fog, not this damn place. Not meeting the one group of Immortals that were desperate to spill my damn blood.

They won't let that happen, I reminded myself. *Phantom won't let that happen.*

"The ground is warded," Vitold explained. "You're supposed to want to leave, it keeps most people away."

Warded. Just like what the Unseelie had carved into my chest. I gripped the armrests and tried to still the pounding of my heart. "Doesn't it affect you?"

He just gave a shrug. "You get used to it after a while."

"Doesn't matter," Arran spoke, drawing my gaze as he nodded up ahead. "We're here."

Through the heavy fog, bright lights shone in the distance. The eerie mist parted, leaving me staring through the windshield at an impressive mansion hidden in the shadows. I scanned the grounds, finding Phantom's Harley parked next to two dark Explorers. Cars I was more than familiar with.

Church pulled up behind the four-wheel drives, killing the engine before climbing out. My body felt slow and heavy, dread weighing me down. So this was what death row felt like. This… heaviness that clung to my bones and welled in my chest.

Vitold stepped out, turned, and reached for my hand. I couldn't meet his gaze, or any of them, for that matter.

"Let's just get this over and done with." I fixed my gaze on the front door as it opened and the towering shadow of the bodyguard filled the doorway.

Church was first, striding forward and climbing the few stairs until he was inside. Arran was next, leaving Vitold to follow me. I met the bodyguard's stony gaze as I stepped through, and caught the sneer.

Fuck me, he was a scary motherfucker.

Footsteps rang out on the tiled floor, the only damn sound in this tomb. I scanned the living room, taking in the leather sofas and dark timber bookcases that lined the far wall. The place was big, expansive and expensive. There had been no expense spared here, not from the paintings that hung on the walls to the sleek lines of the furniture.

"Church." The cold tone of the Vampire sent chills over my skin.

I glanced to where Elithien stood with the others…and *her*.

Ruth said nothing, dwarfed on both sides by her Vampire lovers.

"E." Church reached out, grasped the Vampire's hand in a shake, and nodded to the others.

Phantom stood at the side, an empty glass in his hand. He set that empty gaze on mine, not even glancing at the others.

"E," Vitold murmured. "Hurrow."

The Vampire at Ruth's side gave a nod. But those dark eyes never moved from mine, just bored through me like I was made of nothing more than glass.

All of them stared.

"Carina." Elithien finally acknowledged my presence.

"Vampire," I murmured.

"You know why we've asked you here?" Elithien spoke for everyone, it seemed.

The bodyguard strode past, then turned and leaned against the doorway of what looked like a massive kitchen.

"I have a wild guess," I answered.

He clenched his jaw, the muscles flaring as a spark flickered in those savage eyes. I didn't turn my head, never glanced at Phantom. Instead, I stepped away from Vitold and Arran. If this all went to hell, I wanted them as far from me as possible. The last thing I wanted was for any of them to be hurt…*because of something I did.*

"I get you're pissed off," I started, shifting my gaze from the

Vampire to Ruth. "Fuck knows, I've given you plenty to be pissed off about."

She unfolded her arms and took a slow step forward. There was too much hate between us, the divide too great for either of us to conquer. Maybe this was how it was meant to be? Maybe that moment back in the mansion before the choppers came had been nothing more than wishful thinking?

Her on one side.

Me on the other.

And never the two shall meet.

"We asked you here to get your side of things," Elithien prodded.

I just gave a shrug and held her gaze. "What do you want me to say? I fucked up? I'm sorry for securing the safety of my pack?"

Ruth's lips curled into a sneer. *"Your pack?"*

"My pack," I repeated.

She barked a laugh. "Don't make me fucking laugh, Carina. They're not *your* pack."

I caught the shift from Phantom. Vitold moved carefully, angling his body toward mine. I adjusted my body toward him by instinct. But the movement wasn't lost on Ruth. That sneer seemed to falter as she looked from Vitold to me...then slowly glanced at Phantom.

Surprise widened her eyes. One brow rose as she met my gaze once more. I wanted to say more, to try to explain. But there weren't enough words. This was beyond vindictiveness, beyond payback. This was about my Wolves and *only* my Wolves.

"The deal you made." Elithien steered the conversation away from the heat of anger.

I just gave a nod. "You and Ruth in exchange for the Wolves."

"That was with?"

"Harlan and someone from Homeland Security."

"You made a deal without speaking to us, *or to Phantom?*" Hurrow growled.

I flinched as he stepped forward. The Vamp on the other side moved at the same time. "You put Ruth's life in danger."

Elithien said nothing, just watched me with calculating eyes.

"We should kill you for that alone," Hurrow growled.

There was a growl behind me, low, threatening. I didn't need to turn my head to know it was Vitold. Arran shifted his stance, Church grew terrifyingly still. Phantom said nothing, just stared at a spot in the middle of the room. Rage seethed all around me, the tension heightening as Hurrow and the other Vamp, Rule, stepped forward.

"It's alright." Ruth held out her hand, stopping the movement as she glanced at Vitold, then Phantom. "I thought this was just a fling, just a way for you to get to me again. Clearly I was wrong."

One turn of her head, and she gave a slow nod to her Vampires.

My body trembled, terror cut like icy shards in my veins. I tried to stop the shake of my knees, tried to stop my throat from clamping shut.

"But that doesn't mean I fucking like it," Ruth finished.

I caught the movement a second too late as she swung her hand. The blow landed on my cheek, snapping my head to the side. The shock. The burn. Fire found my flesh as my hair flapped across my face.

Hard breaths consumed me as the temperature in the room plunged.

"You fucking betrayed us."

I slowly shifted my gaze, the searing mark across my face growing hotter as I met her glare. She was wrath in that moment, pure, unconstrained vengeance, as she came closer until she was all I could see. "To betray *me* is one thing, Carina. But to betray those I love, that is *unforgivable.*"

Hurrow and the bodyguard stepped forward. All I saw was fangs from the Vampire and midnight wrath in the bodyguard's gaze. I flinched at the movement as Hurrow clenched his fists. They wanted to hurt me...*to kill me.*

Would Phantom let them? The answer whispered in the darkness of my mind...*I don't know...not anymore.* I swallowed hard with the thought. Panic and shame filled me.

"Enough," Elithien commanded, stopping the Immortals cold.

But it was Ruth I saw in that moment, *really saw her.*

We were mirrored. Both fighting to protect the men we loved.

"I'll fix it," I promised. "Just give me some time. I'll fix it."

"*We* have no time, Carina. *You* saw to that."

"Let me talk to Harlan. I'll tell him I made a mistake."

"And the blood results from the warehouse?" Ruth spat. "The ones you promised not to release?"

"I'll tell them it was a forgery. He knows how far I've gone to arrest you before. He'll believe the lie."

Elithien glanced at Phantom. Hope flared in my chest with the movement.

"You'll have to set up the meet tomorrow," Elithien urged quietly.

The threat in those words filled me with dread.

I gave a nod, searching her eyes. "Give me a chance, Ruth. Give me a chance to fix this."

She sucked in a breath, hate shifting and flickering in her eyes before it dulled. "You betray us again—"

I shook my head. "I won't. I promise."

Elithien stepped closer, reached out to grasp Ruth's hand, and leaned toward me. "The next time you think there's no way out of your damn mess, Carina, call us. I think you'll find out there're a lot more solutions than you realize."

One gentle tug and Elithien pulled Ruth away.

"I need a fucking drink," she muttered. "And ice for my damn hand."

There was a chuckle from one of the Vamps as the tension in the room disappeared. A hard exhale behind me, and Arran mumbled. "Fuck me, that was close."

Movement came from behind me.

But not Phantom.

He just stared at me and, as I turned to meet his gaze, I saw…*nothing*.

5

CARINA

My damn cheek throbbed in the shape of her hand. But the emptiness in Phantom's eyes hurt more than a slap across the face ever could. I glanced toward the Alpha once more, hating how he watched me with that cold, stony stare.

"That's going to bruise," Elithien murmured. "Maybe I could—"

He glanced toward Phantom. Only then did the Wolf show a hint of anything but seething rage. Something passed between them, Vampire to Wolf. Alpha to Alpha. Elithien waited…until there was a slow nod of Phantom's head. Consent given. But consent for what?

"Come on," Elithien gave a jerk of his head, motioning me forward. "Let me get you some ice for that."

Voices spilled out of the open doorway as Phantom refilled his glass from the bar. I searched the Vampire leader's gaze, and nodded. A slap to the cheek like a damn reprimand and it seemed things were back to normal. *For them anyway.* But it was anything but back to normal for me. If anything, the rejection was building.

He had to think about giving the Vampire permission to give me the barest hint of comfort?

Did he hate me that much?

I followed Elithien into the kitchen and found Ruth sitting on the kitchen counter, her legs crossed at the knee, watching as one of her Vampires made her hot chocolate over the stove.

The cold, ruthless bitch still lingered in her eyes, but she was trying to move past it, not meeting my gaze. The freezer door opened and the faint clinks of ice cubes filled the space before Elithien returned carrying a plastic snap-lock bag wrapped in a clean hand towel.

"Here, hold this to your cheek. It'll ease the burn."

I forced a smile, which was more like a wince, as a thank you, and took the ice from the Vampire, hissing as I pressed the cold to my skin. I expected a chuckle from her, a smirk at least, but instead, Ruth just glanced my way and held my stare.

Regret bloomed between us, a kind of sadness for what might've been a compromise…or hell, I don't know, maybe even a friendship. *Because you seem to be running out of those,* Chaos added.

I wrenched my gaze from Ruth, turning instead to Church. My damn knees trembled. Exhaustion pressed close and whispered of slumber. But there was no rest, not until Walker was found safe…and I figured a way out of this fucking mess with Harlan.

"Has there been any word from the search party?" I asked Church as he lingered in the doorway.

One glance toward Phantom and he shook his head. "Not yet, but they're close."

"Pathfinder?" Elithien asked.

One nod from Church and the Vampire turned toward me. "If they're still out there, they'll find them."

"And if they're not?" I prodded.

One savage glare from Phantom, and I bit my tongue.

Still, I'd heard the stories through the FBI, Immortals selling mortals on their own version of the black market. Someone like Walker would be highly prized, not only a walking meal...but a doctor, as well. I pressed the ice against my face and closed my eyes, trying to stop the room from spinning. Walker, Harlan, Ruth and the Vampires, and under all of that, Chaos and the Wolves.

It was too much.

Too much for one night. I was exhausted, and frankly...I'd had enough of Immortals for one fucking night. "I need a car," I announced. "Or a ride. I need to sleep, need to think, and I can't do that here. Take me home."

"Fine," Phantom snapped. "Vitold, take Carina across the bridge to her father's place. I assume that's where you'll be living now."

I flinched at the words, and panic moved in.

Fuck, that stung like a bitch. I held the Alpha's gaze and spoke carefully. "I meant the Hunting Ground."

He cocked his head as a brow rose. "Oh, *my* home? That's where you want to stay? Under *my* roof...with *my* pack?"

Heat burned through me, setting fire to the outline of Ruth's hand. They all stared, wide-eyed, not daring to say a word. But the thought of returning to that hovel, to my drunken father just sitting there in the stench of his own piss, was too big a hole. I sucked in a breath and slowly nodded. "Yes, *please.*"

There was a flicker of satisfaction. But his focus still bored into mine until finally, he nodded. Keys sailed through the air and were caught in the blur of a hand.

I flinched at the movement, lifting my gaze to Vitold as he gripped the keys to an Explorer in his hand.

"I want it back by morning, Wolf," Hurrow muttered. "In one damn piece."

Vitold just gave a wicked smirk. "My reputation precedes me."

"Your reputation precedes us all, Russian," Arran added with a chuckle. "And all the damn cars we've had to replace over the years."

But there was a carefulness about the Russian tonight. One nod of his head was all he gave. "Don't worry, Vampire. I'm in no mood to break your vehicle tonight."

"Thank fuck for that." Hurrow just shook his head as he turned. "By morning."

"It will be returned," Vitold answered, and reached for my hand. "Special Agent."

I glanced around the room, hating how I always ended at Phantom. But there were no words left to be said, none that the jumbled mess inside my head could find, at least. I grasped Vitold's hand and let him led me from the kitchen, still clutching the ice to my face.

I slowed my steps at the end of the living room and glanced over my shoulder. Phantom watched me, hunger darkening those intense eyes. Ravenous, aching hunger. One that burned in my chest, too, a cold, burning fire. The flames licked my heart, searing the flesh with every flick of their tongues.

I wanted him, wanted him to cross the room and take me in his arms. A kiss...a brush of his hand. I was desperate for his affection, needing it like I needed air to breathe.

But he never crossed the divide, instead he severed the gaze, turning to his glass once more. I looked away, wincing for a second, before I went out the open door, leaving the Vampire mansion behind.

Lights brightened the gloom a bit as the door to the Explorer unlocked with a *thunk.* I climbed into the passenger's seat and yanked my seatbelt across my body as Vitold climbed in and started the four-wheel drive. I slid back in my seat, pressed the ice to my numb cheek, and exhaled.

"You alright?" Vitold asked.

I just nodded and closed my eyes. "I'm just so fucking tired, Wolf. Just so goddamn tired of it all."

The engine started with a snarl, then we started moving. I closed my eyes at the motion, letting the crunch of the tires and the sway of the vehicle carry me away.

Walker followed me into the dark crevices of my mind, her smile, her friendship. She deserved better than to be left running for her damn life all alone. *If* she was even alive. I shifted in the seat. I wanted to be out there, searching, hunting. But I'd be useless out there, less than useless against a pack of Wolves.

"Do you honestly think they'll find her?" I asked without opening my eyes.

"Walker?"

I just gave a nod, my throat aching with the lump.

"I don't know. But what I do know is that if *anyone* can find them, then it'll be the Breeds."

"Breeds." I repeated the name, then opened my eyes and found him bathed in the dashboard lights. "Why do you call them that, anyway?"

He waited for a second. Debating, I guess, revealing more of their secrets to me.

"They've always been dangerous, some even Alphas with their own kind, until for some reason or other they entered into a program."

Exhaustion faded. I opened my eyes, shoving upwards in the seat. "What kind of program?"

"DNA testing…and changing."

"Fuck me."

There was a curl at the corner of his lips, but his focus was on the road. "It started off as an experiment, and when that went wrong, they started real trials. They wanted a breed of Immortals who were stronger, more powerful, ones who could hunt and capture better than the rest of us."

"So, you're saying what's out there...this *Pathfinder,* is genetically designed to be more...*Wolf?*"

The half-smile faded in an instant. Vitold flinched, his grip tightening around the wheel. "More Vampire, probably."

"They enhanced them with other Immortals?" I gasped, stunned.

One nod was all I received. I shifted my gaze to the midnight trees whipping past us and exhaled hard. "Jesus, no wonder they're powerful. Crossbreed, that's why the name."

"A *dangerous* Breed," Vitold injected. "*That's* why the name. So, if your friend is out there, then they'll be the ones to find her...and the young pup."

"Wry." I'd almost forgotten about him, so focused on my own damn pain.

I knew enough to know if there was anyone at risk of being killed, it'd be him. A rogue pack wouldn't take too kindly to someone so young...especially a Wolf. I swallowed hard. "I hope they find them soon."

"They will." Vitold reached across and grasped my hand.

The connection was instant, tearing through me like wildfire. I grasped his hand, my fingers entwining with his as that burn moved through my chest. Chaos shifted under my skin, waking with the bond.

She licked her lips and opened her eyes. I felt her waking with the contact, felt her stretching and moving, coming alive as my pulse sped. Vitold's hand stilled in mine, one glance toward me and I knew he felt her, too.

Bright lights sparkled in the distance as I slid my hand along his arm. Corded muscles tensed under my touch. "God, I've missed you."

He jerked his gaze to mine. The glint of silver a spark in his eyes before he turned back to the road. But that hunger was waking inside me, shifting like a beast under my skin. It wanted

Phantom, wanted his anger and his force. But Chaos wanted Vitold, too, and Arran…and Church.

She wanted them all.

Their strength, their sex.

All the sex…

That burn moved deeper the closer we came to the Hunting Ground. Vitold handled the four-wheel drive with one hand, tapping the brakes before he pulled us into the empty lot beside the strip club. If you'd told me six months ago that a place like this could feel like home to me, I'd have probably kneed you in the balls and walked away.

But as Vitold killed the engine and muttered, "See, car all in one piece. I don't understand why the bitching." I leaned across the car seat, turned his face toward me, and kissed him.

His lips were soft, careful. I closed my eyes and waited for his hands on me, for him to pull me across the seat until I straddled him. I waited for the ferocity, for the desperation, and the burn between us.

Because there was burn.

It seethed and licked between my thighs. But there was no pulling me across the cab of the four-wheel drive, no desperate clawing of my clothes. Just a carefulness, one I'd never felt in my Wolf before.

He pulled away, breaking the kiss. I opened my eyes, finding his, confused.

"We'd better get you inside," he said finally.

My heart gave a tremble. Maybe he was just being cautious? It made sense. The last thing we needed was to be out here, occupied, with a crazed fucking female Wolf hunting us down, even if she was Phantom's sister.

I gave a nod and released the buckle of my seatbelt before climbing out of the car. Still, I glanced over my shoulder at Vitold. One scan of the empty lot and he had his head down, striding toward the door. He punched in the code, then opened the door wide, meeting my gaze.

There it was…that guarded look he had.

I forced a hint of a smile and walked through, heading to the living quarters. My boots resounded in the hallway. I opened the connecting door and strode into the kitchen, pitching the melted ice from the cold pack into the sink.

Vitold hovered outside the kitchen, then went to the refrigerator and yanked it open. "You hungry, want me to make you something to eat?"

Hungry? I was beyond hungry. Sickened and starved and too exhausted to do anything about it. I shook my head. "No, just sleep. I want to sleep for a damn year."

He straightened and closed the door. I realized they did that a lot when they were nervous, opened and closed the fridge, hovered around the kitchen.

"Well, you can take my room." He gave a shrug as I strode closer.

"You sure?" A slow nod. Did that mean he wasn't sure? I stopped in front of him, sliding my hands around his waist and leaning my body against his. I caught the flare of his nostrils. "Am I to share your bed, Wolf?"

He just stilled, then slowly met my gaze. One slow slide of his tongue, and I felt the twitch of his cock. He was growing hard, aching for me just as I ached for a kiss…a touch. I ached for them, to feel wanted once more, to feel like I belonged again.

I wanted that more than I wanted sleep.

I wanted that more than I wanted absolution.

I lifted my hands to the buttons of his shirt. "Make love to me, Vitold. Make me feel something more than this fucking divide between us all."

One by one, they opened under my fingers, revealing his bulky, muscled chest.

"Wait," he murmured, and grasped my hands, stopping them at his stomach.

But I lowered my head, my lips finding his warm flesh, kissing him. "You want me," I whispered. "I want you."

"Stop, Carina." The kiss died on my lips. I lifted my gaze, finding that hardness in his. There was a slight curl of his lips, then a slow shake of his head. "We can't."

I flinched. His injuries! *Jesus, I'm such a fucking asshole.* "You're still hurt, aren't you? You're still healing."

He shook his head, a small smile curling the corners of his mouth. "I could be half dead and still want you, *moya lyubov'.*"

I scowled at the words. "You called me that before."

He smiled, and said nothing, keeping all his damn secrets.

I licked my lips. "Alright, then why?"

There was that coldness again, that emptiness that stole the laughter from his eyes and the smirk from his lips, but he said nothing, still searching my gaze.

I pulled away, sliding my hands from under his, and left the warmth of his body. "I see now. Can't or won't, Vitold?"

There was a shake of his head.

"Can't...or won't, Wolf," I growled.

"The Alpha—" he started.

I flinched as though slapped. *The Alpha.* That said it all, didn't it? Phantom hated me so much he refused to let me leave, and yet he refused to let me to stay like it had been before.

Because now it's all changed.

I ground my teeth as agony tore through me. It *had* changed, changed because of me. But I wasn't the only one to blame here. I wasn't the only one who'd made choices they didn't like. "I understand, Vitold."

I took a step away, widening the distance between us. My hands were heavy, my steps achingly slow, weighed down by exhaustion once more.

"Carina..." Vitold started.

There was pain in his eyes, the kind of pain that made this so much more fucked up. "It's alright," I lied. "I'm just tired, Vitold. I think I'll…"

I turned then, leaving the words unsaid, and headed for his bedroom along the hall. My heavy steps mirrored the thud of my heart. I made my way past the study and caught a glimpse of the mess inside through the open door.

She'd been here…the midnight Wolf.

Phantom's sister.

The image haunted me as I stepped inside Vitold's room and stared at the mess of his bed, still unmade. I kicked off my boots, then wrestled with my shirt and my jeans before climbing in and pulling the sheets high.

My cheek throbbed, aching as I pressed it against the pillow. Tears came, slow and thick, running over the bridge of my nose as I closed my eyes. Phantom didn't want me here, and yet he didn't want me to leave.

He wanted me to suffer…

He wanted me to change.

I exhaled hard, letting the darkness finally descend.

And as sleep came, all I thought about was him…and my Wolves.

6

CARINA

I woke to the sound of music blaring through the hallway.

The slow beat rolled through me, familiar and awkward.

"You've got to be shitting me," I groaned and shoved my head under the pillow before I stilled, listening for a second. "Is that Ginuwine's Pony?"

A tortured sound ripped from my chest as I buried myself deeper into whatever I could find. But the thin sheets and soft, downy pillow did little to keep the sound at bay. Instead, it invaded, the embarrassingly enticing sound made me pull my head out from under the pillow and just listen. Until my lips started moving and finally, with a sigh, I shoved up from the bed.

Sunlight spilled through the high windows. I blinked and tried to focus, finding my pants and shirt in a pile on the floor. They were grimy…no way I could wear them again. I needed—

I lifted my gaze to the open closet door and spied a pile of sweats. I was used to wearing their clothes now. Their scent, their feel. Hell, I liked them better than my own clothes. I stood up from the bed, wincing at the ache across my cheek.

It all came flooding back; Ruth's slap, then the drive home

with Vitold. I took a step, moving to the pile of his clothes. Vitold. The ache across my chest came back with a vengeance and with it the agony of rejection.

"Fine," I muttered and grabbed the fleecy sweats from the top of the pile, yanking them on before shrugging into a t-shirt. "You want to break me? Want to make me fucking grovel? You picked the wrong woman, Wolf."

I stomped to the bathroom, switched on the light, and blinked at the glare before I used the toilet. My damn cheek was swollen, the flesh darkening at the edges of the red, raised flesh. A hiss tore free as I gently touched the edges and winced. "Ice will stop the bruising, my ass. I look like I've been beaten, for fuck's sake."

I turned away from the sight, washed my hands, then left the bathroom, and the bedroom, behind. The sharp scent of bleach stung my nose as I stepped out into the hallway and headed toward the music. The study door was closed. I slowed at the sight, fighting the urge to reach out and open the door. I'd invaded enough...for now.

The sinking feeling that had accompanied sleep still lingered, but there was something else now, a hard sense of determination I hadn't felt before, one that seemed to grow with the deep bruise on the side of my face. I left the study behind and rounded the end of the hall, catching movement from the corner of my eye.

Church scrubbed the floor on hands and knees in front of me, shirtless...dark blue jeans riding low over muscular hips. I stopped at the sight, my gaze sweeping along his back as he moved to the sound of the music, rolling his hips as he pushed against the floor.

Bare feet, big hands.

He spread his thighs in a low thrust toward the floor to the beat of the music.

I couldn't breathe.

I couldn't even think as he swiped a brush across the floor and pushed upwards to stand. One glance behind him and he froze, his gaze moving instantly to my cheek before his bright blue eyes darkened. "Did I wake you?"

I shook my head. "No, I was awake anyway." I nodded to the bucket and the brush in his hand. "Couldn't sleep?"

"Not really," he replied, and gave a shrug. "So I clean."

"I can see that." I lowered my gaze to his body. "And dance."

"And dance," he repeated with a low chuckle. "Sorry. This song is..."

"Old as fuck," Arran grumbled as he strode from his room, his curls a damn mess and his eyes bloodshot. "Still, you grind the hell out of it, don't you, brother?"

"Damn right," Church agreed, grinning, until the creak of the connecting door drew his gaze.

His grin died with the heavy thud of boots. I turned toward the sound, finding Phantom's furious gaze settled on me. He took one look at the others and muttered, "I take it you've arranged to meet Harlan?"

That chilling glare met mine once more. There was a cruelty there. I'd never seen him like this, it was almost like he was pushing me on purpose, determined to find the cracks in my resolve. "Good morning to you, too, Wolf," I growled. "It's early, Harlan won't be in his office until at least eight, and until then, I need coffee...or is that not allowed, as well, anymore?"

The curl of his lips was instant, teeth bared with the flexing of his jaw. I turned away from the pathetic display of dominance, or whatever had crawled up his ass, and headed for the kitchen, trying my best to ignore the others as they pretended to be busy with whatever was happening.

"Pack meeting in twenty, Church," Phantom commanded.

I yanked open a cupboard as the sound of Phantom's steps receded, followed by the sound of the study door opening and closing.

"The entire pack?" Arran wondered.

I caught Church's nod and placed a cup on the counter before grabbing the instant coffee. The entire pack? I heaped a spoonful into the cup and filled it with water before placing it in the microwave. How many were there in his pack? More than my four Wolves.

Mine...

Seemed like they weren't really mine, after all. I tried not to think about that and waited for the beep of the microwave.

"By the way, I found your bag." Arran stepped onto the entrance to the kitchen. "It was still in the Jeep from before, so I put it in Vitold's room for you."

"Thank you." I forced a smile as Arran gave a nod and turned. "Arran...can I ask you something?"

My bartender met my gaze.

"Why would Phantom's sister come after us like this?"

The question hung in the air. He gave a careful glance toward Church, then the hallway. "I don't know. I don't think any of us do, least of all Phantom."

"Are we going to ignore the fact that she looked heavily pregnant, and she reeks of Alpha?"

"We're not ignoring anything," Church answered, and scowled. "But we need to know more."

"And this pack meeting will give you that?"

One slow nod of his head and Church met my gaze. "I guess we'll find out, won't we?"

The piercing beep wrenched me from the moment. I yanked open the microwave and grabbed my coffee. Closing my eyes with the first sip, I let the warmth flow through me. "Thanks for my bag, Arran. I should shower."

Their gazes followed me as I headed back to Vitold's room, glancing toward the study door as I went. My duffel bag was sitting on the bed, waiting for me. I'd forgotten all about it, forgotten the moments before that night. I'd driven to the farmhouse expecting answers, or at least another dead end.

I yanked open the zipper, then pulled out slacks and button-up shirts, as well as clean underwear and socks. Jeans and t-shirts were packed underneath, as well as a heavy sweater. It wasn't everything I opened, but was pretty damn close to it.

I went into the bathroom. The pack meeting would start soon and I was determined to find out as much as I could. I needed a way to fix this, to make it like it was before. Chaos chuckled inside my head.

No, not like it was before...I want it better.

I showered and dried, yanked on fresh clothes, and grabbed my phone. I jabbed the buttons, dialing Harlan's phone as I yanked on socks and boots. But it went to voicemail. "Shit."

Trace, Harlan's receptionist, she'd know where he was. I laced my boots and dialed again, this time to his office.

"FBI—" Trace started.

"Trace, it's me, Carina."

"Carina?" Surprise etched her tone.

"I need to see him."

"I don't think—"

"Please, Trace. I need to see him, it's urgent." I closed my eyes and straightened, *please...please...please.*

There was a hard sigh on the other end of the line. "You know he won't want to see you."

"I know, but I have to try. I promise not to—"

"The last thing I need is broken promises from you, Carina," she snapped.

"I'm trying here." I closed my eyes. "Trying to fix this, trying to do better."

There was silence for a second until finally, "If you want to see him, then he's going to be in his office for an hour between twelve and one."

"Oh Jesus, thank you. You won't regret this—" I babbled.

But it didn't matter. I was talking to an empty line. She'd hung up on me.

The door to the study opened and closed down the hall. Footsteps resounded, urging me to stand and slip my phone into my pocket. I straightened my shirt, readied myself for what I'd find, and headed for the hallway.

Voices filled the space, low and snarling. My skin tingled with the energy, standing my hair on end. But it wasn't just here...I glanced toward the connecting door to the club and that rush of energy only grew. Jesus, they were in there. *All of them.*

Power swirled around inside me like I held onto a damn live wire. How many were there in there? Ten...twenty...*fifty?* My pulse raced as Church strode past me. I watched as he opened the connecting door and stepped through.

Arran was next, following the second. Then Vitold, giving me a weak smile as he went.

I turned to follow and reached for the handle.

"Where do you think you're going?"

The low growl stopped me cold. I didn't turn my head, but answered, "There's a pack meeting."

"There is." Phantom stepped to the side and reached for the door instead.

"I thought I could—"

"Thought you could." He repeated, his sneer growing bolder. "I mean, I'd allow it, *if* you were part of the pack, Carina...until then, non-pack members aren't invited."

He yanked open the door, letting the rush of Wolf energy wash over me, before closing the door and leaving me behind.

Just like that.

I wasn't part of the pack, that was clear, not anymore. I took a step backwards. The pain carved deep. He'd said I was one of them. *He* was the one who'd brought me here, made me part of this family...*made me love him.*

Made me love them all.

I winced and stood there, feeling the building storm of power from the club, and for the first time in my life, I didn't know what to do. How could I fix this? How could I make him trust me again?

I turned away from the connecting door and strode toward the kitchen. He wanted to shut me out, punish me. Well, this was punishment enough. I yanked open the fridge and stared at the stacked slabs of meat piled high, and spied something green in the crisper.

"Oh, gross," I muttered as I pulled out the drawer and caught sight of the pathetic, wilted stick of celery. Something was growing out of the end. I fought the urge to gag and tossed it into the trash. "So, there's meat…meat, and more meat. Figures."

My stomach growled as I grabbed the smallest packet I could, then sighed and tossed it back. "He'd probably get pissy if I ate *his* food, under *his* roof, in *his* damn nightclub."

Instead, I made myself another cup of coffee and carried it back toward Vitold's room, until I passed the study and stopped. One glance over my shoulder and that panicked voice in my head whispered, *don't…don't do it.*

I clenched the hot coffee cup and winced. I gnashed my teeth and let out a low groan before reaching for the handle. Phantom had locked himself in here day and damn night since we'd come back. There had to be information in here, something that'd give me an idea of what I was fighting.

I reached out and grabbed the handle, but before I could turn it, I froze.

What the fuck are you doing?

My cheek throbbed, sending the ache across my face. I pulled my hand away and took a step backwards. No, not anymore, not like that. One wrong move and it wouldn't be just a reprimand. One wrong move and I'd be out for good. Phantom might not like me in at this moment, but I was still here, and that was still something.

Instead, I made my way back to Vitold's room and sat on the edge of the bed, taking long, slow sips of my coffee. I didn't know how long it was before I heard them. The door opened, and heavy footsteps echoed down the hall until they stopped at the entrance to the study.

But the door didn't open.

What was he doing?

Was he scenting me? Seeing if I'd opened his closed door and snooped? My pulse sped with the thought, until finally the door opened. I glanced at my phone. 11 am. I'd need to leave soon, drive across the bridge and meet with Harlan.

I still didn't know what I was going to say. What could I do to undo all I'd done? *I made a mistake...I take it all back?* I'd tried that, remember? Didn't work then, I was damn sure it wouldn't work now.

My stomach let out a savage growl. I winced and grabbed my belly.

The door to the study slammed open. Footsteps boomed, coming closer. I shoved up from the end of the bed, still clutching my empty cup, and turned toward the doorway. But Phantom didn't barge in. Instead, the thud of his boots receded, moved back along the hall, and disappeared.

What the fuck was that?

The damn cup shook as I sat back on the bed. I clenched my fist, then shook out the tension. I had to get out of here, needed to get myself under control. I needed to focus on getting Harlan to change his damn mind.

I checked my phone, then headed out, carrying my cup to the kitchen. I needed to find Arran, grab his keys, and use his Jeep, but as I rounded the corner and craned my head to listen for the Wolf, I found Phantom leaning against the counter. His arms were crossed over his chest as he just stared lazily at me. "Going somewhere?"

I forced my gaze from his, stepped around him, and headed

for the sink. "I have that meeting," I answered and washed the cup before drying it. "Is Arran…"

"Out."

"Of course he is," I muttered, then sighed. "Fine. I'll call an Uber."

"No you won't." Phantom pushed off from the counter as I turned. "I'll be accompanying you."

I stopped dead, then shook my head, remembering the last time Phantom was in a room with Harlan. "I don't think that's a good idea."

"Lucky for me, *I* think it is."

"Sure," I snarled. "Because you're the one calling all the shots, right?"

The vindictive smile said it all.

He wanted me to do the impossible with his snarling ass hovering in the background. *Shit.* "Fine," I growled and closed the cupboard. "You want to fuck this up, then go right ahead. Just so you know I'm doing this. I'll hold up my end and do my damn best to get Harlan off the Vampires, but if this all goes to hell because you can't keep your cool, *that* Wolf, is on you."

"I'm driving," he answered digging into his pocket for the keys before striding toward the hallway.

I followed him out to the parking lot, leaving the side door to latch closed behind me.

The sleek black Camaro lit up with the press of a button. My steps stopped at the sight as memories rushed in.

"Is there a problem, Carina?" Phantom murmured, waiting at the driver's door.

All I could see was him, the night he'd driven me here. Aching, *hungry.* Desire punched me now just as it had then. I licked my arid lips, meeting his stare. "No, no problem."

I caught a hint of amusement as he opened the door and climbed in. I rounded the car and slid into the passenger's seat as the engine started with a snarl. The scent of new leather hit me as I inhaled. But under that was desire. It radiated from him…and from me.

Chaos was there, rising to the surface. Heat spread through my body, forcing me to clench my fist around the armrest. I closed my eyes as the car reversed in the parking lot, then lunged forward, and I sent out a prayer to get through this in one damn piece.

7

———

CARINA

We pulled up outside the FBI offices and climbed out. Agents stared as they strode past, making me feel more fucking self-conscious than I was, rocking up to a government building with a huge Wolf by my side...let alone *him*.

Phantom hadn't said a damn word to me since I'd climbed into the car, not even a *'don't touch the leather, it's new,'* remark. Just *nothing*. Seemed like it was becoming the norm where I was concerned.

Shut me out.

Ignore my presence.

I closed the car door behind me and stepped up to the curb, not bothering to wait for him. I didn't have to. As soon as I moved, he was there, stalking forward, his long legs eating the distance as we climbed the front stairs and strode through the automatic doors.

I scanned the guards at the front desk, nodding to one who seemed familiar, and stopped at the counter, unloading the stuff in my pockets before handing over my ID.

"Special Agent." The guard motioned me forward.

I lifted my arms, waiting as he waved the wand over my clothes and nodded. "You're good. But the male—"

"Is with me," I answered, giving him a ghost of a smile. "An informant."

That said it all. Informants were gold here, treated with kid gloves the majority of the time. The guard knew better than to make a fuss. He just motioned Phantom forward, but his brow rose as the mountain of a male stopped in front of him.

"Arms up."

Phantom complied, holding the guard's gaze as the wand swept over his massive arms and expansive chest.

"You're clean," the guard muttered, paling and looking away.

I moved to the elevators, my damn pulse throbbing in the back of my throat. This was a bad idea. A *really* bad idea. Harlan was acting weird as it was, without adding a possessive damn Alpha to the mix. It was going to end in bloodshed, I just knew it.

The elevator doors opened. I stepped in, with Phantom close behind. But the two guys behind us took one look at his sheer size and muttered, "We'll catch the next one."

"Whatever." I jabbed the button, closing the doors.

The numbers lit up, floor after floor.

"You're nervous."

I turned, finding his gaze directed at me. "He finally speaks."

"Why?"

"Why what? Why do you speak, or why am I nervous?"

He didn't say anything, just fucking stared at me. I shifted under his focus. That simmering heat brooded under the surface, always there, reminding me just how into him I was...*still.* I couldn't look at him, or think about him. Not his hard body, or his intense eyes, his soft lips, and big hands...*shit.*

"You're grinding your teeth. You do that when you're scared."

"Terrified, more like it," I muttered as the elevator came to a halt and the doors opened.

"Good," He answered, and strode forward out of the elevator.

Leaving me to fumble and scurry like a fucking kid behind him. I hurried down the hall, having to half-run to step around him at the last second and slow at Harlan's office.

The door was open at the conference room at the end of the hall. I gave one quick scan around me, then opened the door and stepped through.

Trace lifted her gaze behind the desk, her eyes widening at the sight of the monstrous fucking male behind me. "Carina," she hissed and shot a panicked glance over her shoulder to the closed office door.

"I know," I muttered, moving forward, keeping my voice low. "I'm sorry. I didn't know he was—"

"*He's* right behind you," Phantom growled.

This was no time to get pissy...or go back on their words. With a resigned sigh, Trace jerked her head toward the door. "You barged in, demanding to be seen. I had nothing to do with this."

"Scout's fucking honor." I crossed my heart as I passed her desk and whispered, "Thank you."

She stared at me like I'd grown an extra head.

I inhaled hard and moved to Harlan's door, gave a small knock and opened it without waiting for an invitation. If I did, then I'd be waiting forever.

Harlan lifted his head from the mountain of paperwork on his desk. One look at me as his eyes widened, then his gaze grew cold as it shifted behind me. "Chase, no...*no fucking way.*"

"Please." I lifted my hands, pleading as I stepped further inside. "Just hear me out."

There was a curl of his lips and a look of disgust. "Get that *thing* out of my office."

But Phantom didn't leave, he just closed the door behind him, closing us in.

"Don't worry about him." I went closer, reaching out to touch the edge of his desk. "I need you to listen to me. I made a mistake."

The hard shake of his head was instant as he looked back at his desk. "I don't want to hear it."

"The report from the warehouse was a lie. I made it up."

Harlan's head snapped upwards. "Bullshit. Who the fuck do you take me for? I had those tests rechecked, the blood was—"

"It wasn't hers." I straightened. "I wanted it to be, so that's what I told you. Go ahead, run a DNA check on her. You'll find it won't match. It wasn't hers, just some female Vamp at the scene."

He jerked that savage stare to Phantom, then back to me. "Why are you doing this?"

"Because it's wrong." The words resounded as I stepped closer. "It was wrong and I did it anyway. The Vampires are angry, and so is Ruth. They have influence."

There was a bark of laughter.

I rounded the desk and grabbed his hand. "They do *have* influence, Harlan. More than we're aware of. The kind you don't want to ruin your career. But if you're looking for someone to take the blame, then blame me."

"Did you kill Murphy?" He rose carefully, leaving his hand in mine. He was aware of Phantom, that I knew. Tiny flickers of his eyes scanned my face and the rest of the room.

"No," I sighed. "But I wanted to. *You* know that. He was a pig, a sexiest fucking pig who took every opportunity to make me terrified of him."

Harlan leaned closer and twisted his hand in mine. I wasn't the one clutching him anymore, he was clutching me. "Then who did?"

"I don't know," I whispered, the words heavy and hollow in my mouth as those sickening yellow eyes filled my mind.

"*Lie.* Who killed Murphy, Chase?" His gaze bored into mine.

Panic filled me, driving that thrumming in my head. *Think. Come on, Chase...fucking think.* Not the Vampires. Not my pack. There was only one other solution. The truth. "There was another Wolf," I started. "Another pack. They attacked us."

"Wolf, *Wolves*...they're all the damn same," he spat, and glare at Phantom. "Give me one damn reason why I should believe a word you say?"

He turned back to me. But there was a dangerous gleam in his gaze now as he moved closer, sliding his hand along my arm. Heat radiated off his body and that sickening need rolled around under my skin. It didn't want him, it wanted my Wolves. But Harlan didn't know that...nor did he care.

"You want me to call off the hunt, then come back. I want you here, with me. I'll make a special position for you, you can be my liaison agent, work here in my offices, and accompany me on all my out-of-town trips."

He lowered his gaze, taking in my lips, then my neck, and falling to the open neckline of my shirt. "How bad do you want this, Chase?"

How bad do I want this?

That aching pit of emptiness waited inside me. I wanted it more than anything, more than I could possibly comprehend. The last twenty-four hours had sliced me down the middle and exposed the foul, fetid parts of my nature. Love. Desperation. The fight to protect them at all costs. But there was a line they didn't cross...a line these Immortals revered more than anything.

Loyalty.

I reached up and gently removed his hand from my arm. "While I appreciate your concern, Harlan, I have to decline. I came here in good faith to let you know I lied."

His hold grew tighter, fingers digging into my flesh as he moved against me.

My breaths were a panicked rush. One glanced toward Phantom and I caught that lazy, uninterested gaze in his eyes once more. That sight alone chilled me to the bone.

"No," Harlan insisted.

"I-I lied," I stuttered, clutching at any damn straw. "I'll tell everyone, too. I'll contact Homeland, I'll go to the damn press."

Harlan curled his lips, baring his teeth.

I clawed hold of that tiny glimmer, my words a jumbled mess. "I'll tell them you forced me to lie if I have to. You forced me to work with Murphy when there were repeated offenses. Offenses *you* knew about. It'll look bad for you."

"Are you threatening me, Chase?" he growled.

He wrenched his hand from my arm as though I'd burned him. I fought the desperate need to look at Phantom and instead, focused on Harlan. "I don't want to be the bad guy here. I don't want to do any more damage than I've already done by lying to you. But you need to understand that there is no way out of this, none that will look good for you, anyway."

"Fuck you," Harlan spat, and turned away from me. "Now get the hell out of my office."

"I'm s—" I started, but the words were hollow and dead.

I was caged here. A cat on her ninth life, bound by barbed wire and starved. There was nowhere for me to go but to lash out and fight.

"Get. Out," Harlan growled, and turned away, to the spectacular view his office afforded.

I gave a slow nod and turned, catching Phantom's savage stare.

He could glare at me all he wanted.

I was done.

Lower than low. More pathetic than a fucking cockroach. I stepped to the door, yanked it open, and marched out. I felt

Trace's gaze on me as I left the office and headed for the elevators at the end of the hall.

As always, the heavy thud of Phantom's steps haunted me. Fuck, I even heard them in my sleep, thudding...*haunting*. I stopped at the elevator and hit the button, my face growing red.

He'd said nothing, not this entire damn time. Why the fuck did he come, then?

Just to watch me grovel?

The elevator doors opened and I stepped inside. My skin prickled as Phantom moved in after me. "Aren't you going to say something?"

Silence, that was all I received as the elevator sank, taking my stomach along with it. I ground my teeth and focused on getting out of there. When we exited through the foyer, the guards never said a word.

I'd half expected to be arrested and dragged upstairs. God knows I'd pushed Harlan hard enough. I strode out of the building and climbed into the passenger's seat of the Camaro. Still Phantom didn't speak, just started the car and drove us back across the bridge to the Hunting Ground.

The familiar black Jeep was parked in the empty lot. I breathed a sigh of relief at the sight and shoved open the door almost before the Camaro stopped. I needed to get away from him, from that brooding, fucking tension.

Even if it felt like I walked on the edge of a blade. Tension rolled off the Alpha, building like a terrifying storm. I didn't need to be told twice to get the hell away. I strode toward the door, punched in the code, and yanked the handle.

"Where the fuck do you think you're going?"

Jesus, he was right behind me, bearing down like a goddamn freight train. "Anywhere," I answered. "As long as it's away from you."

His savage growl was swallowed by the *thud* of the door slamming shut. I quickened my steps, trying to fight the roaring panic in my head. I'd once believed he wouldn't hurt me...but I wasn't so sure anymore. I wasn't sure about a whole lot of things.

There was a new level of savagery in Phantom, one that shone bright when he looked at me. I quickened my steps, hurrying now as I yanked open the connecting door. Desperation drove me as I scanned the space, finding Church on the sofa, hunched over a map. Arran was there, swiping sweat from his brow as he drank juice from the carton.

Vitold's voice grew louder as he rounded the end of the hallway, his phone pressed against his ear. My pulse stuttered at the sight. Relief was snatched away as my arm was grabbed and I was spun to stare into Phantom's terrifying gaze.

His big hand wrapped around my throat, fingers curled, thumb massaging my vein over and over...and over. There was an emptiness in his eyes, a cruel kind of detachment, one that made me shiver with fear.

"You think you can force me to choose between my alliances and you?" He spoke so carefully, so coldly, so *unlike him.* "You think this...*chaos* inside you is an excuse to lie and betray and *manipulate?*"

I opened my mouth to answer, but one glance at those empty eyes stopped my words. He wasn't interested in answers, not ones I had to give, anyway. I saw it now, saw what this truly was. In his mind, this was already done. *We were done.*

A tremor tore through me at the thought.

There was no excuse I could give him.

Nothing he'd allow himself to hear.

The others behind me were silent. Church shifted his stance, but the others were still, trapped by the same terror that held me here.

"I trusted you."

I closed my eyes with those words and felt my soul tear. It was a killing blow, fatal, raw, like a fist punched through my chest, claws wrapping around my heart. *I trusted you.* And this had been building between us, brewing and growling.

But there was no more faint rumbling of thunder, no more building of bruised clouds. This was the first crack of lightning…the first lash of driving rain, the tremble before the onslaught.

Still, his hand never moved from my throat. The movement of his thumb was feather-light, brushing over the jumping of my pulse. *Go ahead, hurt me,* the thought bloomed in my head. *Just do it.*

I knew what waited on the other side of this. I could see it clearly. *Blindingly clear.* Me on one side of the river…them on the other…*and never the two shall meet.* I'd be nothing but a shell when this was over, even more of an empty shell than I had been before. There would be no life in my eyes, no soul in my body. For all intents and purposes, I'd be dead.

Heart deadened, soul shredded, going through the motions until someday my body decided to give up on me, as well. Maybe I'd start drinking…maybe I'd be like dad.

"No you don't," Phantom snarled. His lips curled, hate spewing rancid and hot from his mouth. "You don't get to pull away from me."

His grip tightened around my throat, pressing against the vein, choking off my air as he impaled me with that savage stare. "You don't get to zone out here. You don't get to deflect the *fucking blow.*"

"Then do it." The words were out before I realized. "Banish me, break me, anything'd be better than *this…*"

"Phantom," Vitold pleaded, and with that one simple word, anguish ripped through me.

It wasn't just my heart on the line here. *It was all of us.* We were connected by more than this fucking shit in my chest. It was deeper than Chaos, hungrier than lust. What we had was *more.* More and more and more and *more.* Phantom's grip tightened, the air held hostage in my chest. Heat flooded my face as he lowered his, his hand still choking off my airway.

It was better this way. A *merciful* ending.

Better than a lifetime knowing what I'd lost.

"Alpha," Arran growled...his desperation resounding in my ears.

"If you only knew what I want to do to you," Phantom warned.

"Do...it." My voice was a choked whisper. "This is fucking killing me, Phantom. You won't look at me, and when you do, it's filled with hate."

Phantom lifted his head, those brown eyes now pitch black as he pressed his body against mine, hard chest smashed against my breasts. His grip eased just enough for a little rush of air. I shuddered, not from the heady, life-saving gasp, but from his rock hard erection pressing against my mound.

Heat bloomed, tearing through me like wildfire.

It wasn't just rage and death in his eyes. There was something else there, something sinister and sick. Something that made my heart beat faster than even the threat to death. *It was the threat of* him. Of his vengeance and his lust. Of his *beast*.

8

PHANTOM

"Do it," she begged me.

*Mine...*the beast roared in my head. *Need to bite...to fuck...to own...her.*

"Hurt me, send me away, I don't care anymore," she demanded with fire in her eyes. "But fucking *look* at me when you do it."

She brought me undone. I pressed my thumb against her neck, feeling the throb of her pulse spike as the image of her naked in my bed bloomed in my mind. I wouldn't be gentle... *couldn't* be gentle. Not now. Not with the beast—

"I need you to..." she started as I thrust against her. She gave a whimper as her eyes fluttered closed. "Fuck me."

But this was a dangerous moment, kill...*keep.* Train or destroy. I *never* wanted to hurt her. But she'd pushed me too hard. Seeing her standing there...*that fucking male's hands on her.*

"Did you like Harlan touching you?"

I couldn't keep the sting of jealously from my tone. She opened her eyes at the words, her brow furrowing for a second. Still the beast howled and thrashed, driving his body against the wall between us. I couldn't control him, not the need or the desperation that raged. One step forward, and she grabbed my arm to keep from falling.

She hit the wall with a *thud*. Her head smacked backwards, shock making her heart race.

"Did you like it when he looked at you like that?"

"Looked at her like *what?*" Vitold growled.

"Fucking bastard." Arran took a step toward the door.

But I didn't care about them, not in this moment. She was *all* I cared about. Gone was the woman I'd carried from the car and into my bed. Now she was a woman with consequences.

"Did you like the way he touched you?"

"I…" she started.

"Did you like knowing I was watching the two of you?" I leaned closer, driving my thighs between hers, forcing her legs apart as I leaned in to whisper. "I wanted to gut him where he stood."

Her moan deepened, hungry and urgent.

"I wanted to strip you and lay you in his fucking blood. I wanted to destroy you."

She stiffened at the words.

I grabbed the wrist on her other hand and lifted it above her head, my right hand never leaving her throat. "I still want to destroy you."

She licked her lips, her gaze drifting from mine. But it wasn't to the Wolves at her back. Not that they'd be able to stop me if I started…no, it was to the hallway. I froze, my blood running cold as I realized where she looked.

"The bedroom," she whispered, and arched her spine, pushing her breasts against me. Her hunger was thick and choking, her need just as powerful now as it'd been that night I'd taken her to my bed. "*Use* me," she whispered. "I don't care…*anything* is better than when you pull away from me."

I closed my eyes to the plea and my beast threw back his head and let out a roar. I was moving before I realized, rocking my hips, thrusting against her. Her desire bloomed sweet and poisonous in the air.

With a snarl, I wrenched my hips back and yanked her arm, forcing her to spin until she faced the wall.

"Fuck me, Phantom," Arran moaned.

I let her hand go, my fingers still gripping her throat. I liked her like this, soft and compliant, not up to her scheming and lies. I liked her *vulnerable.* "Is this what you want?"

I slid my hand over her waist and between her thighs. She bucked at my touch, her response breathless. "Yes."

My fingers found her crease. I bent my knuckles and rubbed, digging my fingertips in hard. She groaned against me, her breath making a damp cloud on the wall, just like she was damp where I manhandled her.

One hand around her throat, one burrowing at the entrance of her pussy.

My balls ached with the heaviness. "I want to be here." I leaned close and growled against her ear, driving my fingers deeper against the fabric between her thighs.

She splayed her other hand against the wall.

"And Vitold to watch while I take you."

A shudder coursed through her. The Wolf grew still behind us. He didn't think I'd noticed how she gravitated toward him, didn't think I paid any attention to them at all. I'd seen it...seen how he looked at her, how that fucking defiance had flared in his eyes when I'd given the command...*no fucking her.*

They'd all hated me in that moment.

Almost as much as they hated me now.

I lowered my head, my lips brushing the side of her neck as I growled. "I want to be hilt deep inside you, fucking you from behind. I want to hear you cry with pain...and then with pleasure."

She thrust against my fingers, her aching desire thick in the air.

"But I won't," I continued, drawing my hands from between her legs and around her throat. "Because you don't deserve it. You need to learn your place here, Carina. We are a pack. We live as a pack, we fight as a pack…we *fuck* as a pack, and right now, you're on the outside looking in."

I stepped away from her, watching as her knees trembled and then buckled against the wall. She turned, rage flaring in those wide brown eyes. She saw me now, saw me for the monster I truly was.

There was a flinch in her stare, a furrowing of her brow. Disappointment and rage were burning in the background, just like Marian…

Marian.

The memory was a blow to my fucking chest, forcing me to step away.

"You…*bastard,*" she spat.

I wanted to feel pain with the words. But instead, I just nodded, resignation quietening the beast in my head, for a moment at least. "Now you finally understand."

With that, I turned, strode toward the connecting door, and punched right through the fucking thing. Wood splintered in an instant as the door slammed against the wall with a *boom.* But I was already gone, striding from the fucking place, leaving the choking scent of her need behind.

I shoved through the entrance door and crossed the parking lot to the Camaro. Lights blinked, locks disengaged. I climbed in and started the engine before backing out, then shot forward.

The tires caught the asphalt as I spun the wheel. I needed to get away from the place, needed to get away from *her.* That fucking woman pushed me more than anyone had ever pushed me before. She infuriated me, drove me to madness.

I shifted in the seat, reaching down to yank the crotch of my jeans.

Need her…her scent, her touch…her body.

"Yeah well, that's not happening."

Want her...now.

"Not. Happening." I jerked my gaze to the rear-view mirror, and met the silver glare of the beast.

Agony carved through my chest, like the savage rake of claws. I groaned, gripped the wheel, and leaned forward.

Want. Her, the beast warned. There was no arguing with him, not where Carina was involved. He'd wanted her from that first moment in the warehouse, and he wanted her still. He couldn't get enough, *never* enough. I fought the urge to turn the wheel and drive like a maniac back to the club. She'd hate me, hit me. She'd spit in my face and dig her nails into my back.

But she'd let me take her to my bed, that I knew without a doubt. She'd let me fuck her, let me lick between those thighs. She'd let me mark her all over again...and again...and again.

My cock pulsed against my zipper, throbbing with the ache.

Until my phone rang.

I pulled it free from my pocket and hit the button. "Mojin."

"Wolf." He muttered, sounding bored. "Thought I better give you a call."

"What the fuck is it?" I growled.

"Testy...testy," he drawled. "I see you're playing hard to get, how's that going for you, by the way?"

"Fae, I'm about five seconds from driving this phone up your ass," I snarled.

He let out a deep chuckle that just pissed me off even more.

"I caught a scent over in Highlands," he went on. "Female... pregnant...and reeks like a fucking male Alpha Wolf."

I winced and yanked the wheel toward the bridge, my heart hammering. "Highlands?" I growled, my mind racing.

There was a muffled sound in the background, followed by a *thump.*

"What the fuck was that?"

"Well, when I tracked her energy, it led me to another pack. I just so happened to follow one as he returned back to his *shithole.*"

I punched my foot against the accelerator and the Camaro leaped forward toward a blue Defender. "And this male…"

"Isn't the Alpha, if that's what you're wondering."

Still, the thought of her with another male, swollen, pregnant. *Sonofabitch.* "I'm on my way," I barked, wrenching the wheel back into my lane, and floored the accelerator. . "Text me the address."

That low, dangerous chuckle filled my ear. "Already on the way…and Phantom…"

"Yeah?"

"Do yourself a favor, and let the pretty little agent back into your bed. No one likes you when you're pissy, let alone *horny* and pissy."

I clenched the phone and opened my mouth to feed the Fae an earful, but the line was already dead. Instead, there was a small *beep, signaling an incoming text.* I yanked the phone away, dividing my attention between the screen and the road, and pressed the address, pulling it up on the map.

"Mess with my fucking sister," I muttered, and pushed the Camaro harder, tearing past a police cruiser driving the other way. "I'll fucking end you all."

They could haunt our streets all they wanted. But neither the fucking cops nor the FBI had a hope of running us out of the city again. My thoughts turned to Harlan as I hit the off-ramp and headed for the fringes of the city.

The bastard had a hard-on a mile fucking long for her, that was easy to see. I'd smelled his lust as soon as she'd entered, and it had nothing to do with the Fae curse in her chest and *everything* to do with her.

But that desire was one-sided. I'd caught nothing but anger and the rancid stench of desperation from her. She was sick with it, fevered and desperate, especially after last night with the Vampires.

I hadn't known they were going to hit her. Scare her, yes. Make her realize how badly she'd fucked up, yes. But that redhead had a temper. Still, I didn't like it. Not the way the blow had sounded on her cheek…or the bruise it'd left behind.

The image stayed with me as I followed the roads to the address Mojin had sent me and pulled up outside a row of old abandoned buildings. Construction fencing encroached on the sidewalk of one of the sandstone buildings, but it was the darkened alley between the two which drew me closer. The black Explorer sat alongside the curb. I glanced into the shadows and inhaled the stench of piss and sweat…*and Wolf.*

Not *my* Wolf, that was for sure. I headed into the alley, making my way past a homeless woman asleep under a looming mess of half a tent and four cardboard boxes. Her feet stuck out of the end, and one black shoe had fallen from her foot, leaving the filthy striped sock exposed.

But she wasn't the one I wanted.

The fetid scent of another pack grew stronger the closer I got, and along with the raw, pungent aroma of male was another. A sweeter scent, one that clung to my nose and made my Wolf whimper.

I knew that scent.

Knew it better than I knew any other female.

I shoved the half-open door aside and stepped into the building.

"In here," the Dark Fae called.

I scanned the mess of discarded tin cans, food wrappings, and rubbish, and strode through the narrow passageway. The place reeked of sex and death. The only thing worse than touching the damn place was knowing my sister stayed here.

"Get the fuck off me."

The command came from further along the hallway. The

beast rose swiftly with the sound. I opened my hand as claws grew. Mojin was standing in my way, blocking me with his massive shoulders and long black coat.

"Let me see him." I forced my way into the cramped space.

The damn bedroom was no bigger than a closet, but blankets were piled high, blankets that reeked of her…*and him.*

Mojin turned at the sound of my voice and stepped to the side, letting me see the pathetic excuse for a Wolf. The bastard sat on the floor, his hands restrained behind his body, his bare legs crossed in front of him. His eyes widened when he looked up and saw me.

"I warned you," Mojin muttered to the Wolf. "I told you you'd want to tell me where she was and that you wouldn't like option two."

The bastard paled and drew his knees closer.

I couldn't stop myself, not already riding that close to the killing edge…not after the way I'd left Carina. I reached down, grasped the Wolf by the back of the neck, and yanked him to his feet. "The female, where is she?"

He couldn't answer, not for a second. Instead, he just stared before finally whispering, "I know who you are."

I leaned closer. "Good, then it'll save me from threatening you. I'm not in the mood for threats."

Danger lurked in those words.

Danger he didn't hear.

Or didn't pay attention to.

"Where is she?" I repeated, clenching my grip around his neck. My nails punctured the skin, leaving trails of blood to slide down to his shoulders. But he barely noticed.

Instead, the pathetic excuse for an Immortal just whimpered. "I…I don't know."

I bared my teeth. "I'm going to ask you one last time… *where…the fuck…is…she?"*

The guy shuddered and shook his head. "She doesn't tell me where she goes, she just leaves me here."

I let out a growl and felt his Wolf cower with the sound. What kind of pathetic fucking male cowers when his mate is in danger? "You impregnated my sister...and leave her to hunt on her own?"

He flinched at the words.

Anger rose like a tidal wave inside me.

A dark wave of savagery.

Of bloodlust.

And vengeance.

I lashed out with my other hand, my claws sank into his flesh. The warmth was instant and the sharp smell of blood followed. I couldn't stop myself. Couldn't stop the beast from doing what he wanted to do.

Bite.

Savage.

Kill...

9

CARINA

I trembled against the wall, burning and *seething*. Aching more than I'd ever ached before. But it was a hollow ache, empty and alone. Unsatisfied, unworthy.

"Carina," Arran called.

I couldn't look at them, couldn't see the sadness in their eyes. Pity, that's what I'd find. I lowered my hand to the wall and pushed off it. The movement rubbed my swollen lips together as I stepped forward. The last thing I needed to feel was that. I closed my eyes for a heartbeat.

"Carina," Vitold whispered, stepping toward me.

I flinched and lifted my hand. "Don't." My voice was husky and raw. "Don't come near me."

I swallowed that burning need and took a step as the green Unseelie glow in my chest throbbed and ached. Hunger consumed me as I made my way along the hallway and stepped inside Vitold's room.

The musky scent of Wolf filled me. It was everywhere, on the sheets, in the air. On me. I closed the bedroom door behind me as a tremor tore free. *He did that on purpose.* The words resounded in my head. *He did this to me.*

To hate me was one thing.

But to be so intentionally cruel?

I clenched my fists and screamed until my throat burned. I screamed my hate, my desperation, letting the shrill sound fill the room, and then I stopped.

Gasping breaths consumed me. I shoved away from the door and stumbled to the bathroom, blinking in the harsh white glare ads I flipped the light on. Jesus, I was a fucking mess. I probed my bruised cheek with shaking fingers, the purple showing through the layers of foundation. I was violent and bitter, ugly inside and out.

One hard swallow, then I twisted the faucet, taking in gulps of water from my cupped hands before I straightened. Flashes of Phantom's face burned in my mind. Curled lips. Silver eyes. Rage and desire, all wrapped up in a brutal mountain of a man.

A Wolf.

No, not just *a* Wolf, *an Alpha.*

Chaos pulsed and glowed under my shirt. A sob lodged in the back of my throat as I lifted my hand to my neck. A shudder ripped through me as I touched my breast. It was more than sex, more than desire that he'd taken from me. He'd taken the one thing I'd been searching for my entire life.

The need to belong was more than hunger.

More than thirst.

It drove me to insanity.

It was there I lingered. There that it bloomed like a deadly rose inside my mind. I stepped away from the bathroom sink, tearing my gaze from the haunted stare in the mirror, and turned for the door. I had to get out of here, out of these walls. And away from *his* memory.

The hallway was a blur. I knew they were there, waiting. Church stepped to the side, carrying the broken connecting door. Concern flared. "Where are you going?"

"Out," I growled.

"Do you want comp—"

I stopped him cold with a savage glare and stepped to the side. He flinched, hurt flaring in those blue eyes, but I couldn't stop myself. I wanted to run, get away from them as fast as I could. I couldn't breathe here, couldn't think. All I could do was *feel.*

"Carina, *wait.*" Church moved fast and grabbed my arm. "You're angry. I can see it in your eyes, you want to hit something, hurt something." He pulled me closer, those strong fingers like a vise. "Hurt me if you need to lash out, just don't go."

"Hurt you?" I snapped. *"Hurt you?* I don't want to fucking hurt *anyone,* don't you get that?" I yanked my arm from his hold.

His blue eyes darkened with sadness. I couldn't stand to look at them, couldn't stand to feel like this, not with them so close and yet *untouchable.* "Just leave me alone, Church. I need to breathe...I can't do that with all you here."

Feeling that chasm inside me.

That pit of darkness that waited.

Opening its arms to welcome me.

I shoved out the door and stumbled into the sunlight, but I couldn't feel its warmth, just the cold, as I stared at the empty spot where the Camaro had been just minutes before.

*You bastard...*the words resounded in my head. But it was that cruelty in his eyes I couldn't forget. The look of a man too far gone to care. I wasn't responsible for it all, but I'd done my part, a part I now regretted more than ever.

I wrenched my gaze from the empty parking spot as the sound of footsteps echoed from behind the closed door. Darkness whispered to me and that ache inside my chest followed, driving me to turn and hurry along the side of the club, then along the front.

I wanted the hate, the edge. I needed my pain to bleed, then maybe I wouldn't feel so empty. I stopped at the edge of the building, to the shadows growing between the buildings…and the Fae who waited. Instead, I glanced over my shoulder, finding the Unseelie compound in the distance. High razor wire fences and a haze of malevolent energy surrounded the place.

The same energy that spilled from the passageway beside the club…drawing me toward the back of the building and toward the Dark City.

That's what the Wolves called it. The hidden, hungry portal used by the Unseelie. The gateway to whatever darkness waited for them in the world between worlds. It called me, that…*hunger. It* called to that glow in my chest, the malicious greed that raced through my mind.

I took a step, sinking into the shadows and leaving the sunlight behind.

Green glow pulsed from under my shirt. My breaths were hard and sharp, making my steps stutter. But I pushed on, making my way to the back of the club, then down the hard decline to the abandoned Unseelie street. Towering cement carcasses stretched ahead of me, and to my left. Buildings that had long been forgotten…if any had even felt the spark of life to begin with. Exposed metal was sticking out of broken walls like spines, gaping empty doorways like midnight eyes.

This place was a monstrous ruin. Abandoned. It was a half-built beast of Unseelie shadows that consumed the light. I kept walking, my steps slower now as I scanned the area for any hint of movement, and from one of the buildings there was a faint pulse of emerald light.

I slowed at the sight, taking in the stony ruin, until a spear of pain cut across my chest.

"Fuck," I moaned, and pressed my hand against my breast.

Only the ache grew bolder, tearing through my heart and reaching down into my belly. I doubled over with the pain, clutching my middle, and let out a deep moan. "Enough," I gasped, and closed my eyes.

But the deep Unseelie hue called me, and inside me, Chaos answered.

I can help you, the seductive call rose. *Make it right with the Wolves, protect the Vampires. All you have to do is give in to me, Carina. Just...give...in.*

That *throb...throb...throb...*beat in time with the pulsing glow. I opened my eyes as the pain eased, and I slowly straightened. Something else came out of the pain, a deep, carnal fervor, one that spread down between my thighs.

That hunger was back in an instant, tormenting and heated, and inside that torment came the image of Phantom. *I licked it... so it's mine,* the Alpha growled.

"Yes," I gave into that emotion.

Need rocked me with the pleasure. *I wanted to destroy you...I still want to destroy you...*Phantom's words made the ache come alive. I burned with that savagery, that unbridled hunger. Pure fucking Alpha.

Still that green Unseelie glow grew brighter, forcing me forward. Frigid air brushed my skin with the lightest touch. The closer I came to the ruined building, the colder it became, until I stepped through the open doorway, shivering.

In the middle of the concrete shell, the lush glow pulsed and ebbed. Shadows and the deep emerald glow fought to consume the space. I clenched my insides and stepped further inside, catching my breath as desire caressed me.

Chaos shifted under my skin, silent and brooding.

A flicker of fear shot through me at that thought. She was always forceful, always demanding and insistent, always *wanting.* But now she lingered in the shadows, like a predator in wait. Power brushed against me like a lover's touch.

The caress found the tips of my breasts and delved between my thighs.

I want to be here. The touch pressed between my thighs as Phantom's faint words drifted around me.

I spun, fear chasing lust away for an instant. But there was no one there. Not Phantom...not any of my Wolves. My pounding heart was deafening as I turned back to that ravenous throb of light.

I want Vitold to watch while I take you.

The words spilled out from the green glow as that unseen touch came back. I licked my lips and took a step forward, my boots skimming the edges of the emerald light. "Phantom?"

Yes, Chaos whispered.

Her voice filled me, carried me, forcing my feet to move as I stepped closer.

Power reached for me, clawing my arms, pulling me deeper as that ravenous urgency grew. Anguish and pleasure waited for me on the other side of the glow, a glow that called to that voice inside my head.

Take me, Chaos moaned. *Now.*

The Unseelie world tasted me, power licking along my skin, finding the remnants of Phantom's touch. With a guttural growl, it reached for me, dragging me deeper into its hold. I tried to stop my body from shuddering, tried to stop that need from igniting between my thighs, but I was helpless to stop it and, as I stepped into the belly of the Unseelie light, my body quaked and shuddered as I climaxed.

"Wait," I cried out, and pushed back against the light. *"No."*

The power released its hold in an instant, leaving me to stumble backwards In a rush. I tripped, my hands windmilling in the air until I found my balance. I stood frozen, watching the center of that green glow darken to black.

"Jesus." I leaned forward and gasped for air.

My body pulsed and quaked, my breaths deepened as I clamped my thighs closed. "What the fuck *was* that?"

Quakes tore through me as I straightened. I staggered

backwards, reaching out to steady myself as I stumbled through the doorway, not daring to take my eyes off that darkened glow. The green was so faint now, barely there. But I still felt that hunger, it brooded and simmered, waiting for me to come closer once more.

"No fucking way." I turned and hurried forward...and came face to face with the biggest silver-haired Wolf I'd ever seen.

The beast stepped forward from the end of the Dark City. The Wolf's fur glistened and dripped with water. *The river,* the words rose to the surface of my mind. His long, slow movements made me stop. I knew these beasts now, knew that disinterested, dreamy gaze was anything but. A blast of power hit me as the Wolf came closer, making me catch my breath.

Panic found me, turning up the thunder of my pulse.

I tore my gaze from the lumbering beast and looked behind him to the only way out of there. But the moment I looked away, the beast started to shift. I'd never seen anything like him. His long strides never missed a beat, he just kept walking forward as he slowly rose to two human legs.

His body stretched upward, morphing into a sleek, powerful male as the coarse fur disappeared into his skin. He was older, with some gray hair touching his temples. But his body didn't have an inch of fat. He was muscular and lean and as my gaze lowered...I saw he was *big.*

"Who the fuck are you?" I muttered, tearing my gaze from his cock to those commanding eyes once more.

"You reek of *him,*" the male growled, never stopping...never slowing. "And need."

His gaze drifted over my body, lingering between my thighs.

There was a sneer of satisfaction, of chilling brutality. "He was always a selfish sonofabitch."

I forced myself to move as he reached for me, tearing myself from the power of this Wolf and this place. But I was too slow and weak. He lunged before I could turn and his cruel fingers dug into the back of my neck.

The tips of his claws pierced the skin as he yanked me forward. My spine arched backwards as he forced my gaze to his and snarled, "Tell me, *mortal*. Where the fuck is my mate?"

10

CARINA

"*Tell me! Where the fuck is she?*" The silver-haired Wolf yanked me close.

So close, I felt the heat of his breath and saw the madness in his eyes, shimmering under the silver shine. I tried to fight him, tried to scream. But those magnetic eyes held me transfixed. Power thrummed through me, a remnant of desire...drawing his gaze slowly down my body.

Confusion claimed him as Chaos shifted inside my chest.

Power rippled from him, terrifying and consuming.

Colder than Phantom, more beast than I'd ever felt before.

Dangerous, that's what he was. Cruel and dangerous. My pulse raced at the thought.

His nostrils flared, drawing my scent deeper. There was a curl of his lips, then that savage gleam in his gaze hardened. He grasped my shirt and, with one savage yank, tore the buttons open, exposing the tops of my breasts and the Unseelie green glow under my bra.

I screamed at the savagery and lashed out, driving my fist against his face.

The blow took him by surprise as the Unseelie glow in my chest kicked like a damn mule, tearing me from his hold.

His claws raked the back of my neck, stinging as I fell and hit the ground hard.

He just stood there as I scurried sideways, the scowl on his face deepening as he looked from me...and at the ruins all around us. "What are you?"

I shoved against the ground and looked toward the empty building where the malevolent green glow had pulsed moments before.

"Answer me," he barked, then stilled. His nostrils flared before those chilling silver eyes slowly widened. "What the fuck *are* you?"

It was like he'd only now noticed me, a mortal standing in the middle of this bestial midnight place, a place filled with shadows and lust.

"What are you?" he repeated.

Panic dragged me back to that night at the farmhouse once more. The night Murphy had waited in the darkness...the night before he'd been torn to shreds and left at the club. Hard breaths consumed me as I stumbled backwards with a panicked glance at the slope up to the outside world and I screamed, *"VITOLD!"*

"Calling for your Wolves?" the bastard sneered, and took a step toward me.

"ARRAN! CHURCH!" The howls burned my throat.

"They can't hear you, and they won't come for you."

I shook my head and stumbled backwards, my shirt flapping wildly. But I didn't care what he looked at...I cared about getting out of here alive. "You don't want to do this."

"Really? I think I do. What the fuck are you? Why do you smell like a mortal but bear the mark of the Dark Fae?"

Keep him talking. "Why are you here?" Anger pushed past the fear. "Phantom will—"

"That sniveling runt?" he laughed, then stilled, his gaze lingering on my breasts.

Calculating. Cruel. I could almost see the foul thoughts in his head. "Where is she?" he demanded again, only this time his voice was deeper, more dangerous. "Where is my mate? I know she's been here."

"I don't know who the fuck *you* are…or who you're talking about."

He just smirked, those wicked canines growing over his lips. "Then maybe I should introduce myself," he growled, slowed his steps for a second, and lunged.

Chaos ripped from my chest with the movement. Shadows and a green glare burst from me with a sonic *boom!* I flew backwards as the Wolf was hit. Air was all I felt until I smacked the ground hard. But this time I couldn't move.

Darkness surrounded me, seeping from my skin like poison.

Sleep now, Chaos whispered. *I'll take it from here.*

I tried to force myself awake, tried to push upwards and fight. But the green Unseelie glow surrounded me. I heard a grunt, then a groan, and the slow drag of someone climbing to their feet as emptiness cocooned me.

Such beautiful chaos you create, Carina. It must be the Fae in you. Faint words resounded in my head.

Flickers of light invaded.

Sparks igniting in the dark.

The heavy thud of my heart was a fist buried deep. A fist of glass, and with each brutal thud, I was cut a little bit more.

I whimpered with the agony and forced my eyes open. For a second, I didn't know where I was…didn't remember. With a groan, I rolled onto my side and pushed against the ground.

What the fuck happened?

I tried to remember where I was, but the towering concrete walls gave me nothing. I pushed upwards on shaking arms and staggered to my feet. Something vague moved through my mind, a memory of empty half-finished buildings like these.

I moved on instinct, stumbling forward before my knees gave way once more.

Where the fuck is my mate?

The roar in my head made me flinch. I shoved upwards and spun, searching the empty road behind me. The Wolf...*the Wolf...THE WOLF.*

Images roared to the surface, driving me forward. I tripped, caught myself, and lunged forward again. Pain ravaged my chest as I hit the steep slope. I ran for my life, clawing the ground and driving my body upwards. Asphalt skidded out from under my boots. I whimpered and kept going, inching upwards until I was out.

But not out of the shadows. Sunlight waited for me in the distance. I lunged toward it, punching my boots against the ground, and tore alongside the club. I knew where I was now, knew what had driven me to that dark place.

And what had driven me out of it.

I reached out, grasped the corner of the building, and threw myself around the corner, straight into a wall of muscle.

"Whoa there!" Church barked as he spun, grabbing me as I bounced. "Carina? What the fuck—"

He froze, taking in my face and my torn-open shirt. His gaze shifted behind me, to the shadows.

"There's a man...a *Wolf*," I cried. "He came after me...Church, he—"

His lips curled, baring his teeth. A barbaric look consumed his blue eyes. "VITOLD!" he roared.

There were others, men who were moving boxes to outside the club on hand trucks.

"What the fuck is it?" Vitold grumbled, striding out the open doors of the club. Amazement filled his gaze as it narrowed on me, his focus shifting to my torn blouse...and exposed breasts.

He flinched at the sight and jerked his gaze to mine. "What the *fuck* happened?!"

"Finis, *that's what happened,*" Church barked, and yanked out his phone. "I can smell him all over her."

My knees were trembling, terror claimed my throat again as Vitold came closer. "Carina? What happened?" My Russian grasped my arms and pulled me to his chest.

I couldn't answer, the words unable to find a way around the lump lodged tight in my throat, but a sob tore free, sounding wounded and raw.

"Did he...did he hurt you?" The words were quiet.

I knew what he was asking...*did he rape me? Did he ruin me?* The idea of that was too much to bear. Tears slipped form my eyes as I shook my head. "No." The choked word was thick and painful.

Church barked his rage into the phone. *"He was fucking here, Phantom!* In *our* house. He...he hurt Carina."

Silence consumed the Wolf.

Silence here...and on the other end of the phone.

"Phantom?" Church muttered and scowled. "Did you hear what I said?"

The screen was dark when he lowered his hand. No caller... maybe he hadn't heard...*maybe he didn't care?* I lowered my head as sobs wracked my body, and gripped my torn shirt together.

"Where, Carina?" Church tried to keep the bite of anger from his tone. "Where was he?"

I lifted a shaking hand, my fingernails crusted with dirt as I pointed to the corner of the building. "Dark City."

He scowled, glancing at the shadows. "He was with the Fae?"

I shook my head. "Followed me. He came after me."

"Carina?" Arran called me carefully. "I felt you...what's going on?"

"Finis was here," Vitold snarled.

"Finis was here?"

"That's what he said," Church growled as he strode forward. "Vitold, with me. Arran, do *not* let her out of your damn sight."

Vitold dropped his hands from around me as I shook my head. "No, Church, don't, he—"

That Wolf was an Alpha...*no*, he was more than an Alpha. *An Alpha among Alphas.* He was powerful, too powerful. "He'll kill you."

But my words made no impact as Church and Vitold leaped forward, taking off in a sprint. "Call for the others!" Church roared over his shoulder.

"Where the fuck is Phantom?" Arran yelled after Church.

But it was too late, they were already gone, tearing around the front of the building to disappear into the shadows. This was all my fault. All *my damned fault.* If I hadn't gone off like that. If I hadn't...

"Mojin. Yeah, it's me. Finis was here. I don't know, man. I just..." Arran lifted his gaze to me as tears slipped down my cheeks. His skin paled as he caught sight of my torn shirt and exposed bra. "You'd better get here fast, brother...and bring the others."

I turned away from those careful eyes.

Turned away as the delivery men came close and spoke to Arran.

I wanted to go inside, wanted to lock the doors. I wanted to crawl into the shower and never get out.

What the fuck are you? I froze with the sound of his voice in my head. I could still feel his hands on me, his fingers crawling over my breasts. His gaze, lingering, seeing me...*really seeing me.* The scream of tires made me flinch and whimper. Arran spun as I lifted my gaze to the midnight beast racing toward us.

The black Camaro being driven by a madman.

Smoke billowed from the rubber as Phantom took the corner hard at the end of the street and hurtled toward us.

"Holy fuck," Arran muttered and stepped away from me,

moving carefully, his gaze riveted on the beast of a car as it skidded to a stop, crosswise in the middle of the street.

The driver's door was thrown open.

Phantom was all I saw.

He was bigger than wrath.

Bigger than death.

Bigger than anything I'd ever known as he plunged toward me.

My stomach dropped at the sight. I cowered from him as he towered over me, crying out as I was grabbed and lifted, my body smashed against his powerful chest. His hands were everywhere, his voice murmuring over and over and for a second, I couldn't catch the words.

Numbness.

Shock.

They slipped away from me, letting his voice invade my head.

"Thank God...thank God...thank God..." he repeated, his fingers digging into my hair and sliding down my back, pressing me against him.

For a second, it was too much, too male, too Wolf...I pushed against him, bucking and fighting. The instinct to survive tore to the surface, until my mind clicked. *It was Phantom.*

It was Phantom.

IT WAS PHANTOM.

My blows became grasps, clawing him harder against me, lowering my head as a wretched groan burst free. "Phantom...*Phantom...*"

"I'm right here," he croaked. "I'm right here. I've got you. I've got you, Carina."

A dam burst inside me, unleashing all the torment and terror.

"I've got you," he repeated. "He can't hurt you, not anymore, not while I'm here."

He held me for a minute, his hands never stopping running down my back and over my shoulders, until finally he pulled away, looking deep into my eyes as he bent down.

"I'm right here," his deep voice resonated. "I'm not letting you go."

But he froze, his eyes on my torn-open blouse. Something shifted in his gaze, something I'd seen earlier. A sickness...and wrath. Raw and terrifying. I remembered the way the gray-haired Wolf spoke of him, calling him a *runt* and a *sonofabitch*. Almost like he knew him...almost like they knew each other well. "Who was he to you?"

Phantom lifted his hand, his fingers brushing the opening of my blouse. Those eyes roamed over me as his nostrils flared wide, drawing in every hint of the other Alpha's scent on my skin.

"Phantom," I spoke again. "I want to know."

"He was once a father to me..." He met my eyes. "Now he will die."

Die?

He dropped his hands and stepped away. One glance at Arran. "I want her inside. Mojin?"

"On the way."

A nod was all he gave before he looked at me once more. "Stay with Arran, do not leave his side. Promise me?"

I couldn't say anything, my mind spinning out of control.

"Carina, *promise me.*"

"I promise."

"Guard her with your fucking life, Wolf," he demanded before stepping backwards, then turning and lunging, leaving the thudding sound of his boots behind.

In the wake of his departure, it all came crashing down. Finis was here...Finis was here...*and he'd almost had me.* My knees buckled under the thought.

"Hey there." Arran was there in a heartbeat, grabbing me around the waist, holding me close.

I turned into his embrace and wound my arms around his neck. "Jesus, Arran...*Jesus.*"

I'd never been a woman to fall apart. Never been so damn weak. I was cold and ruthless. My badge was my purpose, my soul's needs were the farthest from my mind. I was nothing more than vengeance, nothing more than a one-way train to retribution. I'd been a shell of a person. I saw that now. A carcass with no heart. But not anymore.

Now all I felt was my heart.

And it ached and throbbed like I'd never felt before.

"He'll hurt them."

"Finis?" Arran held me against his chest. "One-on-one maybe...but we're a pack, remember?" He eased away and lifted my chin. Tears slipped down my cheeks, slick and wet. "And a pack *always* has each other's backs."

Truth welled in those brown eyes. He forced a slow, sad smile and turned his head, giving commands to the delivery men. I closed my eyes and gripped him tighter, feeling the warmth of his chest against my bare skin.

"There's something that's bugging me..." Arran murmured as the sound of roller doors slammed down on empty trucks. "How the hell did you get away?"

I lifted my gaze, the truth a blur of nothing.

Darkness.

Chaos.

Amongst it all, power I'd never felt before.

Consuming. Changing. *Malicious and evil* as terror moved through me as I answered, "I don't remember."

11

PHANTOM

He'd had her...*touched her*...bared her fucking body to his foul goddamn gaze.

I growled at the thought of that.

Of *him* looking at her...

Just like he'd looked at Marian.

The beast unleashed his rage. *I'll fucking kill him. I'll tear him apart. Like I should've done when I had the fucking chance!*

The howl was brutal and consuming, booming like thunder inside my head until I could barely fucking think. And I needed to think. Needed to see...needed to focus on anything but the crimson hue that clouded my vision.

But the beast was all I could feel, his hate and torment all-consuming, bleeding red into the shadows of the Dark City.

The killing edge rose inside me. I was so close to tearing everything apart. So close to coming completely undone. I charged alongside the Hunting Ground, my steps booming before I leaped into the Dark City and hit the empty cracked asphalt streets with a *thud*.

His stench was fucking there, raw and pungent, like bleach in the back of my throat.

"Phantom!" Church called, then stopped when he saw me.

Hard, savage breaths ravaged my chest as I turned toward my second. For an instant, I couldn't see him, all I saw was male…male around Carina's scent. *Mine,* the beast staked his claim. *She is fucking mine.* Claws pierced my palm, but still I clenched my fist tighter, driving the sharp tips deeper. The hot, coppery stench of my own blood filled my nose.

"Phantom?" My second was more cautious this time. He swallowed hard and took a slow step closer. Still I flinched with the movement, wrenching my gaze toward the buildings behind him.

Vitold charged from the ruins, his gaze unfocused, lips curled, teeth bared. Hunting. That urgency burned inside me. I blinked and tried to force the beast back from the precipice, and slowly my blood-washed world faded back to normal. "Can you track him?" My voice was guttural and strange.

A shake of Vitold's head was a punch to my gut.

"He's gone." Church sucked in hard breaths and answered. "The scent is…fading."

His eyes were wild, panicked and incensed. *We were all incensed.* Fragments of the past rose as I slowed my steps and scanned the buildings. "He has to be here."

"If he is, we'll find him."

I swiveled to the deep snarl that echoed like thunder. Shrike strode from the darkness, coming from nowhere. "Wolf." He gave a nod before his gaze slipped past me.

I swiveled in an instant as a dark, menacing touch caressed my skin, inciting my beast. But it was Mojin who'd come behind me, striding forward with an infernal fucking gaze. He took one look at me and winced. But there was no snarky remark this time from the Unseelie…no, this time he was all business.

"We'll find him," Mojin growled. "And when we do…"

"He's mine," I commanded. *"No one* touches him."

A sting cut through the air. I didn't have to turn my head to know who it was. Church swallowed hard and stared at me. They *all* stared at me.

Easy.

I focused on the cold, fetid air, dragging it deep into my lungs, letting it fill that void inside me. That emptiness that hungered and starved...that beast who waited in the shadows. But he wouldn't wait forever.

"Do it," I growled, and turned to Shrike. "Expose every fucking corner, reveal every fucking lie. If he's here, I want him found, Shrike. *I need him found.*"

"I will, brother." The Dark Fae came nearer.

Darkness clung to him. Shadows danced around his body, swirling around his boots as he slowly stepped closer. He lifted his hands, palms up, then in the space between breaths, *became* those shadows.

Blackness became him. No longer a man, no, Shrike was all Fae. All death. All destruction. Pools of midnight stared back at me and in them, I saw my true reflection.

Just the boy whimpering in the darkness.

Just the boy abandoned by his pack.

Phantom, the woman's plea reached from the past. *You have to run.*

A shudder ripped through me as the Dark Fae in front of me blinked. The shadows spread, darkening this world inch by inch. Church stepped backwards, his eyes growing wide. But the Russian just stood his ground and lowered his head, a brutal sound tearing from his lips. Battle-scarred and desperate to fight.

I could see what she wanted in him, in the Wolf who'd fought a pack to save her life. I tore my gaze from my third as the warrior Mojin slowly stepped past me.

I didn't want to fight a pack in this moment.

Just one Wolf.

One who'd had destruction coming for a very long time.

No, the pup in me whimpered. *I can't leave you, Mom.*

I tried to force the past back as that sinister Unseelie sickness spread outwards. It spilled through the buildings and along the streets, tainting the air with the fetid stench of the unsanctified. It tasted like blood. Old blood, foul and rotting. Brackish and bitter, stagnant and ancient. I tried to swallow the taste, tried to breathe while my gut clenched and my will trembled.

The air around me snarled.

I lowered my head as my beast sniffed and grew still. Danger stalked us through these abandoned streets. The Dark Fae's power was demonic and debased. It grew and grew and grew, until it was all I could feel.

I bared my teeth and let out a warning growl.

My beast watched him with a guarded gaze.

But there was no pulling the Unseelie power back once it was unleashed. No *undoing* what had been done and as I focused on the male in front of me—the one with arms out wide and a midnight stare—I knew that *creature* was better by my side than in my goddamn way.

The ground trembled and shook. Cracks widened to the left of me, racing across the space until the quake finally eased.

"He's not here." The creature who was Shrike spoke.

The sound echoed and stretched, like it moved not through the air *but between worlds.*

"He *was* here," I forced.

"Seems like he got what he came for…*and then some.*"

I searched the endless pools of his eyes. "What does that mean?"

"Chaos." The creature smiled. "Chaos found him. He won't be coming back here anytime soon. But Wolf…" black fangs shone as the Unseelie creature grinned. "You might want to take care of your woman."

Take care of her? The beast in me snarled.

Shadows pulled away from the edges of the Dark City, like the male in front of me had summoned them back home, and as they sank into his body, I realized *he was their home.* White bled into his midnight eyes, the pink blush of skin appeared once more.

"You're welcome to use the portal," Shrike spoke, and there was a flicker of something in his face.

A knowing...a *breathing.* Through the space between us, a connection rose. Brother to brother. Fae and Wolf. But it never invaded, just lingered, waiting for me to reach out with the power of my beast and take what was offered.

My Wolf gave a sharp whine before I pushed my energy outwards, reaching and accepting what was offered. An image rose inside my head. This time, not of the past, *but of the future.* Desire slammed into me, knocking me backwards.

I caught my breath and let out a hiss.

Shrike smiled and pulled his power away, drawing it back into his body with the remnants of the Unseelie darkness. "Your fight is ours, Phantom," the powerful Fae murmured. "Whatever you require."

"He's here somewhere, over in the city." I declared, and glanced at Church and Vitold. "I won't leave a building fucking standing."

Shrike gave a slow nod. "I expected nothing less."

I cut a glance at Church. "Send out the call...*we're going hunting.*"

Church took a hard breath.

Vitold flinched.

But the Fae in front of me...just smiled that terrifying Unseelie smile.

Purpose filled me.

"Mojin, send out the call. Coordinate with the Wolves. I'll be with Phantom" Shrike commanded as he strode toward me, digging in his pocket for keys. "Only one condition Wolf, I'm driving."

Church's brow rose as concern flared in his eyes. But I was already turning to the powerful Unseelie warrior and let my beast growl. "As long as you can keep up."

"Oh, I don't plan on keeping up at all, Wolf," the Fae murmured softly, sending a chill along my spine. "In fact, I'm going to quite enjoy watching you tear the damn city apart."

I followed the Fae as he headed deeper into the Dark City, then turned toward the warehouse. Still, I couldn't shake the fragments of my past. They were too close to the surface, too hungry for the taste of blood.

Phantom, my mom cried. *You need to run, honey...PHANTOM, RUN!*

I was that boy once more, small, weak, and pathetic, staring into the yellow eyes of my mother as the beast in the dark came for us once more. My breaths deepened and hate raged as I strode out of the shadows and back into the light.

A black Explorer was waiting at the curb, doors open, engine running. On any other street on the other side of the city, that might've been inciting a robbery. But this side of the river...and around here? Only a total fucking idiot would steal from us.

I dragged in the scent of Unseelie and winced. "There's a place in Highlands."

Shrike nodded. "The one Mojin found."

I climbed into the passenger's seat and closed the door, my gaze spearing to the street outside the club. The Camaro wasn't there, not anymore. Arran would see to the re-opening of the club...and to Carina.

I thumbed the button for the window and inhaled the air. Finis wouldn't hang around here for long. I wouldn't. I'd be across the river, hiding amongst the mortals.

"My sister was there," I explained as he shoved the four-wheel drive into gear and accelerated.

"But not Finis?"

"No," I answered as we drove past the club. "Not Finis."

My mind chased away flickers of the past as they rose. But no matter how hard I tried to snuff out the fires, some were just made to burn.

Come here, you fucking little shit!

I winced at the roar in my head. I could still hear Finis just as clearly as I had that day.

PHANTOM! My mom screamed, and her terror rang in my head.

Even now…all these years later.

A snarl vibrated in my chest and spilled along the back of my throat.

My nails punctured the leather of the armrest.

Shrike never spoke, just handled the midnight beast through the city streets and over the bridge as we headed for the filthy squalor of Highlands once more.

The scent of blood still lingered as we got close. Black tire marks marred the asphalt, a remnant from when I'd been here before. I yanked the handle as we pulled up hard outside the alley. But it wasn't the scent of my sister I was tracking now.

No, it was the Alpha of all Alphas.

I climbed out and scanned the street. If he'd come after Carina, then he was looking for Marian. Sweat broke out along the back of my neck at the thought.

If he was after her, then that meant she'd escaped, that he hadn't released her to come after me. I walked along the street a bit, and stilled, finding the faint scent rubbed on the corner of the building. It looked like I wasn't the only one who'd found the hovel.

A phone rang behind me. Shrike answered. "Yeah?"

I scanned the dark buildings on the opposite side of the street and lifted my gaze to the skyline. We weren't that far from the heart of the city and the club they called Jewel.

Memories of that night came back with a rush.

The night mortal and Immortal had made a pact.

Not that it had helped.

The Vampire Prince had been slaughtered and the deal between the Costellos and the Vampires had pretty much died with him, until that hot-blooded daughter of Denzel Costello's had come knocking.

"They found another trail, closer to the water…fresher than this one."

I turned at the words and head back to the parked four-wheel drive. But the moment I reached the front of the vehicle, Shrike stopped. He wheeled around, those midnight Unseelie eyes scanning the alley.

"What is it?" Tension spiked inside me.

"Nothing," he answered.

But it wasn't nothing in his gaze.

No, in there shimmered with something ungodly.

Something terrifying.

Something *chaotic.*

12

PHANTOM

*B*OOM!
The beast threw himself at the divide between us.

Need to hunt! He howled. *Need to kill! Let me the fuck out!*

I closed my eyes and inhaled hard. Fists clenched...I wanted to put one through the wall. No, I wanted to put something else through the wall...*the Alpha of Alphas.*

Finis.

I wrenched my gaze from the filthy alley that still reeked from the stench of the weak Wolf's blood.

Blood I'd spilled...

Blood I wanted to spill again.

Memories pushed in, the past waited with a savage bite. The memory of that fateful night all those years ago. The night my father, the Alpha of the Khisfire City, was murdered by his own second-in-command...Finis Blackburn.

Run Phantom RUN! My mother's words resounded from the pit of darkness in my mind. I flinched at the sound. Hate and rage burned in me now just as they had all those years ago as we'd huddled, cornered in the abandoned cabin where we'd taken refuge. Blood marred my mother's face, shimmering black against the moonlight. We'd been running for hours, tired and cold and hungry. Marian whimpered, clutching my side, still far too young to keep going.

No, Mom...he'll kill you.

But she didn't listen, didn't care about the threat to her own life. All she saw was her son...and her daughter. The lifeblood of our powerful line burned in her eyes as she growled, *You have to run, Phantom. You have to be the leader I know you are...you have to do what's right.* Mom's face grimaced as the Alpha's howl rocked the night. She risked a panicked gaze over her shoulder and turned back to me. *Protect her,* Mom whispered as she shoved us through the door into the night. *With your life.*

I flinched from the memory, my heart thundering as the Unseelie warrior just stared at the vacant buildings across the street.

"What is it?" I tried to keep the bark from my tone, but I failed.

I took a step toward the vacant building which held the Unseelie's attention. Shrike didn't answer, not for a long time. Instead, he scanned the broken windows of the empty building across from us, ignoring the flutter of a discarded scrap of paper snatched by the wind.

"Nothing," he said carefully. "Thought I felt something."

My phone gave a *beep.* I yanked it free and glared at the message. "They have a fresh scent by the river."

"Might be how he crossed?"

I clenched my jaw. The river...that's how he'd invaded my territory.

Rage clouded my vision. I was already striding toward the Explorer, a captive of that consuming need to run and savage and tear the fucking city apart. I wanted to get there *now.* Wanted to find him *now.* Wanted to find my goddamn sister...*now.*

That bastard had been to my *home. He'd* crossed the river to invade the Unseelie lands. He'd touched her...*he'd fucking touched her.* My hands curled. I sucked rage deeper into my lungs with every breath.

He'd fucking touched what was mine.

The image of Carina rose in my head, her blouse ripped open, her shell-shocked gaze filled with fear. The way she'd held onto me, clawing my fucking shirt to drag me closer. The thought of him touching even a hair on her head drove me insane.

"You're taking too fucking long," I growled, and kept striding past the open door of the Explorer. "I need to run."

One step and I was charging forward, leaving him behind without waiting for an answer. Not that I'd get one. Wolf. Vampire. Fae. We all knew the beast inside, knew the need to hurt and hate. It was safer for me to run, for the Unseelie, at least.

I slammed my boots against the asphalt. In my head, it was the crunch of leaves under my feet, the cold wind at my back, driving me faster...faster...*faster.* I lengthened my stride and forced myself to exhale.

He was out there...

Hunting for my sister and relishing how Carina had felt in his hands, soft, pliable...*mortal.*

The urge to possess her consumed me. To bite...to mark. To take and keep taking over and over.

I wanted to run and keep on running, past these streets, these blocks. Nothing could stop me, not darkness, nor death. I'd tear the fucking air from my lungs and still I'd hunt, hunt for the thing I wanted the most.

For *her* scent to fill my nostrils and slip under my skin.

I could feel him out there, sense him, too. He was somewhere in this city, hiding somewhere in these streets. I charged past the end of the block and headlong into another. It was more than the pungent, undeniable scent he'd left behind. It was the ripples of the past. The torment that rose as though the past knew exactly where he was…and it was ready.

It was ready to take me there once more. To that night…to *all* the fucking nights. To the blood and the betrayal. And those yellow eyes I couldn't forget. I ground my teeth and lowered my head. My thighs burned, moving heavily until that rush claimed me once more as I pushed myself harder, lunging out of the quiet backstreets of Crown City and into the heavy flow of traffic.

Cars skidded, tires howling. There was a blast of a horn, short and sharp, before a loud blasting bellow of something much larger swallowed the sound. But I was past the point of caring, beyond any measure of self-protection. In the corner of my eye, the eighteen-wheeler barrelled down on me, a gleaming chrome beast.

I ground my teeth, ducked my head, and pushed harder, lunging between cars and across the four lanes, then suddenly stopped in the middle of the highway. The terrifying shriek of brakes echoed as the trailer of the truck swayed, bouncing as the heavy tread of the tires caught and tried to stop the jackknife.

I lifted my gaze to the wide, panicked gaze of the driver as the semi careened toward me with the scream of brakes. Seconds slowed in the instant, creeping forward with the slow thud of my heart. Only one face burned in my mind. Only one curled under my skin…

Carina.

I threw myself forward as that hulking beast of metal hurtled past in a blur of speed. Horns blared all around me as the driver of the semi fought for control, righting the truck at the last second and pulling it back into its lane.

Hard breaths claimed me, driving into my chest. I jerked my gaze back to the glimmer of water in the distance, and kept on going. My steps were slower now, the brush with danger giving way to thoughts of the woman who drove me to the brink of distraction.

I left the blare of horns behind and raced toward the water. A glint of black in the corner of my eye caught my attention. I felt my lips curling as the black Explorer turned and headed for the marker Church had sent me. I drove my boots harder against the ground, determined to beat the Unseelie warrior there.

Towering cranes lifted containers from massive ships into the yard that was once owned by the Costellos. But not anymore. I tore my gaze from the garish yellow and blue insignia of the new company and kept running, heading past the entrance to the shipping yard.

Sunlight glinted off Church's sleek dark blue Dodge Challenger. I slowed at the sight, tearing through the clump of bushes at the dirt road entrance and cut in front of the Explorer as Shrike pulled the fourwheel drive up hard.

The vehicle braked, coming to a stop before the engine died and the thud of the driver's door followed. I slowed to a walk, adrenaline burning in my veins.

"What took you so long?" the Fae taunted as he fell in step with me. "Don't tell me you're getting slow, Wolf?"

I bared my teeth, making him give a low chuckle and lift his gaze to the pack standing at the water's edge. I knew this place, knew it from Arran's description. One deep lungful of the air and the stench of death still lingered. This was the place...the place where Ruth and Russell almost died.

I winced at the memory, catching movement as Church stepped forward. Vitold followed, his head down, the weight of the world on the Wolf's shoulders.

"The scent?" I barked.

One jerk of my second's head, and he glanced at the small rundown building on the edge of the dirt parking lot. "In there, we followed it to the edge of the water."

I looked at the ramshackle building that hugged the tree line on one side. I stared at the busted-open door, feeling a pull. The closer I came, the stronger the scent grew, raw and fetid. Did the bastard have to piss all over the damn place, marking his territory?

I stepped through the doorway, glancing at the busted door until I shifted my focus to the mess waiting inside.

The desk was broken, a chair was embedded in the wall. Every inch of the small space was destroyed. Rage choked the air in a bitter tang. Something had happened here, some kind of mental break. I moved in further, and under the Alpha's stench was another, a softer scent…one I knew only too well.

I moved forward and knelt at a back corner of the room, one littered with forgotten thickly padded winter jackets. *There,* the beast urged. *Can you smell it?*

I picked up a thick coat by the collar and dragged it close. I froze as her scent hit me like a punch to the nose, deep, secretive…and pungent. I took one hard look around the room as shadows filled the doorway.

"It's her," Church spoke carefully.

I lowered the jacket, dropping it where it once lay, before I turned. "Yes."

"Why? Why not come to us, does she think we wouldn't protect her?"

I met my second's angry stare. "I don't know. I don't know any of this."

"We have to find her, Phantom." His voice turned quiet and dangerous. "Before Finis does."

Urgency swirled inside me like a damn tornado, ripping at the seams of my resolve as I strode from the ruined shack as I answered. "I know, believe me, I know."

The water called to me, dark and dangerous. Shrike stood at the edge of the jetty, staring at the riverbank on the other side…*our side.* My boots thudded on the worn wooden planks as

I lifted my gaze, finding the empty streets of the Dark City cloaked in shadows.

"He shouldn't have been there." The Unseelie warrior turned toward me. "The agent I get, what with the brand she carries, but not him...not without invitation."

It was the same damn thing that'd been bugging me. "I know."

"Find him, Wolf," the Dark Fae urged. "Then leave. I want a few minutes with him...*alone.*"

The implications were chilling.

But he wouldn't need to be alone with the Alpha of Alphas. Not by the time I was done with him.

I lowered my gaze, stopping when a glint of something caught my eye, *something yellow.* I knelt and reached between the battered wooden boards, pulling the object outwards. Its metal prongs were bent and twisted, its yellow jewels smashed and cracked. But the sight was a shotgun blast to my chest.

It was hers...

The hair comb was old and destroyed...but it hadn't always been like that. It was once shimmering and beautiful, had once adorned my mother's long midnight hair. Colors faded from the world as I stared at it. I grasped the prongs, straightening them. But I could no more fix this than I could them. *Either of them.*

I closed my fist around the comb and rose as a *beep* came from Church's phone.

"Yeah, *what?* Wait there...we're on our fucking way. *Vitold... just wait right there!*"

I swiveled, catching the movement of the Unseelie beside me.

"He's found him." Church lunged toward the open door of the dark blue Challenger. "It's V...he's found Finis."

But Shrike was already moving, lunging past me with a deep snarl. I shoved the ruined comb into my pocket and followed, panic punching my heart against my ribs as we both dove for the Explorer. Engines started with a roar and we left the jetty behind.

"*Go,*" I urged the Unseelie forward with a growl.

But the four-wheel drive didn't handle as fast as the Challenger. The blue Dodge disappeared in a cloud of dust. *Church was going to get to Finis first...*panic was a fist rammed in my gut. All I could see in my mind was that pathetic Wolf I'd dragged from that locked container. The Wolf we'd seen broken almost beyond repair.

The one I'd tracked my sister to years after she'd gone missing.

I'd failed her then, failed to do the one thing my mother had made me promise to do. I hadn't protected Marian when she'd needed me, hadn't led the beasts away. I'd thought by growing my own pack and my damn reputation, it'd protect her. But it hadn't. It just brought Finis to her door, just as twisted and savage as before, and through the hand of fate, the young, emaciated Wolf who'd been held captive along with her.

I hadn't found her, not when I'd ripped the steel door from its hinges and stepped into a new level of Hell. The stench of fear and piss was choking. Church was almost nothing when I'd carried him from that place; broken, beaten...something deep in his psyche shattered.

Still, I'd carried him back to my house. I'd bathed him, fed him, cared for him, and slowly, when weeks turned into months, then became years, we'd become inseparable. My pack grew stronger with him, Vitold accepted the lead of the stronger male, and when Arran refused to leave and pledged allegiance, we became a pack of four. Four main Wolves... overseeing twenty others in the city. Twenty, who owed me their loyalty, for now...until Finis took again.

And the Alpha *would* take...I knew it in my bones. If I didn't get to him first, the first thing he'd take was Church's life.

"*You're going to lose him!*" I barked at the Unseelie.

Shrike just jerked a savage glare my way. Those dark eyes glinted with the kind of savagery that any other day would've stilled my tongue. But not this day, *not this fucking day.* "I need to fucking tear something apart."

One jerk of the wheel, and I slammed against the door. Shrike handled the Explorer with a blinding blur of speed and punched the accelerator even further. The hulking beast of metal responded, surging forward.

Horns blasted from cars as we pushed in and forced them off the road.

"Where the fuck are we going?" Shrike snapped, and jerked the wheel hard, tearing us from the busy main street toward the taller buildings.

I had no idea. The Challenger pulled ahead and turned hard once more. I pressed my hand against the dashboard as we followed, swinging hard. But the street was empty.

"There!" I pointed to the tight side street.

The Challenger was sideways across the entrance, with both doors open.

I yanked the door handle as Shrike braked hard, throwing me forward. My shoulder slammed into the window before I shoved the door wide. I hung on as we skidded, momentum throwing me out before we came to a screeching halt a hair's breadth behind the Dodge.

But I was already running, lunging between both cars as desperation rose inside me.

Let me out NOW! the beast howled.

I winced and let out a groan with the blast of his howl inside my head. But the putrid stench of Alpha hung heavy and pungent in the air, the scent fresh. He was here...

A thunderous *crash* came from a building up ahead. The sound pushed me harder. I dropped my shoulder and charged through the closed door of the connecting building. Wood splintered, giving away to two hundred and sixty pounds of pure revenge.

I swept my gaze through the space, not caring that there was no consuming Wolf scent. He was here...*I knew it.*

Mine, the beast staked his claim.

"Mine first," I barked in answer, and charged up the stairs, scanning room to room. When there was nothing, I punched through the wall...room after room. I tore the place apart and then tore outwards. *"Church! Where the fuck are you?"*

The answer was a howl in the distance. I lunged back down to the lower floor and out into the alley. A blur of movement caught my eyes...but this time it wasn't the Unseelie.

It was a Wolf...

And not *my* Wolf.

Fetid and raw, the stench of another pack rose in the alley. I didn't know where we were, nor did I care. In that moment, I was vengeance, I was rage. I drove my body forward, slamming through the double doors of some large indoor basketball court, and swung my gaze to the end of the room.

The stench of Wolf was all around me, rising up from the floor of this place. Behind me came the shattering of glass. I pushed forward, charging across the empty floor to a closed door. He had to be here, had to be close.

"Phantom!" Church roared behind me.

But I couldn't stop, not the beast and his thirst for blood, not the adrenaline-laced hate that swept through me. I tore and smashed, ripping doors free before I punched through one interior wall and into another. By the time I was done, the place was in ruins. "Where the fuck *are you!*"

"There." Church was behind me, with hard breaths and wide eyes sparkling with his own barely restrained beast as he lifted his hand to the doors on the opposite side of the building. "He has to be through there."

I let out a bark of fury and strode forward, ripping the damn door off its hinges, and stepped out onto the sidewalk. Movement caught my gaze. Shrike stepped through another door of the building at the same time and met my gaze.

Vitold's scent drifted on the wind, coming from between the packed cars along the street and the brand-new building in front of us. A voice drifted from somewhere deep inside, faint… muffled. I sucked in a breath and lowered my head. My thighs tensed as I drove forward between two parked cars and slammed through the thick metal locks of the doors.

Church followed, Shrike barely a step behind, as I lifted my head and unleashed a howl. The burn lashed my chest and spilled into the back of my throat, filling the air until the sound fell silent. Gasping breaths dragged in the heady scent of other Wolves. Four…*no,* five had been here just minutes before…*and one of them was Finis.*

He was here…*he was here.*

Energy rippled from somewhere deeper in the building. I charged forward, the beast in me clawing the divide between us. He wanted blood…he wanted *all* their blood. Crimson clouded my vision again as I rode toward that killing edge.

And this time there'd be no coming back, not until they were all dead.

And my sister and Carina were safe.

"Phantom!" Church barked.

I swung my gaze toward him as he lifted his hand and pointed to the smear of blood on the wall.

"Wait," Shrike growled. Confusion clouded his expression as he turned toward me. "Something's wrong."

I didn't feel it, not fear or concern. Cold clarity cut through me like a blade as I kept going, pushing deeper toward the rear of the building.

Wolf and mortal. The scent was overpowering, growing stronger the further I pushed into the building. The heavy thud of boots resounded behind me as I lifted my gaze to a door at the end of the hall…and that thrum of energy grew louder behind it.

My beast charged against the barrier between us. He was growing stronger, uncontrollable and fierce. Seconds, that's all I had before he broke through.

"Now!" I growled, and dropped the wall between us.

I was already shifting as I slammed through the door, letting that predatory power detonate inside me, already feeling the shift inside me. Synapses fired and muscles ripped apart, morphing into something else.

The door in front of me flew open, hitting against the wall with a deafening *boom!* Claws punched from my nails as I stumbled into a room packed with mortals.

Mortals who spun in their seats to stare at me, terrified.

"—which is why Madison Shelter for women is so important." The woman's words froze with the invasion, giving way to stunned silence.

I jerked my gaze to the front of the room, to a podium where a woman stood, her gaze fixed on me as I staggered to a halt.

Movement came from beside the woman as FBI Assistant Director Harlan Beneford rose to his feet and barked, *"What the fuck is going on here?"*

The sound reached my ears through the screams and cries of the packed room as Church, Shrike, and Vitold charged in behind me.

Easy, I urged my beast. *EASY…*

But the savagery burning inside me was like a runaway locomotive. Once free of the brakes, it was impossible to pull back. People leaped from their seats in the packed room, and cries of terror and panic rose like a deadly wave.

"Stop right now!" Harlan charged off the stage, his face filled with fury. *"I said STOP RIGHT NOW!"*

I tried to pull the beast back, tried to straighten my body, already half shifted into Wolf form. But my muscles wouldn't obey me. In that moment they had a new master, one who was desperate for blood.

Through the crimson haze, I saw this for what it was...

We thought we'd been hunting Finis and the invading pack of Wolves.

But we'd been set up.

Lured from the safety of the club.

Leaving them exposed...

I wrenched my gaze toward the Unseelie behind me and unleashed her name. *"Carina!"*

13

CARINA

I scanned the boxes of top-shelf alcohol. "You're re-opening the club?"

Arran slipped his hand from my shoulder as the delivery trucks pulled away from the curb in a U-turn and took off. They hadn't stayed long, desperate to get out of here.

Mortals didn't come to this side of the river, and if they did, they didn't stay long.

Except for me...

"Gotta make money," my bartender said with a shrug, and strode toward the stacked boxes. "Anyway, Phantom wants everything to get back to normal."

"I suppose the dancers will be eager to get back to stripping?"

I tried to hide the bite in my tone. But no matter how hard I tried, jealousy flared deep inside me. Things had changed with us, even if Phantom rejected me now. I wanted to be here, wanted to be part of the pack, regardless of how that was.

Arran just chuckled and cast me a cocky grin. "Is that jealousy I hear in your tone, Carina?"

"No." I winced at the lie.

The deep snigger just rumbled in the back of his throat as he picked up two boxes and lifted them without a thought. "Sounds like it to me. Face it, you're jealous. You don't like the thought of other women here."

"Only the naked kind," I mumbled.

Mumble or not, he heard me. That was the problem with living with Wolves…they damn well heard everything.

"You've got nothing to be concerned about, I can assure you. They're like sisters to us, catty, bratty, pain in the ass sisters. God knows we've put up with them for long enough."

"Sisters who are stunning and half naked. Don't tell me there was never a time—"

He shook his head, lifting those gorgeous brown eyes to mine. "*No.* Not *any* time. Not me, not Vitold, not Church. Alpha's orders."

"Alpha's orders," I repeated slowly, and moved closer, reaching out to place a hand on the bulging muscle of his arm. Jesus, there wasn't even a tremble lifting the two boxes.

"Yes." His gaze bored into mine. *"Alpha's orders."*

There was something about the way he said it, some kind of undertone I wasn't getting. "You can't *always* do what the Alpha commands," I protested.

The smile only grew wider as Arran lowered the boxes onto a pile and turned. He took half a step closer, invading my space, all sleek, prowling Wolf. "You don't understand, not yet. But the time is coming soon when you will. I really hope you do, Carina." He stared at my lips before licking his own, the act pure unadulterated lust. "*Really* fucking hope you do, 'cause not touching you…not taking you to my fucking bed right now is killing me."

I was stunned into silence. That took my thoughts in a hard fucking left. I wanted to smile, wanted to brush his words off as just another phrase to shock and awe. Which it had. But there was something more than a dirty remark. There was hunger there, and need.

In an instant, Phantom's voice rose to the surface.

Did you like knowing I was watching the two of you?

That dark, animalistic warning tone rumbled like thunder in my head.

Arran's ravenous gaze burned as he took a slow step backwards. He was a man barely restrained, fueled by need and desire. I took a step before the powerful shake of his head stopped me. "It won't work. No matter how much you want it to. Not until Phantom allows it."

Not until he allows it?

My heart pounded at the words as I opened my mouth to unleash my frustration. But Arran wasn't the one doing this, and the last one I wanted to hurt was him. I left him to pick the boxes up once more and, with a careful jerk of his head, he urged in a quiet voice, "Come on, let me make you a drink while we wait for backup."

I followed him through the half-boarded-up front door and back into the club. Darkness waited in here, darkness and memories. The heavy throb of music rose from the past. I glanced toward the black velvet lounge where Church had danced for me and felt a pang in my chest.

Christ, I wanted that…so fucking much.

Arran lifted the boxes to the counter as I stopped in front of the circular lounge.

"You want to dance for me, Carina?"

I flinched and spun, tearing myself from the hold of the past, and met Arran's gaze. "Me dance? No, I don't think that'd be sexy at all."

He just gave a shrug, those intense eyes burning with lust. "I think it'll surprise you to know what I find sexy."

He stared at me for a second as my cheeks burned before he turned away with a smile and strode toward the stairs.

"You know," he started, beginning to leave me behind. "No dancing, no gourmet meals…it's a damn good thing you're cu—" His sentence ended abruptly.

Irritation grew as I waited. "I'm what, Arran…" I jerked my gaze toward him standing on the middle stair and staring through the busted doorway. *"Please* tell me what I am, I'm dying to find out."

A deep, resounding growl was my only answer, but it didn't come from him.

Pain sliced across my chest as shadows moved in the doorway. *He* stepped through. Damaged. Powerful. *Terrifying.*

"Cute," the silver-haired Alpha answered as he descended. "He was about to say cute, *mortal."*

Arran slowly stepped backwards, not daring to take his gaze from the one they called Finis, the Alpha of Alphas.

"Carina." My Wolf found his voice, his gaze still fixed on the Alpha. "Get out of here…*right now. Run!"*

I stumbled backwards as that agony in my chest turned raw and monstrous.

No…no…no, Chaos whispered, stopping me cold. *We don't run…ever.*

My body shook as Finis descended the stairs, his body commanding. "You going to fucking kneel at my feet, *Wolf?"*

Arran let out a tortured moan and clenched his fists. He seemed compelled by the Alpha's presence, unable to do anything but obey. But he stayed standing, his entire body quaking with the sheer force, which only pissed the Alpha off even more. There was a curl of Finis' lips and a menacing growl that grew louder until it resounded in the room.

Under my skin, power rippled from my chest. Chaos smiled and writhed. The club seemed to darken, like the sun had slipped behind the clouds.

Arran paled as his breaths grew harsher. He cast a panicked gaze my way, and a terrifying desperation glinted in it. Could he feel it, feel the power crawling through my bones and slithering through my mind? The low whimper in the back of his throat told me all I needed to know. He'd fight the Alpha. He might even land a blow or two. But there was no way he could beat Finis…*and there was no way he'd survive.*

Blood.

Death.

The images were stark and cruel in my mind.

Leave him alone, Chaos whispered, and the words flowed from her lips to mine, low and dangerous. "Leave him alone."

Glasses on the bar trembled. The room grew darker…and *darker.*

The clinking of the glass tumblers only grew stronger.

You want more of what I fed you before, Wolf? "You want more of what I fed you before, Wolf?" I took a step closer. *This time I'll shove it down your fucking throat.* The words were hypnotizing. "This time I'll shove it down your fucking throat."

Finis whipped his gaze toward me, his brutal, commanding growl filling the bar. But behind the brutality I saw a flicker…*of fear.* My legs trembled, but I forced myself forward. "You remember what happened, don't you?" He slowly lowered his head, his focus on me. "In the Dark City."

Harsh breaths consumed him. There was a twitch in the corner of his lips before that threatening growl faded. He now knew he wasn't the only predator in the room.

A cloud of darkness swirled around inside my head. Behind it was the truth of what had happened before I blacked out. I focused on that dark mist in my head, driving away the confusion.

The club trembled, shaking the ground. Arran jerked his gaze to the ceiling above as the quaking grew stronger.

"Carina," he murmured.

But it was all right there at the edges of my mind. If I could just—

Finis paled as the quake grew even stronger. He whipped his gaze to Arran and lifted his hand. *"Come to me!"*

He'd kill him, tear out his throat, leave Arran silenced forever, just like Wry.

I couldn't let that happen.

The fog in my head blew away at the edges.

A chill filled me as the power rose.

Yes, Chaos urged in my head. *Take it, Carina...take it for yourself.*

I would take it. I'd take it all if it meant I could protect what was mine. I'd take it even if I was lost to the darkness for all time, *as long as my Wolves were safe.*

"Come. To. Me!" Finis roared, his panic rising to the surface.

The more he panicked, the stronger Chaos roared inside me, until the walls of the club swirled with shadows. The same shadows that welled inside my head. The same shadows I'd seen in the entrance to the Unseelie world.

Fear punched through me, the chilling clarity stopping me cold. I'd be changed if I saw what was behind the dancing black mist...more than I was now. Exposed and raw, my beating heart would be held in Chaos's claws forever.

See me, she urged. *See me now.*

The truth of what she was grew darker and blacker, rising above the wisps, and in the corner of my eye, Finis jerked his gaze toward my Wolf, then lunged, all teeth and claws...*and madness.*

The brand on my chest seared, blazing with the kind of life that ripped a scream from the back of my throat. I was on fire, scalded from the inside, my soul blistered and burned. Through the haze of agony, they collided with a sickening *thud.*

The room was filled with howls of agony and rage. Shadows lashed the walls and smothered the floor, cloaking them from view. I couldn't stop them, couldn't hold on, not to the darkness that consumed my mind...or the unraveling inside me.

My fury trembled the walls.

And shattered the glasses.

Screams invaded. Screams of Wolves as the club was plunged into darkness.

Until there was silence.

Empty, breathless silence as I whimpered and closed my eyes. But I couldn't hold on anymore, not to my own sanity, or to my own soul. The fog in my mind was parting, to leave Chaos truly exposed. It was over, all of it was over.

"Carina," Arran's low whimper reached me. *"No."*

I felt myself rising, my boots left the floor as my eyes opened. I was not myself, *not anymore.* Arran was on the floor, with blood splattering his face and the walls. *His blood,* the thought hit me. I swept my gaze along the stairs, but he was alone. The Alpha, Finis, was long gone...just as he'd run before.

I hummed with savagery and scanned the club, desperate for revenge. Higher and higher I rose, above the black velvet sofas, high above it all. Arran lifted a hand, his eyes wide with suffering.

"Please...*no,*" he whispered as I closed my eyes once more.

"It's alright." I heard the words but they weren't mine...*not anymore.*

Darkness swept through me, cutting colder than any December wind.

14

PHANTOM

"*Stop right there!*" Harlan strode toward the end of the stage, his eyes filled with fury, lips curled in disgust.

But his words were soon drowned out by the screams of terror as mortals ran for their lives. All except the woman behind the microphone. She just stood there in stunned silence.

Church and Arran charged in behind me, their eyes wild and filled with bloodlust as they scanned the panicked crowd.

"He's not here," I barked. "Finis is *not fucking here.*"

The same kind of terror descended on my Wolves. One that hit them like a sledgehammer.

"Carina." Vitold took a slow step backwards. "Jesus...*Carina!*"

"*Go!*" Shrike roared and took a step forward, lifting his hands. The lights in the packed room dulled. "I've got it from here."

I didn't want to leave him, not alone. But one blistering glare and the Unseelie was striding forward, his bellow rising above the panicked fray. "Stop, please calm the hell down," he pleaded. "We are *not* here to hurt you!"

There was nothing I could do, not even if I'd wanted to. I turned, to find Vitold and Church thundering their way back along the hallway. *Please let us not be too late.* I ran like the devil himself was chasing me.

Back along the hall.

Through the quiet building.

Across the streets and the ruined buildings with doors torn from their hinges, until the Camaro's open doors were all I saw. Vitold lunged, but instead of sliding across the hood of the sleek sports car, he headed for the driver's door. Church gave a snarl and hauled ass for the open passenger's door. The engine started, and Vitold punched the accelerator until the beast was howling.

I leaped, cleared the front of the car, and slammed against the seat barely a second before we tore away.

"Vitold," Church urged.

"I know," the Russian growled.

There was an icy clarity in my third as he fixed his gaze on the road ahead. He handled the car like he was built for the racetrack. But he wasn't...he was built for retribution. Or so I'd thought.

But it wasn't revenge that sparkled in his gaze.

It was desperation.

A desperation I felt to my core. Gone was that burn of rage, gone was that hunger for blood.

You bastard...

Those were the last words she'd said to me. Words said in anger. I closed my eyes and held onto the dashboard. *Please be alright...I'll give anything, do anything. Whatever you need me to do. Just be alright.*

I opened my eyes to the flash of red and blue as we tore past the Crown City Police Department and headed for the other side of the city.

"Get the fuck *out of my goddamn way!*" Vitold barked, and swung the car into the steady stream of oncoming cars.

We were Immortal. Our bodies were designed to repair and heal by genetics alone.

But that didn't mean we *couldn't* die.

Just meant it took a lot for us get there.

Kinda like an oncoming bus. A bright yellow oncoming bus with a cracked windshield and thick metal grill. *Just* like the one headed our way. "Vitold."

My third turned his gaze toward me. Something unhinged sparkled in his eyes as he grinned.

"Fuck me, we're all gonna die," Church declared behind me.

My stomach clenched and my heart squeezed like a damn fist. One that punched up from my chest to lodge in the back of my throat as Vitold jerked the wheel hard at the very last second.

I saw the wide, panicked gaze of the bus driver, Thomas…I knew it was Thomas, *because I could read his fucking name tag!* A low, guttural roar came from my third as we flew back into our lane and hit the on-ramp for the bridge.

My breaths were shallow. I didn't have the strength to glance over my shoulder to see if Church was still with us. We were all gonna need therapy when this was over. *A lot of therapy.*

But the streets were quieter heading to our side of the city. Too quiet. No one wanted to cross the bridge, not anymore… not after what had happened with Harlan and the goddamn FBI.

I clenched my fist, letting the thought fester inside me.

Harlan…with his hands on her and concern all over his words.

But I knew what he wanted. What *most* men wanted when they looked at Carina. What that fucking Unseelie beast in her chest wanted them to see. Chaos and Finis. They had collided earlier. She'd said she didn't remember what had happened between them as she'd fled from the Dark City.

A place someone like Finis shouldn't be able to go.

But he had…and that ate at me as we flew onto the off-ramp

and turned hard. I wrenched my gaze higher, finding the Hunting Ground in the distance.

"If he hurt her…" Vitold warned, and punched the accelerator even more.

The Camaro responded with a roar, launching us into the stratosphere. *If he hurt her…if he hurt her…*I reached for the door handle and yanked as the Camaro skidded and turned, stopping hard against the gutter.

Darkness was all I saw.

Fear was all I felt.

And the world faded into nothing.

I lunged past the waiting boxes and through the busted-open door.

Arran knelt on his hands and knees…covered with blood.

"Carina," I forced her name past the fist in my throat.

The Wolf slowly lifted his head, his gaze filled with despair. I jerked my gaze around the club as Vitold and Church lunged past me.

"Carina!" Vitold screamed her name. *"CARINA!"*

"Where is she?" Church descended like the wrath of a god, grabbing Arran and hauling the Wolf to his feet.

Hate raged in my second, darkening the blue of his eyes to black.

"Phantom." The growl came from deeper in the club, where the light didn't reach.

I turned to the sound, watching as Mojin strode toward me.

There was a whimper behind him, a low, tortured moan. Vitold lunged past me at the sound until a massive hand in the middle of his chest stopped the Wolf cold. "You don't want to go back there, Wolf. I'm warning you."

"And I'm warning you, Fae." Vitold's rage boiled over as he tried to push past.

But the Wolf was no match for the Unseelie, no matter how savage he was.

The club trembled, shaking and shuddering. I jerked my gaze upwards, to the spidered cracks that raced across the ceiling. "Chaos."

With the word, the shaking grew stronger, giving birth to a new kind of hell. I'd been so consumed with finding her alive that I'd never thought of *how* she'd survived.

"She's in a bad place. I tried to stop it, tried to ward the darkness as best I could," Mojin said, and took a step closer.

"She needs us," Vitold snapped, and wrenched that savage glare my way. "She needs *you*."

I took a step, drawn by something deeper than rage and fear.

"Phantom." Mojin shook his head.

But it didn't matter, not anymore. Nothing mattered if she'd been claimed by Chaos, her fragile mortal mind shattered.

Her moan rose again, coming from behind the bar. I stepped past the Unseelie, my boots sounding with a muffled thud. Vitold was right there at my side, Church a step behind. Fear bloomed bitter and rancid in the air, dragging a tortured whine with it...until I realized it was me.

Me who was terrified.

Me who was filled with panic and fear.

I stepped around the end of the bar and searched the darkness, stilling on the huddled form on the floor in the corner.

"Jesus." Vitold stopped dead.

"Get away from me," the form that was once Carina whimpered.

But it wasn't Carina anymore, not the Carina I knew, at least. Shadows swirled and lashed across her body...*no, that wasn't right.* The shadows *were* her body.

"She's too far gone, the Unseelie—" Mojin started.

"No." I ended it for him and took a step closer.

Carina whimpered again at my movement and tried to crawl inside the goddamn wall. "Don't. Want. To. Hurt. You."

She didn't want to hurt me?

I swayed at the words. My breath was gone in an instant and for a second, none returned. None filled these barbaric lungs. None filled this pathetic excuse of a male. None gave this carcass life. Because I didn't deserve it. I didn't deserve *her.*

I drove myself forward. Fuck death and wrath and anything else Chaos might do to me.

Her midnight eyes flew open, glinting and sparkling like obsidian orbs.

"No!" She slammed her eyes closed and pressed her face against the wall.

Cold bit with cruel fangs as I moved closer. Shadows lashed and howled, the sound unnatural and piercing. But I never winced at the sound. I just knelt and slid my arms under her.

Agony stung every part of me. I could die by a thousand cuts right now and still my death would be in honor.

"How do we fix her?" Vitold's words rocked the silence.

I pulled her against me, feeling her weight in my arms as her body writhed in a mass of moving shadows.

"I don't think—" Mojin started, staring at me.

Until Vitold took a step, pushing up against the Unseelie. "We don't need you to *think*, Fae. Just tell us what to do."

Memories pushed in, fragments of...*something.* Past the hate and the hurt, the memory of Shrike's words resounded in my head. "The portal, the Unseelie portal," I growled.

Mojin's brows furrowed. There was a flare of panic, then he jerked his gaze to the woman in my arms, a woman who writhed and arched her spine in anguish.

Mojin looked at Vitold, then Church. "You need to bring her back from the Chaos...or risk losing her forever."

Arran stumbled closer. "No, that can't happen."

"Can we get in there?" I asked. "Through the portal?"

Mojin just stared at the woman in my arms. The woman who held our future in her soul. "Get in there? Yes. But withstand what she's become? I don't think you can. I don't know if anyone can."

"Let's do it," Vitold snapped.

There was no thinking. No talking through it. No considering the consequences.

"Phantom," Arran croaked.

The stench of his blood was overwhelming. But the way he said my name…the way they *all* looked at me, as though my one word would crush them. As though one look…one fucking breath of air from my lungs, would tear their world in two.

I lowered my gaze to the woman in my arms and found her staring at me. Those black eyes shimmered like dark, endless pools and I was lost in them, falling head over heels, tumbling into the void she'd become. "Take us there," I answered. "Then leave."

15

PHANTOM

Mojin swallowed hard and nodded.

"Didn't want him to hurt Arran." The dark apparition in my arms whispered.

I swallowed hard and stepped forward, carrying her from behind the bar and across the floor toward the stairs.

"You *saved* me," Arran croaked. "You saved my damn life."

Just like she'd saved mine in the warehouse. The mortal had a habit of doing that. *Just a damn mortal,* the words resounded as I took the stairs two at a time.

Darkness spilled in the air all around us, lashing like a whip. There was nothing mortal about her in this moment, nothing remotely fucking human. She was all Unseelie now, all malicious wrath and unbridled desire.

She let out a moan as I climbed the stairs, leaving the rest to follow in my wake. Sunlight spilled across her face the moment I stepped through the door and for a second, I couldn't walk, stopping in the middle of the doorway.

"Phantom?" Church questioned, pushing in behind and forcing me forward.

"Jesus fucking *Christ,*" my second mumbled.

Vitold was there, his face twisted and tortured as he slowly lifted his hand, then stopped.

"It's still her," Arran insisted as he stumbled forward. I shifted my gaze to his blood-splattered cheek and the bite marks at his throat. "No matter what, it's still her. I'll get the boxes."

Arran moved carefully to the stacked boxes of liquor.

"Leave it...leave it all," I snapped, my voice softening as I looked at her. "Nothing matters...*nothing.*"

I kept on walking, carrying her around the front of the club and down the side of the building until my boots crunched on asphalt. Silence swirled around us, punctured by Carina's low groans as I carried her into the Dark City.

It was deliberate that I didn't come here, not unless I had a reason to. But since the Special Agent had shattered my world, I found myself coming back here time and time again. *So did Finis...*

I tried to push the words from my mind and focus on her. But as I hit the bottom of the steep incline, the faint scent of the Alpha filled my nose, and that savagery came rushing back. I clenched my jaw and lowered my gaze, finding her pained stare.

He hurt you...

He caused you pain.

"Phantom," Church urged behind me. The burn in the back of my throat eased and the growl quietened.

Words were murmured behind me by the Unseelie and in the edges of my vision, a dark fog rose.

"Is this gonna hurt?" Arran growled, and swept his gaze around the abandoned city. "It's gonna fucking hurt, isn't it?"

"Don't be a goddamn pussy," Vitold growled, and gave Arran a glare as he strode forward.

"Hated me..." The words were a hiss, making my steps falter.

I jerked my gaze to hers. "What did you say?"

Shadows crawled along my arms and cascaded toward the

ground. I hissed as the icy touch burned like fire across my skin and the low beep of a phone sounded.

I jerked my gaze toward the Unseelie as Mojin yanked his phone free, glanced at the caller ID, and lifted the phone to his ear. "Path?" He slowly lifted his gaze, his brow creasing down the middle of his forehead. "Yeah, he's right here. No, it's all good. I'll let him know. Yeah, talk to you later."

He ended the call and met my gaze.

"What?" I growled.

"They found Walker and Wry."

Relief swept through me as Church let out a hard exhale and murmured, "Thank fuck."

I swallowed. "Alive?"

Panic jerked Church's gaze up once more.

"Yeah, alive," Mojin responded, and slowly shook his head. "It seems the doc gave our guys a hard time, not knowing we were on their side and all."

I lowered my gaze to Carina, to see her eyes wide and fixed on mine. "Hear that, Special Agent? She's an even bigger pain in the ass than you are."

Carina smiled, but then moaned, her face contorting. Her nails stung, digging into my arm, sweeping away the fleeting reprieve from terror.

"She's slipping," Mojin growled, and jerked his gaze toward the shell of a building in the distance. "You need to get her through the portal."

My damn heart thundered as he turned and strode toward the ruin. There was a second when Vitold hesitated, then he lowered his head and followed. Warmth slipped through my bones as Arran limped and shuffled after him, leaving slow drops of blood in his wake.

The Wolf was hurt...more than the bite on his neck and the pain in his eyes. A hiss drew my eyes back to her as she closed her eyes and arched her back in my arms, and in an instant, we were back there, to that first night when she'd begged and howled in the back seat of my car.

The only difference was, this time her agony was all my fault.

My fault.

I pushed ahead as Church turned toward the others. It was all my fault, every single part of this. My mother, Marian…and now Carina. Bad things happened to the women in my life. They'd happened for my family, and now they'd happened to the woman I loved.

I winced as the words resounded in my head.

I fucking loved *her…*

"Phantom?"

I lifted my head to the deep Unseelie green that spilled out of the concrete shell and across the ground. Darkness surrounded me, but it wasn't a darkness I ran from. No, this was one I welcomed. This would bring me closer to her. The icy burn sank its teeth into my side as I neared the building and the Fae.

"You ready for this?" Mojin murmured.

"No," I said as I stepped up into the empty space and met my Wolves' terrified expressions.

Our kind didn't travel through the Unseelie portal, not it we wanted to live. Was this going to hurt? Arran's question weighed heavy in my chest. I had no doubt it would, no doubt that this was about to hurt like a sonofabitch. "Tell me what I need to do."

Shadows spilled along her arms as Carina let out a chilling growl.

"Nothing," the Unseelie responded, and swept his gaze across the midnight cloud as it rose all around us. "It seems like she's doing all the work for you."

Vitold let out a savage groan and doubled over.

"It'll go easier if you just give in," Mojin muttered.

"Cower?" Vitold wrenched his gaze to the Unseelie, then turned that pained stare toward me.

Carina let out a whimper and threw out her arm, and in the middle of the ruined building, the air shimmered and swirled. A tremble tore across the floor, shaking the walls and what was left of the ceiling.

Chaos, it hummed and burned the air, tasting like foul blood in the back of my throat. I winced at the taste as the tremble grew stronger. Mojin did what he could, closing his eyes, his lips moving in a silent chant.

Until a chunk of concrete broke free from the ceiling and fell.

"Watch out!" Arran lunged, shoving the Fae aside.

The ground, the air…the whole damn building shuddered. Shadows whipped around in a frenzied tornado.

"She's too damn strong." Mojin shook his head. "*Nothing* should be that strong."

"Then there's only one thing to do," Arran growled as he stared into the haze.

Green spilled out of the portal as he took one step, and disappeared.

"Fuck," Vitold growled and, without a fucking glance my way, went after him.

"She needs this, right?" Church sought reassurance without looking away from the emerald hue.

"If you want her to stay intact, yeah. Chaos will take what it wants and leave her shattered."

Shattered. My second curled his lips and snarled at the word before he took a step forward and into the Unseelie world.

"See on you on the flip side, Fae," I growled, and began to follow my pack.

"Phantom." Mojin stopped me with a hand on my arm. "A word of warning; the portal isn't to be messed with. Don't wander away, stay with Carina. It will give you what you need *and only* what you need and don't, whatever you do, let her get the upper hand. You won't like the damn outcome. Chaos needs to understand the bond the pack has over her. Make her bond with you."

"How the fuck am I supposed to do that?" I looked at him.

There was a curl of his lips as he smiled. "Give her what she wants." His hand slipped from my arm, leaving me to step until the burn of the Unseelie wrapped around me and stole me from my world.

Green. That was all I saw.

Shadows clung to the floor and the walls. We weren't in the building we'd left behind...but we were in some kind of building, one where the darkness had eaten the ceiling...and everything else in sight.

"Phantom," Church called, drawing my gaze to an open doorway further along the hall. "I think we're meant to be there."

Carina moaned and opened her midnight eyes. Darkness and desire glinted like shards of glass as my steps resounded. Power shook the walls and the air hummed with something savage and seductive. It was this place, this place of emerald green.

A howl tore through the air, faint...filled with anguish and pleasure. The sound drew my gaze along the long, endless hallway until it was consumed by darkness. The longer I stared the more I felt. Hunger moved through me, the kind that stood the hair on my arms. The kind that made me want to fight.

"Phantom," Church called again.

Only his voice was deeper, his gaze hungry and insistent. Danger lurked in his eyes as he stepped toward me and shifted his focus to her. She unfolded from my arms, reaching up for a hold around the back of my neck to steady herself, and slid from my arms.

Shadows and lust swirled all around her. She wasn't part of

this place...*it was part of her.* I saw it now, saw what Mojin had tried to warn me about, saw the ravenous hunger in her eyes, the same hunger that snarled in the air all around me.

Chaos needs to understand the bond the pack has over her. Make her bond with you.

With Mojin's warning resounding in my head, I gripped her hand and pulled her toward the open doorway.

It was a bedroom...cloaked in greed and addiction. The Wolves waited inside as Vitold stared at the massive bed in the middle of the room and Church scanned everything. The moment I dragged her inside, the door closed with a resounding *thud*...and we were alone.

"Well, we're here." Arran raked his hair back from his forehead.

"We are." Vitold stepped closer and lifted his hand for her to take. "Is this what you want, Special Agent?"

Harsh breaths came from the woman who'd been mortal mere moments ago. But she was far from her mortality now, oceans and oceans apart.

"Yes," the apparition whispered, and slipped her hand from mine to Vitold's.

The act trigged my beast, driving him to crash through the dividing wall between us. I lunged forward, barrelling into my third, and let out a challenging bark. *"Back the fuck off!"*

Rage and possessiveness burned hotter than I'd ever felt before.

Vitold froze, his eyes wide.

*Mine...*the beast in me roared. His fur bristled as predatory need burned in the back of my throat. *Learn your fucking place!*

And the third in our pack slowly lowered his hand.

"Phantom," Church spoke my name carefully.

It was this place. This *goddamn* place. I swiveled toward my second, my lips curling, and watched as he paled and swallowed. This place had weakened the barrier between man and beast. I felt more animal here, more ravenous with the need for *her*. "You. Will. Wait. For. My. Command."

Harsh breaths consumed me. Shadows rolled and spilled along the floor. I shifted my gaze to the only woman who'd ever turned me into that baseless animal filled with jealousy and lust.

Darkness shimmered in her eyes, so black they barely glinted, so black they nearly swallowed me. But the longer I stared, the more I saw her...*Carina*. She was in there, fighting to get back to me. Now I needed to fight for her.

"Is this what you want, *female?*" I growled and stepped forward, flanking her side. She was still and careful. But there was a flicker of a smile in the corners of her lips. "Is this what you want me to become?"

I went for her in an instant, one hand reaching to grasp her throat while I claimed her mouth. Soft, pliable, *so warm...so mine.* I took her hard, forcing that chaotic demon to kiss me back. And she did. Her hands slid along my arms as she unleashed a guttural moan, her fingers spread against my biceps before I tore away, my stare fixed on those endless midnight orbs.

My Carina was in there. I don't know how I knew, but I did. I could feel her fighting to get back to me. I could *feel* her need.

Shadows ebbed and flowed, sliding from around her body to leave pink flesh behind.

"It's working," Vitold growled. "Whatever you're doing, it's working."

"You like it when I'm the beast," I growled against her mouth, then slowly pulled away. "So help me God, he does, as well. He's wanted you from that first damn night in the warehouse. I wish I could figure out why, wish I could get you out from under my skin. But I can't seem to do that, can I, Special Agent? No matter how fucking riled you make me, I still want to fuck you into oblivion."

Her tongue snaked across her lips.

I forced her gaze to mine. "And keep fucking you. Because *that* is what an Alpha does."

She let out a guttural sound, one bridled with desire and unhinged with lust. The beast was shoving against me, forcing my movements.

"*I* eat first." Her eyes widened as my voice turned predatory. "*I* drink first. And above all...*I fuck first.*"

16

PHANTOM

"Do you understand me, Special Agent?"

She just stared at me with that same bestial black stare. *She's in there...just keep going.* A shudder tore through her body. It was more than a tremble, deeper than a quake...it was like something was *born* inside her.

No.

Not born...more like *reborn.* But Carina was in there, screaming and howling like her own beast. Desperation burned in me. I *had* to save her, had to tether Chaos to me...*I had to make her love me.*

There was a twitch at the corner of her mouth before her head dropped backwards and a ravening chuckle slipped out. The deep, guttural sound resounded off the walls to dance along my skin, then moved deeper, into the furthest reaches of my mind...where the beast waited. I winced as my Wolf growled, then panted in response, but I kept my focus on her.

"No."

"No?" I lashed out, grabbed her arm, and dragged her close until I towered over her. "What part of *I'm the goddamn Alpha,* don't you understand, *female?*"

Her lips were pale under the green Unseelie hue, perfect and so goddamn pale. I slid my thumb across the flesh, watching as her mouth opened for me as she answered. "She can't have you."

"She can't have me?"

The glint in her eyes shimmered as Chaos whispered. *"Because you're mine."*

The battle still raged inside her, an unseen war of possession I couldn't see, but still, I had to try to help her. *Make Chaos bond with me...that's what Mojin had said, right? Make an Unseelie creature hungry for a damn Wolf.* Sure.

She kissed my calloused thumb and slowly took it into her mouth.

Make her want me?

Jesus Christ.

"I'm yours, am I, *mortal?*" I growled as she took my thumb deeper, sucking and licking, her tongue dancing around the tip making my cock harden in an instant. She knew what she was doing...knew the kind of temptation she possessed.

Church let out an agonizing groan and looked away, but the damage was already done. I was more aware of *them* now, and so was she. She sucked and licked, over and over, deeper and deeper, until I grasped her wrist. She wanted control, wanted to be in charge, and never once took her gaze from mine.

Don't let her get the upper hand. My cock twitched, punching against my zipper as she let out a seductive moan. Christ, I wanted her. A cold sweat broke out along the nape of my neck. But to give in now would mean I was giving in to Chaos, and that's not who I wanted at all.

I released her arm and grabbed her throat, feeling the muscles work under my hand as I leaned in to growl, *"If* we do this...we do it *my* way."

Her tongue stilled against my thumb, leaving me to pull it free of her mouth. Spittle came with it, the long, thin string reminding me of something else I wanted in there, wanted it sliding down the back of her throat, wanted it glistening on her lips. Stay in control. *Stay in control...*

She just stared at me with that same fucking stare. The one that said you can *think* you're in control all you want...but we both know the real Alpha here...*and that's not you.*

I lowered my gaze to her splayed-open shirt. "Take it off."

She didn't hesitate, just opened it wider, tugging the tail from the waistband of her pants. *That's right...*my beast was forceful. "I want you naked."

Her shirt hit the floor before she reached behind for the clasp of her bra. But she was taking too long...*and she knew it.* A snarl spilled from my chest as I lashed out with my claws. Instinct raged as the razor-sharp tips carved down the middle of her bra and never once nicked her skin.

Elastic released, her breasts bounced with the force as the garment pulled away. I was mesmerized by the movement, tracking the soft peaks of her nipples, peaks that hardened under my gaze. The green glow captured them, kissing the perfect dusky pink. I swallowed hard as the beast inside pawed at me. He wanted out...he wanted *her.*

"Y-your pants." I tried to force the tremble from my voice but there was no mistaking it.

Her fingers moved achingly slowly reaching for the button. Harsh breaths came from behind me. *Mine,* the beast warned. I was nearing the edge, that dangerous moment when an Alpha could turn on his pack if he wanted something he wasn't willing to share.

So help me God, in that moment, I was re-fucking-thinking it.

They'd already had her, already bonded with her, and I wasn't talking about that Unseelie bitch inside her. I was talking about their fucking *feelings.* I dragged in a deep breath and scented their lust as she jerked down her zipper.

One glance their way and I knew she could smell them, too.

"You hate me right now, don't you?" I murmured. "I can see it in your eyes. But you want me just as much. It's a cruel kind of torture, isn't it? To hate and need at the same time."

"You don't need…" she whispered, and pushed her pants down over her hips.

I lowered my gaze, my focus moving to the sheer black lace panties as my Wolf bared his teeth. "Don't I?"

"Not like I want you."

I met her gaze as her pants hit the floor at her feet. My grip eased around her throat. "Tell me, *mortal,* how much do you want me?"

That smug glint in her eyes dulled with desire, making my pulse stutter. There was truth in there, more truth than I'd seen since we'd been here. The kind of truth that made her vulnerable…and it was alright that she didn't answer. I'd already heard her loud and clear.

"Ask me again," she said as she slid her fingers under the waistband of her panties at her hips.

"What?"

"Ask me again if I liked Harlan touching me."

Hate flared with her words. My heart rate spiked, my breaths deepened. There was a curl to my lips as I ground out the words, "Did you like it when he looked at you like he wanted to fuck you?"

"Yes," she answered, stopping me cold.

She was playing me, trying to rile my beast into reacting. And it fucking worked. A savage bark ripped through my mind, making me wince. He pawed at the barrier between us with a terrifying frenzy. I'd lose control if he got through, then I'd be nothing more than a barbaric monster driven to the killing edge. I'd fuck her, just like I said. *But I'd hurt her, too.* I wouldn't be in control, not then, not with the rut driving me.

Still, that didn't stop the words from coming. "Did you think about his hands on you?"

"Yes."

A whine came from behind me and movement made me wrench my gaze back as Church took a slow, careful step forward. "Phantom. You have to stay in control."

But I didn't hear him, not really. His words skimmed across the darkness of my mind and drifted into nothing. I jerked my gaze back to her. "A Wolf not good enough for you anymore, mortal?"

"A Wolf doesn't want me," she answered carefully, meeting my eyes. "Not anymore."

With a savage sound, I grabbed her, spun her to face the pack, and yanked her hard against my chest. She lifted her gaze to the rest of my pack, to their hungry gazes and heaving chests.

"I don't want you?" I ground my cock hard against her ass and trailed my hands down her stomach. My pack's steely gazes never wavered, fixed on her. "Look at them, they want you."

"But not you, right?" she moaned, and arched her back.

My fingers crept lower…and lower…and lower, until they danced along the ridge of elastic. "I can smell their hunger, scent their need. It's choking, like a beast of its own."

She let out a low guttural sound, riding the length of my cock. One brutal yank and I ripped the sheer lace panties free, leaving her naked to their gazes, and dropped the shredded garment to the floor. She lashed out and grasped my wrist, her hips driving harder and harder against me.

"They'd tear me apart just to get to you," I growled against her ear, "*if* I let them."

She slipped her other hand behind her, fingers reaching for the button of my jeans. "Phantom, *please*," she begged…*fuck, I loved it when she begged.*

"Say it again," I snarled. "Tell me what you want…*beg for me.*"

I gave a slow thrust, driving home my hunger. She gave a whimper as the shadows whipped and thrashed against the walls. A tremble tore free, shuddering the floor under my feet. I glanced at the walls, then the ceiling. No cracks, no fissures of any kind. This wasn't the mortal world, this world wasn't so goddamn fragile.

That scream of desire cut through the air again, coming from somewhere along the hall. My Wolf reacted to the sound, throwing back his head with a desperate howl of his own.

Hunger.

Desperation.

Primal fucking desire.

I closed my eyes. "Say it, or I leave you here and *no one* touches you."

A low moan. "No..."

My claws drew back slightly, leaving just enough to lightly drag across her abdomen and trail down. "Then tell me what you want, Carina. Or consider us finished."

Agony stabbed through my chest at the thought, and that's all it was...*a thought.* The real thing? *That* would fucking kill me. Desperation rushed to the surface, making my voice ragged and raw. "Tell me what you want."

"You," she answered as the shadows merged into one monstrous dark beast that occupied half the room. "I want you."

"How do you want me, female?"

She let out a tormented sound as I trailed the claw of my index finger over her mound and gently slid it between her lips. Pleasure, that's all it was. All pleasure, with the threat of pain. Her head rolled to the side, exposing her neck, and it was too much for me to keep the beast at bay. Fangs punched through, forcing me to bite.

The very tips of cruel fangs designed to rip and tear pressed against her jugular. She shuddered as my finger slipped lower, my claw retracting just enough to let me touch her. Slow, careful circles, and I found the place that made her shudder... and whimper with need.

"I want you inside me," she groaned. "Jesus Christ, I want you inside me."

The words swirled around inside my head. My fangs pressed harder against her neck. I could feel her pulse through the tips, thrumming...*thrumming.* One bite would be all it'd take. One bite and the torment I felt inside would be over. Love...loss... darkness forever. I wrenched my head away, revulsion colliding with that agonizing flare of love.

Still, she didn't lift her head, just rocked her hips with the rhythm of my finger as I circled her clit over and over again.

"I want your mouth," she whimpered. "Right where your finger is. Your tongue...*fuck yes, I want your tongue.*"

With a savage snarl, I pulled the beast back from the edge, and his claws with it. My fingers left a slick trail along her belly. "Is that what you really want, mortal?"

Her shudder was what I needed. I turned her around to face me and, as I stared into those brown eyes that bled into black, I slowly dropped to my knees. *Fight, Carina...fight to come back to me!*

Her lips parted. The look was predatory, but I didn't break her stare. Instead, I leaned closer and kissed the remnants of her desire on her belly. Salt bloomed against my tongue as I gripped her hips, holding her steady, and moved lower.

Panting breaths made her chest rise. Green glowed against her skin, darkening at the peaks of her nipples. I pulled her against me, my tongue finding the place she needed me to be. One hard suck of her clit made her head drop backwards as she let out a hard, shuddering sigh.

"Fuck yes," my mortal cried.

Her hand went to the back of my head, fingers splayed between the short strands of my hair. But I needed no encouragement to go where she needed me most. I lowered one hand to the back of her knee and lifted her leg, sliding it over my shoulder.

Growls echoed from two of my Wolves behind me.

Jealous…

Possessive.

The sound made me smile…*and hunger even more.* I speared my tongue into her core, pushing the muscle deeper, driving harder, until there was no place on her body that didn't smell like me. *Maybe one place.*

Fingers and tongue, I slid two inside and felt her buck against me. Her fingers fisted my hair as I worked her body, thrusting deeper and sucking. Wolf against Unseelie. My beast drove his power higher until the air hummed with the strength of his claim.

The growling of my Wolves ended.

One whimper and they were mine…

Just like she was mine.

I gave a hard lick and pulled away, my fingers still working inside her, thrusting, *fucking.* "Do you get it now, Carina?" She rocked her body, holding on to the back of my head and pushing her hips against my fingers. "Do you get where your place is?"

But it wasn't Carina who stared back at me when she lowered her gaze. It was the endless darkness…the unbridled *Chaos.* Her lips curled as she answered, lust and devotion raging in her eyes. "At your feet, *Wolf?*"

I pushed her harder, curling my fingers, feeling the shudder tear through her as her climax barrelled down. "No," I answered with a smile. "By my side. It has *always* been by my side."

With one hard shudder, she slammed her pussy against my face, her cries of, *"Yes!"* booming through the room.

Yes…

Yes.

Slick against my fingers. I wanted her more than ever. So much that it was painful. So much that it could tear me apart.

But as I slid my fingers from her body, I knew she needed to learn her place. "Now, my *Chaos...*" I snarled, and rose to my feet, towering over her once more. "Get on your fucking knees."

143

17

CARINA

I swallowed hard at the command. His gaze burned through me, drawing the last tremor free. He canted his head, waiting...*waiting.* I licked my lips as Chaos gave a hard exhale and finally released me from her clutches.

The weight lifted as her stranglehold eased.

"I'm waiting," Phantom growled.

"I think she's gone," I whispered as I exhaled long and hard. "I think she's finally gone. Thank fuck."

His smile was chilling as he placed his big hand on the back of my head. "That's good, Carina. That's *very* good. But it doesn't change a damn thing."

The *Alpha* in him raged.

Pressure on the back of my head made me stiffen. This was all a game, right? All an act to break her hold over me? A chill swept through me as he pushed harder, forcing my knees to buckle, and never once did he look away.

"By my side," he whispered, that silver shine glinted in his eyes like shards of glass. "Or not at all. The choice is yours."

My gaze trailed down his mammoth body as I knelt at his feet. His erection bulged against his zipper. The sight of it made me tremble. I looked up at him. He was a god in this moment, a savage, *bestial,* predatory hunter. There was no give in him, no weakness he'd show…not to me.

He'd once told me he wasn't a rapist and everything inside me knew that was the truth. None of them would hurt me, most of all Phantom. If I didn't want to do this, all I had to say was no. The vision of that played out inside my head. He'd remove his hand from my head and he'd step away. One command to the others, and they'd let me leave.

Leave his world, his life…his bed.

The choice was clear, either run *with* the pack, or not at all.

A ripple of power slipped through me, making me catch my breath. But this wasn't the bitter cold of Chaos. This was warm, soft, and urgent, all at the same time. This was the bloom of deep spices in my nose and down my throat. *This was Wolf.*

I reached up and unbuttoned his jeans. Satisfaction sparkled in his eyes. The slow slide of the zipper tore away faster as the bulge of his cock pushed free. My tongue snaked across my lips as that Unseelie green turned his boxers black.

Warmth waited for me just through the fabric. His cock twitched as I trailed my fingers along his length. Jesus, he was hard…so goddamn hard.

He was hard for me.

A surge of adrenaline ripped through me, making me even wetter. I yanked down the elastic, leaving that monstrous thickness to spring free. Instinct took over as I opened wide. I wanted this more than I'd wanted his mouth. Hunter. Predator. *Protector.* That's what I saw when I looked at him.

Pain and loneliness.

A weight he carried alone.

That's what it meant to be the Alpha.

But I could help him carry that burden.

I leaned close, keeping his stare. The thick head of his cock slid along my tongue as I pushed it deep. He never once forced me, never once hurt me, just rocked his hips forward. That slow thrust drove him deeper until he bumped the back of my throat.

Still, I wanted more.

He let out a groan as I wrapped my fingers around the base, my thumb dancing along the pulsing vein underneath. A flare of panic surged to the surface as he pushed deeper, rocking all the way. My nostrils flared at the slide of my hand against that tight, slick skin.

As he pulled backwards, I licked the head of his cock and tasted the delicious salty tang that danced across my tongue. Dear God, he was breathtaking…every single inch of him.

"I want you by my side, Carina," he repeated. "I want you as my mate, but I can't have you breaking the pack. Do you understand me?"

I swallowed hard and he let out a savage groan. One nod was all it took. One nod, and that darkness in me rippled with excitement. She wanted him, just as much as I did. His Wolf, his power…*his body.*

She wanted them all.

"Now be a good mate and swallow," he growled, pressing gently on the back of my head.

Heat roared through me at the touch. I wanted this…*craved* this, to be wanted, to be obsessed about, *to be used.*

One driving thrust and he filled me, stretching my lips wide until they could go no further. I pumped his length, driving my clenched fist all the way to the base, and felt him jerking in my mouth.

Warmth spurted, sliding down the back of my throat. He kept himself there, pushed all the way to the hilt, as I swallowed.

"Jesus fucking Christ," he groaned as his fingers tangled in my hair.

But my hand never stopped working him, even as he softened and pulled out. I wanted more…*so much more.* My core was hot and aching, needing more than his tongue.

"Church," the Alpha called as he looked down at me. "Vitold…and Arran. Our mate is in need of servicing."

Only then did he look their way…only then did that primal force in the air around him change.

Church rose to his feet carefully and took a step forward. Vitold was next, followed by Arran. I understood now. There was a succession, one built with loyalty and blood. Phantom untangled his fingers from my hair and skimmed his thumb across my cheek. Love shone in his eyes now, the kind of love that rocked me where I knelt.

"My Queen," he murmured, and turned his hand over, his fingers waiting for mine.

I took his offering and rose to my feet.

"The pack," he murmured, and shifted his focus behind me, "takes care of its own."

I turned, sensing motion, and my hand slipped from his as Church yanked his shirt free with one powerful move and reached for me. Hard muscles rippled under my hands as he gripped my waist and lifted.

I spread my fingers along the base of his neck and held tight. "Are you going to dance for me, Wolf?" I whispered.

"Dance? No, *mate*, I'm going to fuck you."

"As I fuck you," Vitold contributed, coming alongside us.

"And I get to watch," Arran growled. "Fuck me, I get to watch."

Vitold grasped my chin and turned my head, moving closer to take my mouth. Remnants of Phantom's release still lingered. Vitold gave a guttural growl as the salty taste surfaced and swirled along his tongue. His grip on my chin tightened, then slid to my jaw.

Hunger raged in his eyes as he pulled away. "The bed," he urged.

Church manhandled me like I was nothing, striding forward only to tear my hold from his neck in one forceful motion and throw me through the air until I landed in the middle of the soft bed.

They were on me in an instant. Arran lunged across the bed to claim my mouth as Church undid the buttons of his pants and shoved them low in the corner of my eye. Pure muscle. Pure *devastation*. I groaned at the sight of him and Arran swallowed the sound before he broke free.

From the other side, Vitold moved closer, already naked as his shirt dropped from his hand.

"Didn't take you long," I teased as fear mingled with lust.

"Do you blame us," Church growl in response and climbed onto the foot of the bed. "We just sat there and watched you take the Alpha, and all the fucking time I was wishing it were me."

"And me," my Russian agreed as he climbed onto the bed.

"And me," Arran murmured, sliding his thumb along my lips.

My pulse sped as all three of my Wolves reached for me.

"Mine," Church breathed, staking his claim, and lowered his gaze to the juncture of my thighs. "I've waited long enough."

Vitold bowed his head and eased back, leaving the second of the pack to move forward on his hands and knees. Strong thighs moved between mine before he reached up, placed one big hand at the side of my head, and leaned over to kiss me.

My pack...

All mine.

Church's hand found my breast as he claimed my mouth. The kiss was hungry and urgent. I flattened my feet against the bed and bent my knees, drawing them higher to widen for him

"Are you ready for me, *mate?*" Church growled against my mouth.

I was more than ready, desperate and aching even at the thought of him. A hard surge of his hips and that delicious length pressed against me. I moaned, arching my spine. My fingers went to his head as he slipped lower.

"My God, you are delicious," he sighed, and kissed the hard peak of my nipple.

Warmth consumed me at the touch of his tongue. I lowered my gaze, watching as the green hue danced across his lips as he took me deeper into his mouth and thrust his hips against me.

"More," I whimpered as Chaos rose under my skin. "I need you."

His mouth curled in a seductive smile as he slid one hand between us, shifting himself as he thrust upwards, ramming into me with one inhuman blow. My eyes fluttered closed as all thoughts left me. I was nothing more than an animal in that moment, nothing more than *need*.

I heaved my hips upwards as he pulled out, only to slam home once more. I wanted to see him, wanted to scrutinize the exquisite beauty of the way his powerful body moved. I opened my eyes to the glint of steel in the Unseelie darkness and watched as his muscles flexed and rolled with inhuman perfection.

"This what you need, Carina?" Church gasped, his forearms bulging with the force of the thrust.

The way he said my name sent shivers along my spine. I liked it, liked the way he said my name, and liked the way he looked at me, all territorial hunter. "Say my name again."

As his cock drove deeper inside me, inflaming that desire, he growled, *"Carina."*

I drove my hips harder as he glanced at Vitold. Something passed between them, unspoken...and commanding. Vitold reached for me, sliding his hand along my cheek, the pressure turning my head toward him. "Now, let's see what you can do to me with that beautiful mouth."

A surge of heat moved through me as Church picked up his pace. But my Russian was already rising, already moving closer, his cock rigid and ready. I was more than eager. I wrapped my hand around his length, taking him into my mouth as my climax sent bolts of lightning through me.

I cried out my release around Vitold's cock, taking him deep and hard. With a bestial sound, Church stilled and emptied deep inside me. My senses were on fire, desperation driving my fisted grip along Vitold's length.

"Jesus Christ, I'm not going to last, *moya lyubov*," his words not much more than a groan.

His gentle fingers cupped my jaw, and the caress made me open my eyes to his gaze. He liked watching me, liked staring at the place where he and I joined.

"Harder, Vitold." Arran growled.

The slick slap of skin on skin sounded. I reached for him, replacing his hand with mine.

"Up." Vitold commanded.

Church slid free, leaving Arran to take his place as I turned over and kneeled on all fours. My body was on fire, pulsing and quaking. One look down the length of my body, and I found Phantom watching, that seductive, possessive smile curling one side of his mouth.

"Mine," Arran growled, and slid inside me.

"Mine," Vitold repeated and cupped my mouth as I turned back to him.

Mine, Chaos whispered in the darkness of my mind and as that Unseelie power rose inside me, I knew there was no more fighting the draw of my pack. She was in...*all in*. There was only desire pulsing inside her mind now...and it started and ended with my Wolves.

18

CARINA

"*C*arina." I opened my eyes to find the green glow of the Unseelie world once more, and Church's piercing gaze. He gave me the ghost of a smile and murmured. "We have to go."

Exhaustion moved through my body, weighing down my tired muscles and aching bones. I wanted to close my eyes, to drift off to that deep, dark slumber once more, but there was something in his eyes. Something that dragged my thoughts to the surface. Something that forced me to push up from the bed and find the real danger in the room.

Phantom slowly paced from one wall to the other, green and black swallowing him with the movements. I swallowed hard. "Did something happen?"

"No. Nothing happened." Church reached his hand out to me. "But we need to get back home."

I gave a slow nod as the events of the last few weeks resurfaced in my mind. Chaos had consumed me, she bled into every aspect of my life, but she wasn't the only danger we had. In the wake of her power, when the remnants of her Unseelie lust had faded, everything else came crashing down.

Finis.

Marian.

Walker and Wry.

My pulse gave a stutter. *Walker...they'd found her.* I licked my lips and scooted across to the other side of the bed where my clothes waited, neatly draped on the foot of the bed. Vitold and Arran stood silently, watching me with hungry gazes.

"I'm sorry," I muttered. "I don't know how I fell asleep."

"I might have an idea," Vitold answered, his voice dangerously seductive.

I risked a glance his way as fire burned in my cheeks. An ache spread between my thighs as I yanked on my pants, then my bra and shirt. The ruined remnant of my panties was nothing more than ripped strings. Claws-one, underwear-*zero*. I was going to have to find more robust clothing, especially around Phantom. Maybe chain mail might do it?

I tugged on my boots and tried to fix the gaping front of my shirt as best I could. "How do we get out of here?"

They all turned to me, even Phantom, mid-way across the room as he muttered. "I was hoping you had an idea about that."

Me? I glanced toward the open door and the darkness that waited outside. A deep, resounding *thud* carried through the air. The longer I stared at the emptiness outside this room, the deeper I felt that pulse. This place was alive, hungry and still, like a predator waiting...

"I don't know." I whispered and took a step closer to them, trying to remember how we'd gotten down here in the first place.

The portal.

Remnants slipped into my mind and in the vastness, Chaos shifted from her slumber. She was slow, lazy...*sated.*

"We need to get out of here," I murmured.

"I know," Phantom answered behind me.

"No, we *need* to get out of here *now*." I demanded, driving my need to her.

"*I. Know,*" Phantom growled.

His urgency spilled through the emptiness, bringing Chaos wake fully. She rose through the dark, her movements still slow...*achingly slow.* I turned to my Alpha and lifted my gaze to his. "Tell me again. She hears you...*she obeys you.*"

There was a shimmer in his eyes, a recognition, before he gently grasped my shoulders. "Get us the hell out of here, *now.*"

That resounding boom tore through me. There was some kind of connection we shared now. One that hadn't been there before that flowed from Wolf, to Chaos...*then to me.* She obeyed him, and that thought alone was terrifying.

Through the doorway the Unseelie darkness growled. I closed my eyes as the urgency resounded, rambled the walls inside me, and spilled outward. She was there, pushing her power out into the air, *forcing* that portal to the Dark City open.

"Touch me," I groaned. "You have to touch me to get out of here."

The air in the center of the doorway shimmered, rippling with power...*her* power. Phantom rested his hand on my arm and the connection tore through me, hungry and urgent. Church's touch blazed like electricity through me, but Vitold's was darker and dangerous, resounding deeper. I squeezed my eyes closed, waiting for the last connection, until it finally came, and the pulse of Arran's touch at the small of my back sent a chill racing along my skin.

There was a bark, a savage roar that came from Arran. My heart punched hard and desperation surged as I felt myself being ripped out of the pulsing emerald Unseelie world and thrown forward.

My arms flew outward as I stumbled, but strong hands caught me and pulled me against him. Phantom glanced around at the pitch black. I caught the movement of his head as he lowered that silver shine to mine.

"Jesus, the landing sucked," Arran grumbled.

"You're such a pussy," Vitold responded.

"Where are we?" I asked as I focused on the shapes around us.

"Looks like we're back where we began," Phantom answered, his hand sliding from my shoulders as he took a step forward.

The portal? I followed him, feeling that strange hum between us. It was a flow of energy, a current that pulsed like a tide.

"Carina?" Church called my name.

The moment I turned, that current inside me changed, becoming a different tone, something darker, sounding filled with angst and sadness. That was the only way I could describe it. How did sadness sound? It sounded like a heart breaking, and that's what Church felt like to me.

"Is something wrong?" Concern bled into Vitold's tone. The moment he stepped forward, that hum changed once more.

"I...I don't know," I answered, shifting my gaze from Vitold, to Church, then Phantom...and finally Arran. "I can feel you."

There was a smirk from Vitold as he took a deep breath and pushed out his chest. "I tried to be gentle, but I fucking wanted you—"

"Not *that* kind of feeling, Vitold," I explained, watching his chest deflate. "I *feel* you, like some there's some kind of connection between us."

Church jerked his gaze to Phantom. But there wasn't a hint of surprise on the Alpha's face.

"You know, don't you?" I questioned. "Something happened to me down there, something *changed* me."

"Yes" Phantom answered, and turned to me. "Something *has* changed, Carina."

"What?" Vitold growled.

"What is it?" Arran asked, moving closer.

We all looked at Phantom as he answered. "I made Chaos love me."

Jealousy kicked in my chest. He *made* her love him? Harsh breaths consumed me as my mind raced. That was why she was quiet. That's why she was *calm.*

"I had to force the connection. It was the *only* way we were going to survive. I had to make her subservient to me and in doing so...subservient to the rest of us."

Subservient.

The word rang out loud. I looked into that shadowed part of my mind, searching for that waiting hunger that'd plagued me from the moment the damn Unseelie curse plunged into my chest. It was still there, breeding and brewing like a storm on the fringes. But there was no bite to the storm anymore...not where the Wolves were concerned.

Phantom moved closer and the outline of his hand moved against the dark before the brush of his fingers came at my jaw. "I had to seal the bond between us. This was the only way. Just don't...don't do anything to break it, because breaking it means breaking us forever."

Breaking us...

I tried to swallow as his words hit home. "I won't."

One nod of his head, then he gave me a sad, soft smile. "Good. Now that's covered."

"Wait..." Church protested. "Now *that's covered? What* the hell was covered, Phantom?"

My Alpha's smile grew wider, his focus fixed on me. "Looks like we have an Unseelie mortal woman connected to our pack's tether."

"She can sense us?" Church muttered.

"She can." Phantom leaned down to whisper against my ear. "And *we* can sense her."

Excitement blazed to life in my veins. My pulse was erratic, spiked and thready even as the Alpha jerked his gaze away.

"You made it." Mojin's voice filtered through the darkness. Black on black shifted. "Was starting to think Chaos had won after all."

"How long?" Phantom growled.

"Twelve hours."

"Jesus *fucking Christ,*" Phantom snapped.

"Don't worry. The world hasn't burned down...*yet,*" the Unseelie muttered, and cast a careful glance my way. "Is she sated?"

"She being Chaos? If so, then yes," I answered.

The asshole had the nerve to smirk. "Thank the Dark Queen for that. Now, back to the real world."

He turned and stepped out of the ruined building. Phantom followed, leaving Church to glance my way. With one jerk of his head, I hurried after the Alpha and the rest of the pack came behind us.

"Path is due any second," Mojin spoke as we walked. "The rest of the search is over, the Breeds have other obligations, it seems."

"That's good." Phantom's long strides made me hustle to catch up. "The young Wolf?"

"Territorial, it seems," Mojin commented.

"Any sign of Finis?"

"No. Not a damn thing, but I have Honor and Ruin canvassing the streets."

I lifted my gaze from the cracked asphalt to the Fae. *There were more of them?* The thought sent a shudder of fear coursing through my veins.

"I need to get back out there. She has to be found." Desperation bled into Phantom's words.

"I know, brother...*I know.*"

I had taken him from the search to find his sister, taken precious moments that could have saved her life...and everyone's around her. That knowledge weighed heavily as we headed to the rise and climbed our way out of the Dark City.

"Still, nothing explains how Finis got here in the first place," Mojin muttered.

There was an edge to his tone, a hardness that made me wince.

"The place is warded by Fae, so Fae had to have allowed it," Phantom answered. "If you're sure of your guard, Mojin, then there's only one other place to look."

The Fae warrior gave Phantom a chilling stare as we crested the rise. I had a sick, sinking feeling about whatever stood in the Fae's way. Vampires I could understand, Wolves I knew...but the Unseelie was a whole different Immortal creature altogether. One I wanted to stay clear of.

"Catch ya, Wolf," Mojin snarled, and strode away.

The silver glow of the moon captured his movement. I jerked my gaze over my shoulder to where we'd come from. There was no moonlight there, no soft ambience to find your way. It was as though the power held there consumed it all.

"Carina," Phantom called my name, jerking me to the present. "You alright?"

I forced a smile and nodded. "Yes." And followed as he headed back along the side of the club.

The place was just as we'd left it. Boxes of liquor stacked still outside the open door and even though it'd only been hours since we'd left, it felt different somehow. Changed...or maybe it was me?

The lights flickered in the club, brightening to spill through the open door. I turned and followed the pack inside, making my way down the stairs and stopped at the end of the bar. The air was tainted, dark and festering, and as I shifted my gaze to the place where I'd huddled in terror in the corner, a deep-seated rage shifted into my mind.

The foul stench of *him* lingered. Finis had tried to take what was mine, had tried to hurt what I loved. Footsteps sounded and stopped behind me.

"He didn't win," Arran murmured, and slid his hands around my waist, drawing me against him. "He won't ever win while we have each other."

"No, he won't," I agreed, and turned to stare into his gaze. "Because I won't let him."

Music came on, the beat hard and edgy. I leaned forward, kissed Arran, and stepped out of his arms. But I didn't walk through the connecting doors to the living quarters. Instead, I opened the cabinet, grabbed a broom, and got to work

We all did, silently cleaning and fixing in a kind of determined silence. Arran carted the boxes of bottles to the bar and I unpacked them one by one into the shelves underneath. The work was cathartic, giving me space in my head. I was done with the FBI. Maybe I'd been done for a while, just going through the motions until something better came along.

I lifted my gaze to Phantom as he worked on the shattered front door, and Church as he scrubbed every inch of the club, and Vitold as he talked on the phone, then ended the call. He lifted his gaze to mine. A surge of pride shone in his gaze. *We were a pack.*

Headlights shone through the open door before they ended an instant later. I placed the last bottle on the counter and stepped around the open end of the bar as the others turned toward the thud of car doors. An ache tore through my chest with the sound of frantic steps.

"Chase!" Walker screamed my name.

I lunged, driving myself across the floor as she flew through the open door and down the stairs. Her eyes were wild and wide, scanning the bar.

"Walker!" I roared. *"Walker!"*

Her frantic gaze swept toward my movement. She was filthy. Her clothes were torn and bloody, her hair a mess of knots. She looked...*haunted.* Haunted and hollow from the inside out and thinner than I'd ever seen her before.

The sight drove me forward as I raced around the tables, opened my arms wide, and collided with her. Huge sobs were wrenched from my chest. Her body trembled as I held her close. "Walker. Jesus, Walker. Thank God you're safe. I never...*never thought I'd see you again.*"

She lowered her head and sobbed, clinging to me like I was her salvation. I guess I was in that moment. I was the only one who knew the kind of terror she might've lived through... because I'd lived through the same.

"I didn't think I was going to survive," she cried, "didn't think I was going to make it through."

"You did." I gripped her tightly and lifted my gaze. "You did make it through." I slid my hands to her shoulders and pulled her gently away to stare into her red-rimmed eyes.

"I must look god-awful," she muttered.

"You look like hell," I answered. "And you smell even worse."

She barked out a laugh as clear snot slipped from her nose. I pulled her against me once more. "I fucking love you, Walker."

Only then did I lift my gaze to the young Wolf who watched us from the across the room, the one surrounded by my pack. But it wasn't me the lean, muscular male watched with ravenous eyes.

It was her...

Gave our guys a hard time, didn't realize we were there to help, Mojin's words came rushing back to me. When Walker finally straightened and looked me in the eye, I saw a change in her, a hunger I'd never seen before. She turned her head, wiped the back of her hand beneath her nose, and met the young Wolf's gaze. But the way Wry looked at her was more than careful, more than relief. It was downright possessive...*what the hell had happened between the two of them?*

19

CARINA

"Eat more." I pushed the plate toward her and scowled at the barely touched steak.

She shook her head as she leaned back. "I can't, Chase."

I glanced toward Church, who just leaned against the kitchen counter with his arms crossed over his chest. She'd barely eaten, and had barely said a word, as well.

"You're sure you saw the Alpha dead?" Phantom's words drew my gaze.

He stood next to the young Wolf, watching as he fisted the thick steak in one hand and held the plate underneath to catch the drips, not that there would be much, the way he savaged the half-raw thing. It was his third in a matter of minutes.

There was a nod as his throat muscles worked. I could almost see the thick wad forced down as he glanced toward Walker. He kept looking at her. At first, I brushed it off. After all, they'd spent over a week running for their lives in the middle of nowhere. Then they'd fought, ate, slept near each other, and even though Walker hadn't actually said the words, I knew deep down, they'd killed together, too, just to stay alive.

Still the younger Wolf watched her, not like he was afraid,

more like afraid for her. I forced a smile as she met my gaze and stabbed the steak. "Fine, one more bite." And while she hacked and sawed at the slab, I glanced at Wry.

He was young, nineteen maybe, still carrying that spark of purpose, where every breath was more than oxygen flooding his blood, it was life…it was drive. He hadn't been tempered by the world…not quite. Not even with the jagged scars across the base of his throat or his haunted eyes.

"Need to find you a place to stay," Phantom thought aloud.

"There's always the Fae," Church answered behind me.

Wry shook his head vehemently.

"No?" Phantom's brow rose.

Another shake.

"You can't go back to the club."

A nod, this one insistent and those brown eyes burned a little brighter. The scrape of a chair sounded as Walker rose to her feet. "Maybe I can stay with him."

It wasn't a question. It wasn't, *can I stay with him?* Surprise flared through me as Walker glanced my way, her cheeks reddening.

"You want to stay in a strip club in a dangerous part of the city?" Phantom queried slowly.

"Point to me a place in this city that isn't dangerous, and I can give you a list of all the shootings, stabbings, domestic violence, and all manner of other disgusting fucking things we do to each other," Walker snarled and stepped forward. "You think I'm afraid of the big bad wolf when he comes through the door at me? Buddy, I've been stitching, gluing, and packing up intestines for long enough to have a score or two of my own to settle when *any* fucking asshole *dares* come at me."

Phantom was silent.

Church's brows rose.

Vitold just smiled and lowered his gaze, shaking his head,

and cast me a look that said, *yep, two fucking peas, man...two fucking peas in a pod.*

But Wry...*he fucking beamed.*

His chest puffed out, and the frantic nodding of his head was practically giving *me* a goddamn concussion. Phantom just looked from the steely glare in Walker's eyes to the young Wolf beside him. "Okay...*that was unexpected,*" he breathed.

Walker sucked in a deep breath and shifted her weight from one foot to another, her eyes softening as she glanced at Wry. "Yeah well, just so you know I'm not afraid to step up to the plate when needed."

"Heard that about you," Church murmured and stepped closer, reaching around to brace his hands on either side of the counter around me, boxing me in with his massive chest. "Heard you can hold your own."

"When I have to...just hoping I don't have to," she answered.

"Me, too, *mortal.*" Phantom gave a slow nod, pride gleaming in his gaze. "Me, too. Well, if no one else has any objections, then I guess we'll head to Wild...and by *anyone,* I mean you, Carina. You got a problem with this, then speak now."

Walker jerked a panicked gaze my way. Her breath caught, waiting...*waiting.*

"None whatsoever," I answered, that knowing burning through as I gave her a smile and a wink. "Just a heads-up though, stripper soundtracks can get old pretty quick, so you might want to invest in a set of good headphones."

Church leaned to the side to glare at me. "What's wrong with my damn music, female?"

My heart gave a flutter at that low, warning snarl. I'd never get used to them calling me *female.* Not ever. Heat flared through me as I remembered the way he'd danced, the thick muscles of his hips clenched tight as he thrust against the floor. "Not a goddamn thing."

He gave a slow thrust behind the counter, driving his cock against my ass as he growled, "Damn right."

"Then Wild it is." Phantom gave a nod.

But Walker just watched me, her gaze slowly moving to Church's hands splayed on either side of me. I caught the shift in Vitold's gaze as he watched her watching me, then slowly headed toward the kitchen.

"You alright, *moya lyubov'*?" He stopped alongside me.

I gave him a smile and nodded. He captured my jaw and tilted it up. The kiss was possessive and hungry, claiming a little more of my soul than he had before, then he broke away. "Just checking."

He left me, opening the refrigerator door, but not taking a single thing out.

Men.

But Walker followed the movement, glancing from Church to Vitold.

"You alright, Doc?" Phantom asked.

She jerked her gaze toward him. "Sure," she stuttered.

"Good, then. Wry, you and the Doc can ride with Church. Let's get you set up."

Church leaned closer and gave me a kiss on the back of my neck, along with a playful nip. "You and I aren't anywhere near finished, Carina. You want dancing? I got just what you need."

He pushed away then, leaving me to grip hold of the counter for dear life. One wink my way as he strode out of the kitchen and left, made me weak in the damn knees. Vitold closed the refrigerator and strode after him.

Wry and Walker followed, my best friend giving me that same careful glance she had moments ago. Confusion mingled with a flicker of annoyance. What was her problem? Didn't I just hear her wanting to stay with Wry?

"Ready?" Phantom slowed, catching my glare directed toward Walker.

"Sure," I answered, followed him out of the living quarters, and headed down the hall to where the vehicles waited in the parking lot.

I tried to shake off her condescending stare, turning my focus to the bigger threats waiting for us in the dark. Chaos shifted under my skin as the doors to Phantom's Camaro unlocked. I climbed inside, watching as Arran and Vitold climbed into the Jeep and started the engine as we left the Hunting Ground behind and drove across the bridge, heading for one place that still gave me nightmares. I turned my thoughts to finding Marian.

Phantom had told me about the hair comb and the abandoned office he'd found. He'd kept his fear in check, allowing rage to take its place when he'd described the jacket his sister had used as bedding. But I saw the terror in his gaze, and the way his fists tightened. I may not belong to the FBI anymore, but I was a decent investigator and I'd hunted more than my fair share of scumbags.

My thoughts turned to Ruth as we hit the off-ramp and sped through the streets, heading to the strip of nightclubs in the city. I'd been wrong to send Harlan after her to spare the Wolves. I couldn't blame her if she didn't forgive me. I glanced across at Phantom as he handled the car effortlessly. Not even my Alpha had forgiven me...not yet.

I could spend the rest of my damn life saying sorry and it'd still *never* be enough. Actions spoke louder than words. It was the way of the pack...*the way of the pack*. Phantom turned the corner and pulled onto the street. The moment he did, my heart thundered.

Gunshots rang out in my head, followed by the sound of shattering glass. Panic filled me. The thunder of my pulse filled my ears.

"Breathe, Carina," Phantom murmured, the deep sound of

his voice invaded as he pulled up into the parking lot and killed the engine. "You're safe now...just breathe."

Headlights cut through the darkness, illuminating the inside of the car as my Alpha turned toward me. "You alright?"

I forced a nod and swallowed, pushing back the memories of the past. A metal fence surrounded the rear of the club. The blackened walls were gone, pulled down, some taken for evidence. I tried not to look at the spot where Murphy had been found, his body mauled by teeth and claws.

Those torturous feelings rose, dragging a flare of agony with them as I closed the car door behind me. I swallowed relief for the fact he was gone and wrestled with the guilt that rose with it. *Good,* Chaos murmured. *One less piece of shit to contend with.*

Car doors opened and closed all around me. Boots crunched on asphalt behind me as hands slid around my waist. *Arran.* I leaned back against him, letting his scent wash over me.

"You alright?" he whispered.

In my head, I was still screaming his name, still gripped by fear, still thinking he was dead. But he wasn't and we weren't back there anymore. "Yeah," I said as I breathed a sigh of relief. "I think I am."

Lights came on inside the club. I turned as Vitold and Church headed for the front. But Wry was there...staring at a spot on the ground, and Walker stood next to him. She reached out slowly and her fingers carefully brushed the back of his hand. The gesture so damn intimate it was uncomfortable to see. I took a quiet step backwards, but still caught the shift in the young Wolf's gaze. He wouldn't let someone come up behind him again, not like he had before, and as he turned his hand and took Walker's in his, I knew he'd do anything to keep her safe.

Just like my Wolves had done for me.

Love.

That's what had brought us together. That's what made our

pack...our pack. I turned then, leaving them standing in the dark and let them have their moment. God knew they deserved it. The front of the club hadn't even been touched by the fire. But a faint acrid stench still lingered in the air inside. I stepped through the open doors and along the corridor that led me into the seating area. This place was bigger than the Hunting Ground. A dance floor was to my left in the distance. The dancers' stage was to my right, and in the back was Arran.

He glanced my way as I neared, that careful stare scanning every emotion in my eyes. Phantom was on the phone. I could hear his voice spill through the club as footsteps came from behind me. Walker and Wry strode in, hand in hand, my best friend taking in the bar and the tables and finally, the stage.

"I have Hunter and the rest of the outer pack on their way." Phantom slid the phone into his pocket and met the young Wolf's stare. "They'll take turns keeping watch."

One hard shake of his head and Wry dropped Walker's hand.

"Look, it isn't safe," Phantom growled, and stepped closer.

Fingers moved carefully as Wry turned to face Walker. Sign. He was trying to sign. Phantom just scowled, his gaze shifting between Wry and my best friend. "This is happening."

"Hold up," Walker commanded, lifting a finger and stopping the Alpha cold. "I can't...Wry, you're not making sense."

The young Wolf slammed his fist into his palm and shook his head in frustration before he turned to Phantom. His long legs consumed the distance between them in a heartbeat. He was shorter than the Alpha, barely. Wiry muscles in his arms were corded and strained, but Church had said he'd been even thinner at Wry's age, barely more than skin and bones, and look at him now, six foot three of gorgeous muscles and strength.

Even without the brawn, Wry was commanding. He lifted his gaze to Phantom's and met his Alpha's gaze. Seconds felt like minutes, until the stare was strained.

"You sure?" Phantom murmured.

One simple, forceful nod.

"You know what happens, right? What happens if you come under attack?" Phantom shifted his gaze to Walker.

Another nod from Wry, only this time slower. Something unspoken passed between them, until it dawned on me. Walker would be here. She'd be vulnerable...she'd be a target for an attack.

"Then you keep the doors locked. I want daily updates...*nonnegotiable, Wolf.*"

Wry nodded carefully.

"This club needs to get back to business. I want the doors open a week from now, so you have a lot of work to do. I *will* be checking on you."

"So will I," Church growled.

"And me," Vitold added.

"And me," Arran chimed in, glancing my way. "With Carina."

My heart thundered as I glanced at Walker. I didn't like this, not with a vicious Wolf from the Inner Circle after blood. Footsteps echoed through the hallway. Wry was already lifting his gaze and stepping to the side, directly in front of Walker.

The act was so powerful and protective, something Vitold had done for me countless times, placing himself between her and possible danger.

Jesus, those two were really serious. I was almost shocked, not because of the age difference, but because Walker had never shown any interest in love.

"Phantom." I shifted my focus to massive older Wolf headed our way. He was stocky, moving with the kind of long, lithe grace Phantom and the others had. I could tell he was a fighter, one of those Phantom had spoken about, the ones who preferred to live in the outer reaches, a leader of his own band of Wolves, but owing loyalty to one Alpha...and right now, I was praying that Alpha was Phantom.

"Hunter," my Alpha nodded acknowledgement.

"I have my men waiting outside." The male scanned the room and stilled on me.

"Been a change of plans." Phantom strode forward, meeting the battle-scarred male. "How do you feel about hunting the Alpha of Alphas?"

Hunter stilled, then slowly turned his head, his scowl deepening. "You mean Finis?"

Panic rose as I searched the older Wolf's gaze. Phantom was risking everything by telling him. He wasn't part of *our* pack, but a member of the outer pack. I glanced at Church, then Vitold, and Arran searching for a hint of concern. But there was none.

"I've been waiting a goddamn lifetime to bring that bastard to his knees," Hunter growled.

"I need him alive." Desperation deepened Phantom's tone. "He's after my sister."

Surprise flared in the older man's eyes. He glanced over his shoulder at Church. "Marian's *here?*"

A low snarl came from Wry as Phantom nodded. "Yes, she's here somewhere…and she's pregnant, heavily pregnant."

"Jesus." Hunter raked strands of long brown hair back from his face and winced.

"So, I need the bastard alive, Hunter. I need him alive and broken."

Hunter gave Church a careful glance. "Oh, the bastard will be broken, I can assure you of that. Text me the coordinates. If the bastard is out there, we'll find him."

20

CARINA

*H*unt him...the words echoed as Hunter left the club. Chaos was moving in the darkness of my mind and rose to the surface. *Hunt,* she whispered. *Hunt for my Wolf.*

Hunt for her Wolf indeed. An ache flared across my chest as that Unseelie green pulsed. I knew the sensation so intimately now and the flood of power that came with it.

Hands moved slowly, the slap of flesh on flesh drew my gaze as Wry signed.

"He wants to hunt," Walker spoke carefully, her gaze on the Wolf as his hands gestured.

"No." Phantom shook his head. *"Not negotiable.* I need you here, need you focused. We need a command post, a place for the others to come and go. I *need* your eyes and ears keeping track of everything until we find her."

The young Wolf stilled, his brown eyes glinting with purpose.

"We can do that, can't we?" Walker said carefully, cutting Wry a look of pure purpose. "We can be here when they need to rest. We have food, water, bedding."

A slow, careful nod from Wry.

"That's settled then," Walker finished.

But Wry wasn't done, that determined stare never once breaking from Phantom's gaze.

Tension rose, sending shivers up my spine as Phantom took a step toward Wry. "You got a problem with that, Wry?"

Male against male. Wry held his gaze, then finally shook his head.

"Doc, here, can keep the bastard alive until we find out what he knows about Marian."

Wry threw his hands in the air, fingers flying, until Phantom cut him off with a shake of his head. "Don't bother. You think you're the only one with vengeance burning in his fucking veins? You think getting your damn throat ripped out is the worst thing that can happen to you? You don't know what retribution is yet, *pup.* Take a number and get in fucking line."

Hate seethed in Wry's gaze as Phantom turned away and the rest of the pack followed. I glanced at Walker as desperation mingled with exhaustion in her eyes.

"Try to get some rest." I reached for her, drawing her against me to murmur, "We'll be back as soon as we can."

She barely hugged me back, just gripped me weakly before I stepped away. "Be careful out there, Carina," she murmured. "Try to remember we're not one of them."

I winced at the words, gave a small nod, and followed my Wolves out of Wild and into the night once more. Not one of them? No, but I wasn't one of my kind, either. I didn't think I'd ever been, not really.

Raised to be alone and lonely. My purpose was nothing more than a desperate need to be consumed by something. Better than to acknowledge the gaping, empty hole in my life. My thoughts turned to my father as I headed for the Camaro. Phantom was already inside, the engine rumbling with that throaty growl as I climbed in.

"You ready for this?"

There was an edge to his tone. A tremor. The question wasn't if I was ready—I turned to find his piercing gaze in the dark—the question was, was he?

Where you go, so do I, Chaos whispered, and the words echoed. "Where you go, so do I."

Silver glinted in his stare, headlights splashed against the dashboard as he shoved the car into gear and reversed. We followed the others, heading deeper into the city. In the side mirror, Arran's black Jeep speared off. A quiet descended, one not born from an emptiness, but from predatory hunger, that beast that scented and watched…listening to everything.

The hairs on the back of my neck rose as Phantom slowly turned, driving down quiet backstreets and past darkened houses. I caught glimpses of the others. Midnight blue shone under streetlights a street in front, before Church's car turned again and was gone.

Cell lights brightened. Phantom drove and texted.

"You know I can do that, right?" I lifted my gaze to his.

"Text?"

"No, Wolf. I can drive. It's kinda what I'm trained for, you know?"

Surprise shone in his eyes. He didn't like giving up his precious control, I saw it now. But one nod and he pulled the Camaro over to the side of the road and climbed out. I scooted over, slid around the gearshift and into the driver's seat.

Nerves filled me as I adjusted the seat forward and checked the mirrors as Phantom climbed back in. "Hunter's on Lions Parade, thinks he might have a scent."

"That was fast." I shoved the car into gear, and swung around.

Tension rose, snaking through me as Phantom's phone brightened once more. I pulled out and punched the accelerator, cutting swiftly through the streets. Red and blue flashed up ahead. I slowed, signaled, and turned, only to find several cop cars parked on either side up ahead. My gaze shifted to the unmarked. FBI without a doubt. FBI and Crown City PD gathering in the streets. Something just felt *wrong*. I slowed the Camaro, catching one of the officer's gaze as we slowly drove on by before, barely a minute later, Phantom gave a snarl.

"False alarm," he muttered and scanned the street outside his window.

"He's hunting your sister, right?" I turned, heading into the more dangerous part of town.

Time seemed to slow to a crawl. Street after street. I kept my focus on the darkened buildings, wondering who and what was hidden inside. This part of the city was no pretty Brighton Park. There were no sculptures, no flowers, not even the city sweepers dared come here.

This was a place where the cover of darkness was a blessing in disguise where shady deals went down among even shadier people and no one looked at you twice. Red and blue lights flashed as a police cruiser pulled over, cutting off a group of three young men as they walked along the sidewalk. "So, if you we're him, where would you go?"

"Not here, that's for sure," Phantom muttered. "Too much attention. I'd look for the quiet places, the neighborhoods that keep to themselves."

"But out there, you're too far away. Out there, you're at risk of being seen," I argued, the agent in me rising to the surface. "You'd want a place that was central and quiet. A place abandoned, a place where you could come and go as you wanted."

"And leave no trace behind," he responded.

My pulse raced as I turned the Camaro once more. "And how could an Alpha Wolf do that?"

Phantom turned his head, that piercing stare carving through me as though I wasn't even here. "By covering it up."

"With another Immortal's scent." I turned again and drove

my boot against the accelerator, honing in now...*like I scented prey.*

Phantom slid his thumb across the screen of his cell and lifted it to his ear. "Hunter, the warehouse behind Jewel. Yeah, that's the one. I think he might be using it to cover his scent."

I couldn't believe I was going back there, to the place where it had all begun and, even as the images of that night filled my mind, Chaos smiled her chilling smile and rubbed her hands in glee.

The place where I found you, she whispered. *The place where you became mine.*

"Not yours, bitch." I snarled, and nosed the Camaro along the darkened street heading toward the ruined Jewel. "You...*are mine.*"

Chaos smiled at the words and let out a purr. The sound rolled like thunder as the headlights washed across the corner of the warehouse. Deja vu hit me like a truck as I kept driving, focused forward, and never once turned my head.

Phantom was frozen, barely moving, barely breathing. I opened my mouth to speak.

"Keep going," he murmured. "Park two blocks over and we'll double back."

Two blocks? I eased off the accelerator and let the car coast while Phantom's fingers flew across the keyboard, punching in coordinates. I didn't need his words, that was answer enough. He *felt* something, enough to make us walk two blocks back at the ass crack of dawn.

Exhaustion pushed in as I tapped the brakes and pulled the Camaro onto a side street and parked. Headlights off, and we plunged into darkness. "He's there, isn't he?"

"Is or was...I couldn't tell. His scent is faint."

"But it's there?"

"Yeah," he glanced my way, his Wolf's eyes glinting. "It's there."

He waited for a second, long enough for headlights to illuminate the road behind us, before he climbed out. The soft *thud* of car doors followed. I eased the driver's door shut and lifted the keys to Phantom. He just shook his head. "You keep them. If anything happens. I want you to go straight to—"

"Wry…" I answered as he stepped behind the muscle car and stopped in front of me.

"No, not there. Go straight to the Vampires. Do not fucking stop, do you hear me, Carina? Do not fucking slow. You drive like the devil himself is after you."

The Vampires? Heat bloomed in my cheeks as I shook my head. "I don't think that's a good—"

A low snarl resounded in the back of his throat, stopping my words cold. Steel shone brighter in his eyes as fear washed over me. One hard swallow, and I nodded. "Got it," I murmured as the others headed our way.

Panic washed over me as my Alpha turned to the others. Church, Vitold, Arran.

"Arran, you're with me. Church and Vitold, I want you to head three blocks east and then turn the corner. If he's there, I want the bastard boxed in."

Phantom's phone brightened. He glanced at the screen. "Hunter and his team are coming in from the north."

An icy fist clenched in my stomach. There was something about this that didn't feel right. I didn't want us to split up, didn't want us spread too thin. If we had more men…more Wolves, it might work. Maybe we should wait for the others?

I took a step forward, the words on the tip of my tongue, but Church and Vitold were already striding away and sinking into the darkness, leaving Arran behind. I cut a glance to the Wolf as panic swirled inside me. His gaze fixed on mine before he mouthed, *you alright?*

I wanted to shake my head, wanted to tell him about the panic that gripped me. But it wasn't my place, not to voice my concerns, not when I was already skating on thin ice within the pack. I gave a nod as Phantom left the alley and headed for the street.

I followed, scanning the darkness. But this time not just with my sight. I let the hunger flow through me, let it seep from my mind and flow out into the air. Chaos was a hunter, an opportunist...a danger, and not just to me.

"As long as you protect the Wolves," I murmured, and kept walking, "I don't give a shit."

That resounding purr of foreboding grew louder. The Wolves. I shifted my gaze to Phantom walking ahead, then dropped my focus to the pavement, catching movement behind me. She belonged to the Wolves now, and they belonged to her.

A flare of light up ahead. Phantom's steps slowed as he scanned his cell, then in a heartbeat, his steps quickened and before I knew it, we were running, the sound of our steps like thunder in my head.

Chaos rose quickly, sweeping through the darkness of my mind. A beast herself, she drew in the night around me, tasting...*sensing*. I clenched my jaw, hissing with the bite of pain as that Unseelie glow spilled from my chest.

There...the snarl raced through my mind. Sharp, *bitter*. That foulness filled my nose and slid down the back of my throat. I swallowed hard, dropped my head, and dug deeper as Phantom started to pull away.

"There." Arran jerked his head toward movement as I lunged from the gutter and hauled ass across the street.

Church and Vitold were a blur cutting across the same street in the distance before they were gone. I pumped my arms, my thighs on fire, but still, I was barely at a stroll compared to them. "Go..." I wheezed. "I'll catch up."

"Not on your fucking life," Arran growled, placing his hand in the middle of my back. "Now *move your ass, Special Agent*."

His words spurred me on and I pushed harder, tearing past

familiar darkened shops, and lifted my gaze to the street ahead. There...in the distance. That sense of foreboding rose, the feeling growing stronger and stronger as the deafening sound of shattering glass filled the night.

Arran growled and lunged, racing ahead, his long, lithe movements suddenly powerful, filled with purpose. My hand went to my hip on instinct, but there was no gun, not anymore. A howl of rage ripped through the silence before movement came from my right. Phantom lunged, his eyes wide and blazing, his hands shining black. "It's not him," he roared. *"It's not him!"*

But he was here...*somewhere.*

Phantom whipped his head toward movement as Church ran toward us, his boots pummeling the asphalt. More movement came up ahead. The dark blur made my heart stutter and stop, but before I knew it, Church was barreling over to me, grasping my arm to pull me closer. "It's alright, it's just Hunter."

Hunter.

The older Wolf lifted his gaze to mine as the washed-out streetlight found his face. For a second...just a second, I thought it was *him,* the Alpha of Alpha's...the one who'd come for me in the Dark City and I'd been helpless to fight. *Where the fuck is she?* Finis's roar resounded in my head as I sucked in great gulps of air.

My lungs were on fire and my legs were numb. Momentum was all that drove me forward...that and desperation. I turned the corner with Church and caught sight of the warehouse... Panic kicked in my chest as memories of that night rose. Blood, death...hunger lingered at the edges of my mind. But I couldn't think about that now, couldn't let that terror shake my present. *Focus...that's all you have to do, focus and fucking survive.*

Church's gaze jerked toward the dark alley as we sped past. His hand slipped from my arm as he slowed.

"Keep going!" he growled.

He left me as I raced ahead toward the towering mountain of steel. But I wasn't alone for long. A *boom* rocked the night. Steel howled as claws punctured the walls from the inside. I stumbled as those claws shredded thick steel like a damn tin can and Phantom strode out.

He threw one look at my terror, took a step toward me, and stopped. His eyes shimmered silver, his bloodied hands were curled into fists. But it was his face that gripped me with terror. Shadows welled in the hollows of his cheeks. He looked like a ghost, a wrathful spirit consumed with vengeance.

He jerked his head, nostrils flaring, as Hunter strode through the darkness, heading toward me. "The goddamn place *reeks* of him."

My Alpha gave a nod, his lips curled as he scanned the dark. "He was here, not more than a few minutes ago."

But it was that gaping tear in the warehouse wall that gripped me. Shadows and the stench of death waited inside. Something pulsed in there, something fetid and foul. Something that beat like a rotting heart...*thud...thud...thud.* Chaos let out a hiss as I stepped forward, leaving the two Wolves behind.

There, Chaos moaned as a gust of wind tore through the gaping hole and slammed into me. *Right there.* I turned my shoulders and stepped through the shredded steel.

"Carina?" Phantom called.

But I was already in the grasp of that scent, already drawn deeper into the spell of the past. "In there," I whispered. "I can feel something."

Footsteps echoed behind me as I left the faint spill of the streetlights behind and sank into the dark. Hate rippled...hate and something else, something darker, something *deeper.* Chaos let out a tortured moan and the sound tore from my lips.

"What is it?" Phantom asked.

But I couldn't tell him, couldn't voice the horror that

gripped me inside. I could only walk deeper, listening to that sickening *thud...thud...thud* of that raw, fetid thing *pulsing.*

"What the fuck is that?" Hunter growled.

The interior lights of the warehouse came on with a flicker. They were faint at first, until the illumination hummed and brightened to a harsh glare that made me wince. *Boom...boom... boom...*that sluggish pounding grew louder, and with it, Chaos's low tortured moan deepened as I crossed the massive space.

Painted orange marks still marred the concrete, drawing my gaze to the darkened blood splatter. But that wasn't what called me, not the remnants of that night nor the tortured memories that still lived in my head. It was something else, something *newer...*something that made Chaos thrash with agony.

Something that made the Wolves behind me growl in fear.

Footsteps boomed like thunder as Phantom strode past me, his gaze drawn to the same darkened corner at the end of the warehouse.

"Phantom?" Church called behind us, and Chaos threw her head back and howled with pain.

Thud...thud...thud. That festering thing called me closer. I couldn't do anything but obey.

"Phantom...what is that?" Church's voice trembled as Phantom pushed forward, his hands fisted at his sides, body canting forward as though he *fought* to step closer...as though the very thing that beat with savage darkness also made him want to turn and run.

Like it made me want to turn and run.

Phantom let out a moan as he neared the end. Black on gray, something glinted in the shadows. Something that sparkled like metal...something that smelled of *death.*

"*Get...away,*" Phantom growled, desperation burning in his words. "Church...Church, get away."

"What is that?" Church strode past me, his gaze riveted on the *thing* in front of Phantom.

My steps slowed as that glint of steel hanging from the wall sharpened into focus. Phantom reached out and for a second, I wanted to scream *STOP!* I wanted to howl with rage. I wanted to tear the world apart with fury. I wanted to protect—I turned my body to Church and lifted my hand...I wanted to protect.

Links clinked in Phantom's hands as he drew the thing closer through the shadows until the overhead warehouse lights shone against the steel. They were shackles. Thick, heavy, the links so round they reminded me of the Costello shipping yard. But those shackles weren't designed to moor a ship. They were designed to chain a human...*or a Wolf.*

Church let out a sound that ripped through my soul. He froze, shaking his head.

"Get away from here," Phantom cried out. "Church...*get away!*

But there was no stopping my Wolf, no changing the present as he went closer, staggering on trembling legs. "That's my blood...*my* blood."

And in an instant, I knew what had drawn me...what that foul beating thing had been all along.

It wasn't a heart.

It was hate.

It was cruelty, and savagery...it was *a trap.*

21

CARINA

"**N**O!" Phantom roared and spun to face us.

He shoved his arm forward and dropped the shackles. His eyes were wide, terror shining, as the cuffs hit the concrete with a *clang* and the sound echoed through the warehouse. "Get away from here, Church! *I said...get the fuck away!*"

But it was too late, Church was already reaching for the shackles, already unleashing the terror in his mind. The terror that had been Finis's plan all along.

Chaos screamed as that unseen connection blazed to life between us, tearing memories from Church and slamming into me. Snatches came through. Terror, desperation, a life barely holding on. The stench of that place came with it, putrid and rank, burning my eyes, welling in my belly...because that's all there was for him.

The stench. The darkness...and *the end.*

Just air...just the stench of his own shit and vomit. Vomit that had long ago hardened and dried.

How long have I been here? My belly clenched tight with his words as they filled me like they were my own. A sob trapped in the back of my throat. *How long...how long since he took her away?*

Marian. Her name filled me as it had filled Church. The girl who had been locked away in there with him. But *he* came back for her, and tore her away. Her screams still haunted me, terrifying and shrill, filling my head. *"Phantom! No...no...no... Phantom...PHANTOM!" she screamed.*

Phantom. She called for a ghost that wasn't here. A ghost that'd never come. There was no one here. No one, until *he* came once more. The Wolf who smelled like death. The Wolf who'd broken my bones and beaten me bloody. The one who'd shackled me. I lifted my head, unable to see in the darkness. But I could feel, and I could hear.

Clink.

Clink.

Clink.

Chains rattled. Sharp edges carved my flesh. Warmth ran free and the metallic scent of blood filled my nose as it ran down my hands and over the shackles.

I'm dying...

The thought surfaced as I stared into the emptiness. Harsh, ravaging breaths were all that remained now. A moan, barely a whimper, rebounded against the box I was in. *No air...no air... only a matter of time now...when the Wolf power in me fades away.* I closed my eyes, wishing it would come faster. Death, death...no more pain.

"Marian!"

A faint scream slipped in. I clenched my eyes closed. *Stop that...stop that. No one is coming for me...no one.* Just like *he'd* said, like he'd *promised*. The sound of his laughter swirled around inside me as that call came once more.

"Marian!"

A moan escaped. Fire followed, searing through my chest as I lifted my head and opened my eyes.

"Marian! Marian, where are you!"

"Here," I croaked, and sucked in a breath, dragging it from the empty pit of my soul. A pit I was falling into…a pit that was my end and with my last ounce of strength, I roared, *"I'M OVER HERE!"*

"Marian? What the fuck."

Fists beat the steel container. I yanked my arms, but the shackles just bit deeper and the gnash of metal followed. But I didn't care, didn't feel a thing. *"Please!* Get me out of here!"

There was nothing. *Nothing.* No sound of the male. Just silence. Just cold, empty silence. Grief rose like a wave to consume me. It was a trick…always just a trick. Warmth slipped from the corner of my eyes this time. I sank into that loneliness, swallowed by the darkness…until the howling screech of metal filled the space.

Light.

Just a flicker.

Faint like the glint of stars. Just *like* the glint of stars. Cold air rushed in, sweet, cold air.

"Jesus fucking Christ." The male gagged. "Marian…*is that you?"*

I licked my lips, tried to force the word through the burn in my chest, a burn that swelled my throat. "Help…*me."*

The shriek of steel came once more as the side of the container peeled backwards. More air rushed in and I closed my eyes and opened my mouth to the sweet rush.

"My sister," the male croaked, forcing my lids to flutter open. "The bastard took my sister."

I could barely see him as he leaned into the cramped space. There was nothing but the silver eyes of his Wolf. Nothing but revulsion and horror. "He…he kept you in here?"

"Gone."

The male's brow furrowed. "What?"

"Gone," I whispered, and moaned as the shackles snapped tight when I tried to move.

His gaze snapped to the steel chains above me before he swallowed hard. "Fucking hell. Just wait…just wait right there."

He stepped away, leaving the open side of the steel container to swing closed once more, locking me in. I whimpered, "No. Don't leave me…*don't.*"

The side was yanked open once more and he was back, this time with heavy cutters in his hand. He took one look at my arms stretched high above my head and murmured, "This is gonna hurt, so hold on."

A *snap…snap,* and my arms fell, smacking the floor. Agony roared through my shoulders, tearing me apart from the inside out. Then he was closer, the cutters tossed to the floor of the container with a *bang!*

"Easy," he murmured, those wide eyes fixed on me. "Jesus Christ, I don't want to hurt you." He slid one arm under my legs and the other under my back.

"Dying," I whispered as the world swam and darkness rose once more. *"Dying…"*

"NO!" Church roared as his memories blazed in my head.

I stumbled backwards and slammed my hands against my ears as Chaos howled with rage. *Kill him…*she roared. *I'm going to fucking kill him! I'm going to tear him apart and feed him his own black, pulsing heart!*

Her rage was consuming, driving me to stumble backwards as the warehouse walls rattled and bowed.

"Carina!" Phantom roared, his gaze wide as the ceiling of the warehouse peeled backwards with a shrill shriek.

"Carina!" Vitold was there, grasping my shoulders, and pulled me against him. "Control it…control the beast, Carina."

But it was Church the beast fixed on…Church as he dragged those broken blue eyes toward me, then turned and lunged. He was a blur in the darkness, racing toward the gaping hole we'd come through.

"Church," I yelled, shoving Vitold aside, and ran after him.

Pain and desperation drove me to follow. I charged after him as he smashed through the torn-open wall and into the night.

"Carina!" Phantom roared. "Carina, no!"

But this was one time I couldn't obey...*not even if he* was *the Alpha.* I lowered my head and pumped my arms, racing through the torn wall and out into the night. My pulse thundered, the sound deafening in my ears. I tried to listen, tried to track which way he'd gone.

"Carina!" Arran called behind me.

But I couldn't focus on him, not when Church's desperation was screaming inside my head. Chaos swirled all around me, dragging shadows from the corners of the buildings. *Find him,* she commanded and the dark apparitions scattered like hunters searching for prey. But it wasn't prey we wanted. It was the Wolf who owned our heart, who'd marked our soul...who'd filled our minds and made our bodies hunger.

It was Church...Church who was in agony. Church who was consumed by the memories of his pain.

I turned along the street where I'd come from, took two steps and stopped. No, not this way. The power inside me trembled, dragging me toward the small dark alley. I followed that tremble of power and left the bright glow of the streetlights behind.

Finis could be out here. His scent still lingered, raw and rancid, a tinge of bitter excitement as he waited for us to find the shackles. I swallowed hard and kept moving, glancing over my shoulder as I left the streets behind and sank deeper into the alley.

"Church?" I called him. "Church, please, it's me."

Harsh breaths were all I heard, shadows slipping around me, crawling along the walls as I passed the end of the massive warehouse and kept on moving. Instinct was taking over now, forcing me to push deeper and, as I lifted my gaze higher, I caught the corner of Jewel.

The Jewel. Maybe that's where he was?

"He's hurting." The growl came from in front of me. Phantom stepped out of the darkness and into my path. One shake of his head stopped me in my tracks. "You don't want to see him like this."

"Let me past, Phantom." I demanded as I tried to step around him.

But the male filled the space, all broad shoulders and dangerous stare. He shoved his arm out in front of me, barring my shoulders. "I'm telling you now...it isn't pretty."

"He's my *mate*," I snarled, and lifted my gaze to his. "If it was you out there, you think I'd stop to get to you? You think I wouldn't tear the fucking city apart and *anyone* else who stood in my way?"

He stilled, then slowly lowered his arm. "No, you wouldn't."

"Then let me pass, Phantom."

His forehead creased as he exhaled hard and slow. "Just...be gentle."

I didn't have time to answer him, didn't have time to sooth his pain. Not when Church was all I could feel...and when the haunting memories of his past were so close to the surface. I left Phantom behind, feeling the weight of his gaze on me as I glanced along the back entrance and caught the back door of Jewel ajar.

Church...Chaos moaned as his agony wafted through the door. He was all I could feel, all I could sense. His pain was choking, filling my head, wrapping around my throat until it squeezed the life from me. Just like it'd been for him all those years ago.

My Wolf...

Turmoil and rage were packed way down deep, no wonder

he was so tortured. He needed my power, needed my darkness and my strength. He needed Chaos to be just as dominant as she was. He needed to fight to find release...and as a low snarl bloomed from the darkness, I knew he needed Chaos now more than ever.

"Can you help him?" I whispered.

Help? Maybe...but I can fight. I can rage and ravage and hunt...I can find this Alpha and tear him apart until I wear his blood...is that good enough? Her desperation curled my lips and clenched my fists.

Kill. The need consumed me as I stepped through the doorway and into Jewel. But this wasn't about me, wasn't my pain to soothe, wasn't my retribution. It was Church's. Church with his terror so close to the surface.

Moonlight slipped from the high windows to flood the room with the faint silver glow. I used the light, and made my way carefully around chairs and tables as that tethered connection between us grew stronger and stronger.

"You shouldn't be here," the low growl made me flinch.

I scanned the darkness, my focus drawn to the shadows at the edge of the room. Church stood with his back to me, his arms up, braced on the wall.

"You should go," he snarled, and clenched his fists. "I'm not safe to be around."

"I know," I said, and took a step closer.

Chaos pushed against the barrier between us, her need pulsing and beating, growing stronger and stronger, drawing him toward me. My Wolf spun, his eyes blazing with pain and rage. The scrape of a chair came next to me toppled by unseen hands, and fell backwards, hitting the floor with a *thud*.

Church glanced toward the sound as I stepped forward, and another slammed to the floor and slid along until it hit the wall. Shadows raced, spilling along the floor as the building gave a tremble.

"You're not the only one not safe to be around, Wolf," I murmured and moved closer. "Not the only one who wants to tear the world apart right now."

His breath slowed, and his gaze burned.

"I can't control her," I warned, and clenched my fists as one of the high windows shattered.

Shards of glass rained down as I lifted my hand and stepped even closer. "She wants blood, Wolf. She wants blood and death and she doesn't care how it happens."

His cheek twitched under my fingers. Breath caught as those blue eyes raged with pain. "I'm ruined, Carina, broken and ruined."

"You think I'm not?" I moved against him. "Like calls to like, remember?"

Behind us, another window shattered as I slid my hand lower, sliding down the hard ridge of his jaw to splay against his throat. "You want to fight, or do you want to fuck?"

His jaw clenched as I gripped his throat. I felt the tremble as his moan tore free. Those blue eyes blazed with the kind of dark fury that both excited and terrified me. "Fight or fuck, Wolf. It's up to you?"

22

CARINA

"Get away from me," he warned, lips curling, his fangs on full display.

The hairs on my arms rose with the deep, savage sound. But even as I shuddered, Chaos was rising to stake her claim.

"You want to hurt me?" she murmured, and the words resounded between my lips. "Or do you want the kind of release you've been craving? The kind that will leave those *fucking* memories behind?"

Hard breaths scattered my hair. "Can't…leave…them…behind," he growled, and the sound vibrated underneath my grip. "Not for a goddamn second…*not ever.*"

I moved closer, until I pressed against his towering frame and slid my hand around to the nape of his neck. "Then don't you think it's time to take control? Don't you want that? Control, *power.* I can give it to you."

His lips trembled and curled, teeth bared in the dark.

I lifted my other hand and with it came a tremble that carved through the building. Enough to rattle the walls…and shatter the windows. The deafening *cracks* ripped through the space.

"He can't hurt you, Wolf, not now...not anymore. Not with Chaos at your side."

He reached for me, his hand sliding along my throat, the webbing between his thumb and forefinger forcing my chin up until I met his gaze.

"I don't want to be gentle," he growled, that bestial stare boring into mine. "I don't want to be kind. I don't want to care about your needs...I just want to be..."

"Brutal," I answered for him. "You want to be raw and savage and brutal. You want to be empty."

Pain darkened his eyes. "Yes," he murmured. "That's exactly what I want. I just want to be empty."

Power crack;ed through me and lashed the air like a whip. Chairs and tables exploded into shards of wood that battered the walls and the floor. "Empty?" I reached for him, pulling him down to me. "I'll make you feel more than you've ever felt before. More than hunger, more than pain...more than the darkness that eats your soul."

I yanked his lips hard against mine. That was all it took for the dam wall to shatter inside him, all it took for that battle between his rage and his need to break. I felt his Wolf charge to the surface and unleash a chilling snarl into my mouth. My tongue ran over the tips of his fangs. Ones that pressed against my tongue and filled my mouth—fangs that *were growing*.

My shirt tore with a sickening *rip* and cold air danced across my back. Church shoved me away with the kind of brutal strength that took my breath away. His chest heaved with unmerciful breaths as he stared at me, his beast glinting in his eyes.

"You...you don't want this," he insisted, his voice deep, guttural and strained, hovering between Wolf and man. "You don't want me, not like this."

I lowered my gaze to the tips of his fingers, where long, wicked claws grew. Fear punctured my defenses, just like his claws would breach my skin. "You're wrong about that. I want you more than I've ever wanted you."

A shake of his head forced me to move. I stepped back a step, tearing the remainder of my shirt free and casting it to the floor. "You think you can scare me away? You think letting your Wolf free will make me turn and run?" I yanked the straps of my bra down and my breasts bounced, slipping free. "You don't scare me. I want you, Wolf. I want *you*."

He lowered that animalistic gaze to my body and a ripple of *otherness* tore through him like a shiver. Man and beast. That's what I dealt with now. The man who battled the monster...but only one of them could touch me. Only one of them could take what he wanted, until with a guttural roar, he lunged.

Church was a blur as he grabbed me in an instant and lifted my feet from the floor. Claws dragged across my skin as he grabbed my bra and cast it aside.

"Want...*you*," that inhuman voice promised as he took me down to the floor, laying me on some shattered furniture.

Shadows lashed and pulled along the walls as my head hit the floor. Darkness moved like it obeyed a new mistress now... and that mistress smiled, forcing my back to arch for his gaze. "Bite me," I urged. "I want your fangs on my skin."

There was nothing left of the man in his eyes now. Nothing that could bring his hunger back from the edge. I lifted my gaze to the raging beast in his eyes as he braced his paws on either side of my head, towering over me.

"Ever been eaten by the big, bad Wolf, Special Agent?" the beast in him growled.

He lowered his head and dragged the tips of those fangs across my chest.

My nipples hardened instantly and I knew he could see the way my body reacted, knew he was aware of every goddamn tremor and catch of my breath. Warmth spilled over the swell of my breast as he moved his head, his tongue dancing across the hardened peak. I clenched my fists and closed my eyes as the sharp points of his fangs followed, finding my tender flesh.

A moan ripped free, making me squirm, and heat flared, driving deeper and deeper with every flick of his tongue.

"Bite me, she says," he murmured as the vibrations danced across my nipple. "You have no idea what that does to me...and my Wolf."

"I have an idea," I denied breathlessly.

I fought the tremble, clenching my fist closed before I opened my hand again and reached for his face. Hard lines replaced had his perfect cheeks. He was morphing as I touched him, bones shifting under his skin. There was a catch of his breath and that predatory gaze moved down me, lingering on my breasts.

"Take off your clothes, Carina."

My belly tightened, but I never hesitated, finding the button of my jeans without my gaze leaving his face. One push of the button and slide of the zipper, and I was shoving my jeans low, sliding them down my thighs as I kicked off my boots.

Fur the color of desert sand slowly carved through his skin. Bones shattered with a *crack,* making him twitch and close his eyes with a groan. But when he opened his eyes again, it was Church's blue eyes shining through.

Church who whimpered, "Can't...stop...him. Wants you too much."

I grasped his face, feeling the long bones of his snout as his face morphed. Shadows consumed what remained of Jewel around us and, as Chaos's power unleashed inside me, they spilled out. Gone were the walls...gone was the floor. Instead of the ruined bar, we were in the middle of a forest, one with towering pine trees above us and soft earth at my back.

Church lifted his head and stared all around us. Confusion tormented him for a second until he found my gaze once more. "You?"

I pushed upwards. "Me."

He leaned backwards, sitting on his heels, his beast fighting for control. But both craved freedom...and me. I pushed upwards, climbing to my hands and knees, and rose to stand. I stepped out of my jeans, my hands sliding over my hips, catching my panties, and slowly drew them down. "It's just us here now, Wolf. No one else. You want to take me like a beast? Then take me."

His forehead creased. Agony twisted his perfect features. The shake of his head was nothing but a lie. I slid my panties lower and stepped out. Cold danced across my skin, making my nipples harden even more as I moved closer. I touched his cheek, feeling the bones shift and morph under my touch.

One twitch of his lips, and an inhuman snarl came spilling out of his lips to surround me. He took one step, pushing me backwards. I stepped, unable to see where I went, and stumbled. I jerked my gaze behind me as Chaos took over, playing out the game he so needed me to play.

"*Run*, Carina," Church growled.

But it wasn't Church who was in control. Chaos reigned as she took control of the vision around us. I found myself charging for the towering pines as an unmerciful howl came behind me.

Trees towered above me. I reached a rise before I was hit from behind. I shoved my hands out and hit the soft forest floor, my fingers sinking into the leaves and earth. But he was behind me, his breath blasting against the bare skin on my back.

"You shouldn't have come here." He leaned down, his words a growl against my ear. "Shouldn't have offered what you did."

I closed my eyes with the tremor as heat tore through my body and welled between my thighs. This was what he needed, this pretense of control, hunting what would make him lose himself...and right now that was me.

"Don't hurt me." My words echoed through the vision.

"Hurt you?" He dragged his lips down my spine. "I want to fucking tear you apart."

I dropped my head with the shiver. This was a dangerous game we played. But I knew him...and I knew his Wolf, too. He'd fought to protect me, put his body on the line to make sure I was safe. He wouldn't hurt me, no matter what he said.

"Then do it," I answered, rolling my bare shoulders and lifting my hips until I hit against his.

Skin against skin. I didn't have to turn my head to know Church was back now, from the heat that rippled from his body as he leaned down. "You make my beast dangerous, Carina. You make him fucking savage. He wants you, wants to do things to you no man should."

His hands on either side of my body blocked me in, until he pulled one away. The slow slide of a zipper filled my ears. I curled my fingers, driving them into the dirt. Cold kissed the tips. The vision knew everything. The smell of the trees...the feel of him above me as he sank his weight on mine.

"He wants to fuck you, Carina, wants to bury himself so deep inside you that there'ill be no one else like him. You make him possessive and zealous, you turn into him into something savage...something predatory...and that scares me."

It scared him, just like it scared me. But right here, in this pretense of a forest, there was just us. There was no Finis, no warehouse, no battleground of terror to wade through. There was just this heat between us, a heat that'd been building, and it was here now, every savage aching desire.

"You really want this?" he asked, lowering his forehead to my shoulder and gently thrusting against my ass.

"I really want this."

Another thrust against my ass. Only this time, he pushed deeper, pressing his chest against my back as he rocked. Fear mingled with desire. He was so close to his Wolf, so close to the beast pushing free. I arched my back and lifted my hips higher. Bestial. Dangerous…*driven.*

Panting breaths against my neck, he drove his massive thighs between mine…then pushed against my knees, splaying my legs wider. His hand left the floor beside me, and a sharp claw danced along my spine all the way down to the swell of my ass.

"You…are…*mine,*" he growled.

Power rippled all around us. That green Unseelie glow spilled out of my chest and bled against the forest floor as he slid his hand between my legs, his claw retracting as he went. Danger and the promise of pain made my pulse speed as he slid his finger along my crease.

"Do you know what the rut is?" The dangerous snarl sent a ripple of desire through me as he grasped my hips and yanked me against him.

He lifted my body, slamming my back against his chest. "It's when a Wolf is consumed by their mate. When they can't stop themselves from fucking. When all they can think about is that warm, soft place between their thighs."

He slid his hand between my legs again and splayed my thighs wider. I was trapped now, suspended by his strength and that heated breath. I ran my hand over the corded muscles of his arms, then reached behind me over my shoulder. God, he was fucking hard, driving between my ass cheeks as I arched my spine and ground my body against his.

"I'm holding him back, Carina," he cautioned in that ragged growl. "But you make my beast want to sink to that debasement, you make him want to ride this perfect fucking body until I lose control, and I *can't* lose control, Carina. Not now, not ever."

I cried out as he drove inside me, my body clenching with the invasion.

"Cant. Ever. Lose. Control." He punctuated the words with brutal thrusts.

I clawed a hold on the back of his neck. Terror rose inside

me as he wound one massive arm across my middle, pinning my body against his...not that I ever wanted to leave.

"Hands out," he commanded as he lowered me to the ground once more. His grip eased, the thrusts turning slower as he lifted me on his powerful thighs, driving into me from behind.

He was a savage.

A *Wolf.*

His thick cock slammed into me, making me tremble and shudder. Making me bow my head and hold on. Strands of my hair lashed my face with the onslaught. Chaos rose to the surface, letting out a sensuous moan. "That's it," I cried out, and squeezed my eyes closed. "Take me."

His cock grew thicker inside me, hardening and swelling, the sensations rubbing part of me that made my body tremble and my will weak.

"Don't..." he warned as I clenched inside, needing more... needing so much more.

But his words weren't his own. His Wolf commanded his body as he drove me forward until my breasts pressed against the cool, soft forest floor. Still he didn't slow, didn't ease, just drove his tilted hips upwards until there was nothing but him.

Him driving me against the ground.

Him filling my body with his.

Him violent and bloodthirsty, snarling against my ear.

Him owning me...

"You...*are...mine.*"

Stars sparked as that bulbous base moved deeper, stretching me...filling me until, with one final thrust, he stilled. Warmth spilled inside me. Muscles clenched, holding on as he let out a dangerous sound, one that rolled like thunder across my skin.

"Don't move," my Wolf commanded. "Don't you dare move."

Deep breaths claimed me. I lowered my head to the ground as the thunder of my heart filled my ears. He was still inside me, still hard...still *very hard.* A slow, eager thrust and he tore a moan free. Slick and wet, he moved inside me, never drawing completely free…just enough to easily drive back home.

He fucked me, pressing his hand against my back to hold me against the ground.

I was lost to the feel of him, to the smell and sounds we made, to the cold, soft ground underneath me, and the way he made me shudder and shake. Desperation filled me, making me writhe and moan. "Harder," I whispered. "Fuck me harder."

Pain flared for a second as he pulled free, then his cruel grip against my arm yanked me until I rolled. But then he was back between my legs, grasping my hips…and looking down between us. I followed his gaze, catching sight of the thick base of his cock. One that wasn't normal for a mortal…*but it was for a Wolf.*

I clenched my ass as he rammed inside me, forcing me wider and wider.

Still I couldn't get enough…we were animals in this moment.

Animals alone in the dark.

Bare and brutal.

And utterly in love.

23

PHANTOM

I turned at the sound, dragging my gaze from the shattered window of Jewel as an unmerciful roar came from inside. The walls trembled, and energy pulsed. Chaos was at work inside and the savage sounds of a hungry Wolf and Carina were almost too much to bear.

Steel links clattered in my hand as I met Vitold's gaze. Dark, sunken eyes, pale, thinned lips. The male looked as haunted as I felt. "Let's go."

Footsteps were all I left behind. Carina would save him, would bring him back from the abyss. She'd draw him deeper into her—I fixed my gaze on the streetlight in the distance—the way she drew all of us deeper into her.

The sweet scent of blood welled in my nose. Old blood, fetid blood. I clenched my fist around the stained shackles and kept on walking. Pain lashed across my chest. The point of a blade pressed against my heart as Vitold took another step, then slowly pushed to a run.

Run, the beast urged. *Hunt. Kill. Kill him...I need to kill something.*

The sting of claws against my palm was instant, the bite

bringing me into focus. *Find him.* The urge was overwhelming. I tried to push the need aside, tried to focus on Marian, as movement came from my side.

"We searched the entire area, Finis is gone," Hunter snapped, and jerked his gaze to the alley behind me. To that dangerous Unseelie power as it rippled from what was left of Jewel. "What the fuck is that?"

"That is none of your damn business." I kept on walking, letting the old warrior keep up.

A nervous glance behind us and he dragged that confused and pissed off look to me.

Hunt, my Wolf insisted, baring his teeth, and I clenched my fist tighter. My teeth ground as a low warning sound slipped free. The stench of Church's blood made my Wolf savage and dragged all those memories to the surface.

The night I'd found him dying in the middle of an empty field.

With the stench of my sister's blood all over him.

I tried to shove the memory away, tried not to let my emotions get the better of me. Marian, that's all I cared about right now, finding her and keeping her safe. Then I could hunt. Then I could—

"You left this behind." Arran stepped out from the shadows and into the light as I hit the corner and left the alley behind.

I jerked my gaze from the glint in his hand, forcing myself to look away. "No, I didn't. Put it away."

Still in the corner of my eye, I caught the Wolf's fang swing and the flicker of energy it still possessed. I jerked my gaze to Arran's, terror and hate driving to the surface.

"It's our pack," Arran whispered, and lifted the fang into the air.

But it wasn't *just our pack, was it?*

Wasn't just a token of the ones we'd left behind.

Carvings marked the enamel, etched with a steady hand. It

was a fang from *the Alpha*, the only fucking Alpha that ever mattered...*my father.* Arran stared at me, the leather thong wound tight around his fist. He was just a runt when I'd run that night. Just an insignificant runt. But he'd searched for me, and found me...the last male of our line.

The night Finis murdered my father in cold blood filled my mind as I lifted my hand and took the Alpha's tooth. It was a show of dominance, of fear, fangs ripped from the dying Alpha's mouth and worn with barbarity. I never thought I'd see it again.

But now I had...because he'd left it for me.

Hunt! screamed my beast. *KILL HIM...KILL...HIM!* My breaths consumed me as I curled my finger around the tapered edge and grasped the fang in my fist. My eyes closed on their own as the faint hum of power came from the last remnant of my dad.

"We have to find him," Arran whispered, his words nothing more than a choked hiss. "We have to find that sonofabitch. He won't stop, not until he has her."

"Or he's dead," I answered, and opened my eyes. Cold fury moved through my veins. "Or until he is dead."

Blue and red lights danced in the darkness along the street. Police cruisers gathered in packs. The air was filled with a dangerous promise. One I heard loud and clear.

The mortal enforcers were gathering arms and circling their prey, waiting for the moment to strike. "We need to scatter."

Arran and Hunter lifted their gazes to the commotion in the distance as unmarked Feds joined the fray.

"It's happening," Arran murmured.

"It's happening," I repeated. "Maybe not tonight. Tomorrow or the day after."

"Are they coming across the river?" Hunter cast a careful glance my way.

"Yes."

I'd felt their hate brewing for months now. First, it was the fire, then the attack from the other Wolves. Harlan was the mastermind behind it all. I was willing to stake my life on it. "Hunter, keep scanning the street. Tell your guys to stay out of sight. I want to know if there's even a hint of Finis or my sister."

"Will do," he answered, his gaze still fixed on the cop cars up ahead. "And if these bastards attack?"

It was a good question, a damn good question. Mortals against us. There was no doubt who'd survive. But the fallout from that...what was left of the Inner Circle and the savage bastards who waited in the wings would be swift and merciless. We'd not only have the fucking mortals to battle...we'd have our own kind, as well.

"Keep an eye on them," I instructed. "Any hint of them coming across the bridge, I want to know about it."

One nod from the older warrior, and he stepped to the side, then slowly sank into the shadows. He was gone in an instant, keeping to the darkness, where our kind hunted the best. I felt his pack more than I saw them, each Wolf had his own energy signature, resounding like a tone through my Wolf. He knew them all, and commanded each of them with bared fangs and a sense of power, one that was under threat.

"What are we going to do?" Arran murmured, watching the cops as they pulled back out onto the dark street into U-turns and drove away.

"The simple answer?" I watched red brakelights flare. "We find Marian, *then* we find *him*."

"And about them?" He stared at the herd of flashing lights leaving.

"That I don't know, Wolf." I took a step, leaving him behind for a second.

Vitold waited at the corner of the warehouse, took one look at the disappearing cop cars, and shook his head. "This is about to get bloody, you know that, right?"

I said nothing and strode past the Wolf. I knew it. We *all* fucking knew it. I just needed for the war to wait until I found my sister…and killed the one I'd waited my entire life to exterminate.

Waited…the word resounded in my mind as I made my way to the Camaro and climbed in.

I'd run that night, run like my mother begged me to do. I took Marian's hand and together we raced through the darkness as fast and as far as we could. I carried her when her knees buckled, heaved her into my scrawny fucking arms and kept on going, finding salvation in the darkest corner of the smallest cave, there we waited until we dared run again.

I kept her safe for a year, kept us moving from town to town, kept us surviving, living on smaller prey and keeping our faces unseen, until one night, she just packed up her things and left… and I never saw her again. Never saw the few items my mother had given her…not until today. I lowered my hand, slipping it into my pocket, and withdrew the comb.

The busted yellow stones reflected in the streetlight. I slipped it onto the dash and started the engine. So many fucking questions, so much rage. I didn't hear a word for months, until one day I came across an old Wolf who'd once been part of our pack and he told me the truth. Told me she'd gone back there, to the terror I'd fought so hard to leave behind. He told me she'd been taken in by Finis, told me she was kept in his tent…and under his control.

Fury had consumed me. I shook my head, ripped apart from the inside by agony and fueled by rage of the memories. I'd tried to track them down. But before I came close, Finis up and disappeared, taking my sister with him…and ultimately became our leader and took his seat at the Inner Circle.

It wasn't fear of him that kept me from the bastard, it was *her,* Marian. No one had seen her, not since Finis had taken her from the pack. But there were rumors, whispers of a female kept prisoner and moved from place to place in the dead of night.

Still, I kept searching, kept trying, until I got a bead on a location at three am by one of the Breeds. That call had had me gunning my fucking engine, tearing through the streets like a goddamn madman. I'd hunted and searched, finding my way to the middle of nowhere…and an open field. That night, I'd pulled an emaciated Wolf from a fucking steel shipping container, a Wolf who'd still reeked of my sister's blood.

He was dying. He'd been beaten and starved, and the horrors inflicted on him shone in his dead, haunted eyes. For years he wouldn't come out of his room. He was alive, breathing, eating, but not living. Never living.

Until one day, he did.

It was slow at first, trust and alliance didn't come easily to Church. But years passed between us, years of loyalty, years of me training and hunting for my sister and taking him along until the trail grew cold and there was no word of her. All I could do was wait. Make myself important, make myself known.

Finis watched me from the safety of a seat at the Circle, and I watched him from my new home here in Crown City. Now I had a chance…it might be the only one I'd get.

Hunt him, my beast raged.

That hunger burned as I shoved the car into gear and pulled away. Hunt him, hunt him and save her. Save her like I hadn't saved her before. Those yellow eyes came back to me, and the swell of her belly. I left my pack behind and turned down the backstreets of Crown City, keeping away from the mortals and did what I did best, what my beast needed me to do.

The cold morning air of Crown City held many secrets…I only need two of them.

My sister safe and by my side.

And the body of my enemy at my feet.

24

———————

CARINA

Movement rocked me. The sound of an engine pierced the darkness and dragged me closer to the surface. I cracked open my eyes, to find Church behind the wheel. He glanced my way, sensing me somehow, and forced a soft, sad smile. "I'm taking you home, it's alright, go back to sleep."

Sleep, Chaos murmured in a drugged tone. *Sleep...*

But I let her sink down inside my mind, and stared at him, at my Wolf. "Are you alright?"

He cut a glance to the road ahead, then to me once more. "Yeah, I'm alright."

A ripple of fear cut through me. One that chilled me to the core. I focused on him as that tremble grew stronger and the unshakeable feeling I was being watched grew bolder. I shoved up from the passenger seat and glanced out the window as sunlight spilled over the horizon.

"What is it?" Church's brows furrowed as he glanced into the rear-view mirror then at me once more.

"I don't know," I answered, sinking into that feeling, and waited.

But there was no whisper from Chaos, no tremor that

usually preceded her rage. Just the unknown touch of another. "I feel like someone's watching me."

"No one's watching you, Carina...only me." Desire swept through his tone as his gaze skimmed my body.

Memories of what had happened between us back at Jewel darkened that predatory gaze. His lips parted with a quick breath as I glanced at the middle of the bridge behind us then turned to look out of my window.

"You're safe with me," my Wolf insisted. "Close your eyes, let me take care of you."

I eased back against the seat, my gaze still on the permanent darkness that cloaked the land leading to the Hunting Ground. The place they called Dark City...the place that filled me with dread. I wanted to close my eyes, wanted to tear my gaze from the shadows as we hit the end of the bridge and sank into the land of Wolves and Vampires...and the dark ones they called the Fae. But I couldn't relax, not until we turned left and headed toward the strip club.

Even then, my gaze was drawn to the towering warehouse further down the street.

"Carina?"

I met Church's gaze.

"Your pulse is racing," my Wolf questioned, pulling into the parking lot next to the club.

Exhaustion waited, weighing down my body. I exhaled, letting the tension go. "I'm alright, just tired. More than I'd realized."

I let that eerie feeling go as Church killed the engine and leaned across the seat. "You used a lot of energy last night, it's only natural for you to be exhausted. You need to eat and sleep."

"Phantom?"

"Still out there, he won't come back." His voice deepened as pain moved through his gaze. "Not until this is over."

I wanted to be out there, wanted to be right alongside him,

hunting and hating. But last night, Church had needed me the most, and right now…I needed sleep the most.

"Wait right there," Church commanded, slipping out of the car and rounding to my side.

He yanked open my door and grasped my hand as I climbed out. It might take me forever to get used to someone opening my door and reaching for my hand, but after almost losing them, forever seemed like a perfect plan to me.

We'd find Phantom's sister. I knew we would. Maybe that's who I'd felt back there, in the Dark City? Maybe she was just waiting to pounce again? Church strode to the back door and punched in the combination for the lock. One glance over my shoulder and I followed him inside.

Our footsteps resounded in the hallway. "Are we the only ones here?"

One nod of his head confirmed my suspicions. "Don't worry, Mojin is hanging around. We'd know it if anyone else was here."

Mojin…the Fae. A tremble broke out as Church stepped through the busted connecting door to our rooms in the back.

"I'm going to take a shower," I muttered. "Then I'm going to crash."

I left my Wolf behind and turned along the hall, making my way past the study to Vitold's room. My duffel bag was still on the end of his bed. But it was his closet I headed for, grabbing a cotton t-shirt and pair of boxers before I went to the bathroom.

I took my time, meeting my dark eyes in the mirror as I undressed, until I felt the weight of my Wolf's gaze watching me removing the clothes I'd shed for him hours ago. Church strode toward me, yanking his own shirt over his head as I reached for the button of my jeans.

"Will you let me take care of you?" he murmured, casting a careful glance to meet mine. "Please."

I gave a small nod and dropped my hands. This wasn't just about sex anymore, it was about mating, about caring and comfort for him more than it was for me. It was about showing him how much I wanted him. "Of course."

He took a step and sank to one knee. Those big hands trembled as they worked the button of my jeans, then the zipper. He shed my clothes with careful hands, rising to unclasp my bra, and lowered his head to kiss the top of my shoulder. "Let me start the shower."

I turned to watch him as he turned the faucet and adjusted the temperature before taking off the remainder of his clothes. I let him wash me, let him run his hands over my body. I let him care for me the way a male cares for his mate, and after my hair was shampooed and conditioned and my skin was squeaky clean, then he turned to himself.

"Will you let me take care of you?" I asked, reaching for the soap.

A shake of his head and those blue eyes darkened as he pulled away. "No...not yet."

I dropped my hand as a flicker of sadness rose. "It's alright." I gave him a soft smile. "This is enough...for now."

Relief swept across his face with a hard exhale. "It's just hard for me."

"I get it." I moved around him, letting him stand under the spray. "We have time."

"Yes. We do." There was something promising about the words. Something I carried with me as I stepped out of the shower and grabbed a thick towel, using it to dry myself.

"Will you sleep in my bed?"

I caught his gaze in the mirror as I pulled up Vitold's boxers. "Sure."

He turned off the spray, shaking his head and casting water from his head before grabbing my towel. Barely a sweep of the fabric across his skin later, and he was casting the towel aside and grabbing my hand. There was an exhaustion in his slow, languid movements, one I felt to my soul.

He grasped his phone and hit a number with one hand as he towed me through the bathroom. "Anything?" he asked into the phone. "Yeah, she's fine. We're both…fine. Just an hour or two. Wake me if you get a scent and, Phantom…thanks, brother."

My belly trembled with the words, and my heart raced as he lowered his hand.

"Anything?" I asked.

A shake of his head as we made our way along the hall and turned. "No, but they're out there looking, like I should be looking."

"You need to rest. We all need to rest. We'll take the graveyard shift."

The words made him chuckle as he strode bareass naked toward his room. I lifted my gaze to Phantom's open door next to Church's and felt a pang of sadness. He was out there, hurting, hating. The need to be with him was consuming, making my own words taste like ash in my mouth.

Sleep, how can I sleep knowing he was out there? Knowing he needed me at his side? That cold tremor of awareness cut through me once more, making me shiver.

"What is it?" Church murmured as he dropped my hand and climbed into his bed.

Darkness and power…and *lust* moved through the air. But it wasn't the same sensation as before, this one wasn't focused on me, more like brushing my energy before it was gone once more. "Nothing, just felt someone."

"Mojin. It's just Mojin. He's guarding the place, still pissed off at how Finis walked through the Dark City."

I sank into the mattress and slid under the cotton sheets. "I thought only the ones who were marked could get through the wards."

"They are." He met my gaze, rising up to rest his head on his hand. "They're supposed to be, at least."

So maybe that's why I'd felt something in Dark City as we'd

driven here? Maybe Mojin had been the *touch* I'd felt? I breathed a sigh of relief and curled my spine, dragging my knees to my chest. "Makes sense." I sighed as that bone-weary heaviness moved through me.

But Chaos was quiet…*too quiet.* In that moment, I didn't care, closing my eyes instead and sank down into the darkness. Church shifted beside me. I was aware of him, the brush of his hand against my knee, the hard slide of his body as he moved closer…and closer until finally, nothingness rose up and in one consuming bite, swallowed me whole.

"**Y**ou're awake," Vitold whispered.

I cracked open my eyes and slipped from the darkened world of Wolves and men. With a deep breath, I licked my arid lips and asked, "What time is it?"

"Almost six."

I scowled and my heart sped as I shoved upwards. "Six at night?"

There was a smirk from the Wolf as he pushed off the doorframe. "You were pretty out of it, Carina. Muttering something about Unseelie. Anyone else might think you have the hots for the damn Fae." He stopped and scowled, his voice deepening. "You don't though, right?"

I chuckled and slid my feet to the side of the bed. "No, I don't have the damn hots for the Fae. If anything, they fucking terrify me. Give me damn Wolves anytime."

He strode forward, grabbed me around the waist, and lifted me into the air. "That's good, my love," he grinned, pulling me against him and burying his face in my hair. "Very good. 'Cause I really like the dude and I'd hate to have to tear him apart."

I stifled a laugh and wrapped my arms around him, taking comfort in his warmth. "You've got nothing to fear there, Vitold.

Nothing to fear at all. The only thing you need to be concerned about is getting me to Phantom. I need to be out there, helping him."

He lowered my feet to the floor, those brown eyes darkened in an instant. "No, you don't want to be out there, Carina. Trust me, it's safer here."

"Safer?" Anger flared. "You think I give a shit about being safe?"

He just scowled.

"Our Alpha is out there, he needs us."

"My orders were to keep you out of it."

"Keep me out of it," I repeated. "What *it* am I to be kept out of, exactly? The part where his sister is in trouble or possibly hurt, or the damn Alpha of Alphas, who has a fucking hard-on about terrorizing me." But there was no explosion in his eyes, no flicker of fear. That wasn't it...no, that wasn't it at all. "What the hell aren't you telling me, Vitold?"

He swallowed hard and combed his fingers through his hair. "What makes you think I'm hiding anything?"

"Oh, fifteen years of FBI training and interrogations has made me pretty fucking good at knowing when I'm being lied to."

The heat of desire was quickly dying away, leaving behind that hardness I'd built my life upon. The same hardness that had made me merciless...and almost ruined my future with the Wolves. But here it was, roaring to the surface in place of the deep, pulsing drive of Chaos.

Chaos...

She was quiet, too quiet for far too fucking long. I felt the emptiness like I'd feel the loss of my damn arm. "What the hell is going on, Vitold? And *this time* I want the truth."

He took a step backwards into the hallway. The small shake of his head only drew that hunter in me closer to the surface. I closed in, stepping through the doorway, driving him backwards. "You can either tell me, or I can go out there and find out for myself."

"No." The word was a growl. "I have orders."

"Orders? What am I, a fucking dog?" I forced through clenched teeth.

Pain and rage lashed across his gaze. "No, you're *our* fucking mate and you'll be protected like a mate. It's not good out there, Carina. The city…the city has turned, and it's not good."

I searched my mind for answers. The city has turned?

Images of police patrol cars filled my head. It was the only thing that made sense. The only reason Phantom would keep me locked away. He was afraid I'd go to them, he was afraid I'd betray him all over again.

The thought hit me like a slap. "He doesn't trust me."

Silence was a cruel fucking answer, but that's what I got.

I gave a slow nod. "Alright, I deserve that."

"It's not dangerous, not yet. But we can feel it brewing."

"And me standing here in your fucking boxers is going to keep me safe?" I snapped, then instantly regretted it. "I don't care about them, Vitold. I don't give a shit about their battle or their world. All I want to do right now is to find Marian. So, let me ask you a question. Did our Alpha specifically tell you to keep me locked in here?"

My Russian Wolf thought about it for a minute before he shook his head. "No."

"Then what exactly did he say?"

His hard exhale set alight that spark of hunger as he muttered. "I'm going to regret this, aren't I?"

"Not at all," I lied, and dragged my shirt over my head. "In fact, we're going to do the complete opposite of what he *thinks* I'm going to do. I'm going to find his sister…and bring her back."

I left him standing against the wall in the hallway.

Left him watching me with a mixture of pride and utter fear.

Because I meant every word I'd said. Chaos was quiet inside me and without her, that investigative hunger blazed to life. I had an idea, it was a long shot. But it might just give me the one thing I needed to earn their trust back.

All their trust...the Vampires included.

25

CARINA

urry, that urgency spilled through my veins. I left Vitold behind and went toward his room, excitement and fear filling me. But a few steps along the hallway and that pressure on my mind came once more, that…uncomfortable feeling of being watched.

I jerked my gaze over my shoulder, to find nothing behind me, just like before. Only this time, that feeling grew stronger until the pressure wound around my head like a band, ensnared in a trap I hadn't known was there. The white walls around me blurred.

"Vitold." I threw my hand out and stumbled.

Something was wrong. *Something was very wrong.*

"Carina?" my Wolf queried as I stumbled. He came around the corner and lunged in a blur of panic. *"Carina!"*

You DARE use my power? A savage male voice cleaved through my head. I slammed my hands over my ears and rocked with the force.

Vitold caught me instantly, pulling me into his arms. "Carina! *What the fuck is going on?"*

But it was Chaos writing in the emptiness…it was Chaos

battling that formidable dark power that dragged me under like I was nothing...*like she was nothing.* I reached for Vitold as her screams grew louder. "Something is hurting her. Something is..."

Use MY power? The male's voice boomed and I howled with the pain. My shrill scream bounced against the walls as Vitold wrenched my jaw higher, panic fill him as he stared into my eyes.

But Chaos was lashing out with her sharp claws inside my head...

Chaos howled and raged.

And the battle for control begun.

My strength! The male blasted the words through me. *My portal!*

"*Get out!*" I screamed as my outer world was filled with the thunder of footsteps. "Get out...get out...get out!"

Shadows swept along the hallway, like the light was being strangled from my world. I felt him, that deep Unseelie glow spilling from the center of my chest, as out of the darkness Mojin descended like a vengeful, wrathful God.

"What the fuck is it?" the Fae snapped, those dark, soulless eyes fixed on mine.

He grabbed me, tearing me from Vitold's arms, his gaze sliding to that emerald flicker from my chest. There was a second when my Wolf's lips curled and his warning raged inside my head...*I really like the dude and I'd hate to have to tear him apart.*

But there was no savage battle of Wolf fighting Fae. Instead, Vitold let me go. "What the fuck is happening to her?"

"I don't know." Mojin's focus slipped from the glow in my chest. His energy pulsed against my skin and pressed against my mind, probing, searching for a way in. "I can't quite...there's something in there, something stopping me."

Get the fuck out, Seeling! The male in my head roared, and sent out a blast of power. Mojin's hands were ripped from me as he was thrown clear along the hall.

Shadows howled and scattered as he hit the floor with a sickening *thud.* But Vitold was already there, pulling me into his arms. "What the fuck just happened?"

I tried to answer…tried to speak. But words failed me as further along the hall, Mojin lifted his head, hate sparkling in the abyss of his gaze. He slowly rose to his feet and, with a look of determination and outright fear, he charged toward me, lifting his hands in front of him.

"Mojin, *NO!*" Vitold jerked his gaze toward the movement and howled.

But it was too late, far too fucking late to fight. The Unseelie warrior's power punched through me, cutting coldly and cruelly through my mind, until I was choking on his strength, sliding under as the feeble hold on my own sanity slipped. Chaos howled and clawed her own throat, battering against that unfamiliar male's choking hold until I started to feel myself shatter…and fall…

Until, with a howl of fury, the unknown male inside my head was gone.

Mojin wrenched his hands away, harsh breaths consuming him as he snatched his power away. He was the one who stumbled now, and he was the one who fell to his knees, his eyes widening as he stared at me.

Pain pulsed inside me like a fist gripped tight at the base of my head.

Lights throbbed above us, burning and searing, until I closed my eyes and let out a whimper.

"What…the…fuck…was…*that?*" Vitold snarled, glaring at Mojin.

My moan deepened, burning through my chest as Vitold's grip tightened. He dragged in a huge breath. My Wolf's hands were on me, pulling me closer and lowering me to the floor.

But Mojin never tore his gaze from mine as he answered, "What the fuck did you do?"

"What the fuck did *I* do?" I tried to shove against the floor.

He pushed forward, ignoring the warning snarl from my Wolf. "No bullshitting, Carina. What the fuck did you do?"

"I didn't do anything!" I snapped, pain mingling with fear until my voice was thick with tears. "I didn't do anything."

"Unseelie." Vitold shoved himself upwards and took a step toward the male, claws punching through the tips of his fingers. "What the fuck did you do to her?"

Hate against hate, the Unseelie male rose on unsteady feet. "I just saved your mate's life. *That's* what *I* just did, a fucking thank you would suffice."

"Who was that?" I whispered, even though I didn't really want to know.

There was a shake of his head as Mojin turned.

"Please."

The warrior stoppled and looked over his shoulder, finding Vitold, then me. "Someone you don't ever want to mess with. Someone *I* don't even want to mess with. But now that you have, it all makes sense. I couldn't work out how Finis walked through Dark City. Now I have my answer."

"Who?" Vitold took a step closer.

"The only Fae that could grant him the ward to walk through our world without us knowing and the only *bastard* who *dared* call me a fucking Seeling."

Vitold flinched and paled in an instant. "Timor."

"Timor," Mojin agreed. "The fucking Unseelie Prince."

A tremor coursed through me with his name. Not just any Unseelie…but a goddamn Prince. "What does this mean?"

"Nothing fucking good," Mojin growled, and glanced at Vitold's claws. "Guard her well, Wolf. This shit is far from over."

He left then, stealing the shadows as he went. The thud of his boots still rang in my ears long after he was gone.

"He's fucking kidding, right?" I whispered, and jerked a panicked gaze to my Wolf. "Another goddamn Unseelie in my head? As if *this*," I yanked my shirt up to expose the glowing green jewels in my chest. "And goddamn Chaos that lives and breathes inside me isn't torture enough?"

"It's not a joke, Carina." Vitold shook his head. "This is serious."

"Do I look like I'm laughing?"

But there was real fear in his eyes, real fear shimmering and glinting. This changed everything now? Goddamn it. I couldn't let this ruin my one fucking chance at fixing this thing between us, couldn't let it bring me undone. I sank into the darkness of my mind and sent a whisper to the wind. *Are you there?*

Chaos moaned, the sound deep and wretched. But she was there, and right now, that's all that mattered. She was there and could rest while I tried to think of a way around this and do what needed to be done. My body trembled and a throbbing ache speared my skull, but I forced myself to my feet. "This changes nothing." I forced my feet to move, wincing as that agony cut like a knife. "I'm going out there, with or without you." I exhaled. "It'd just be better with, Vitold."

"Of course I'm with you, my mate." He was there, holding my arm, pulling me against him. "But I can't fight what I can't see, and right now, you're a ticking time bomb."

I met his gaze, desperate to kiss those perfect lips. "Then we need to hurry. I think I know the first place we need to look."

He let me go, watching as I braced myself against the wall and made my way into his room, yanking his shirt over my head as I went. I hurried, dressing into clean black jeans and grabbed a clean t-shirt from Vitold's pile, sliding it on over my bra.

Green jewels glittered as I tugged the shirt down. For a while, I'd almost become used to it, used to that inhuman hunger inside me, used to that voice inside my head. The one who promised protection and instead gave me nothing but pain.

But that thing…that man who cut through me like I was nothing. He terrified me.

"You ready?"

I lifted my gaze to Vitold as he stood in the doorway wearing a leather jacket. Underneath it, his chest was strapped with guns and knives. In one hand was a shoulder holster, adjusted as small as it could go, and in his other a Glock, a switchblade, and my own jacket to match his.

"Damn," I exclaimed as I crossed the space between us. "Give me leather and steel instead of flowers and chocolates any day."

He smiled, and when he did, my heart fluttered. He was gorgeous, even sad and worried like he was. I slipped on the holster and let him work the webbing, adjusting as he went, until he was satisfied. "It's clean and checked." He handed me the gun. "There's a fresh clip and a knife. I want you to shoot first and ask questions later, got it?"

"Got it," I answered, sliding the magazine and blade into place and slipped on the jacket.

The night felt different, humming with a kind of savage tone. One I felt deep in my marrow as we strode out of the back of the Hunting Ground and across the darkened parking lot again. I climbed into Vitold's black Explorer and yanked my seatbelt closed. "I want to head across the river and take Lexington and Fifth."

He shot me a look as he backed out, then shot forward. "That's just past the main part of the city."

I gave a nod. "Yeah, I know."

With a look of confusion, he drove. That hum of energy throbbed louder as we left the club behind. I glanced into the side mirror, catching a flicker of green in the darkness coming from the Unseelie warehouse. Something was happening, something more than the arrival of Finis and Phantom's sister looking for revenge. That terrifying ache still lingered in the back of my head, like a migraine that wouldn't leave.

"You in there?" I murmured, the words echoing through the darkness.

Yeah, I'm here, Chaos answered, sounding hung over as hell. *Just keep that bastard away from me.*

"You alright?" Vitold turned when we hit the end of the street.

"Yeah, I think we're good," I answered, lifting my gaze to the sparkle of the city lights.

I'd wasted an entire day sleeping. But now, even though my head still throbbed, that desperation was coming back, hunting these streets like a fucking beast. We passed a cop car as it headed toward the wrong side of the river. The cop behind the wheel turned to watch us as we drove past.

The movement put me on edge. I scanned the few cars we passed, finding two unmarkeds, Detectives maybe, *or Feds.* I glanced across the river, catching the lights sparkling on the inky water. "Doesn't feel right."

"No, it doesn't," Vitold agreed and pushed the Explorer harder. We hit the off-ramp before we turned, cutting across empty lanes until we could find the first exit, and headed into the city.

Lexington and Fifth was past the throbbing heart of the city, deeper into the business part that had traded space for a quieter flow of traffic. Still, there were plenty out this time of the night, probably mostly workers finishing late and heading home.

"Want to give me a clue what I'm supposed to be looking for?" Vitold slowed as we drove along the street.

Accountants' and lawyers' offices were broken up by fast food restaurants and a massive Starbucks. But it was the eight-foot-high fence line that surrounded a darkened expansive building that caught my attention. "There." I motioned to the corner.

"A vet clinic?" e asked.

"A very big vet clinic," I replied as he pulled over, parking the four-wheel drive farther along the street to not draw attention. "She's hurt, bleeding, in pain, and maybe delivering her baby. Where would you go?"

He climbed out and I followed. The weight of the Glock wore at me, but not as much as Vitold's words. Any other day and any other Wolf, I might shoot first. Hell, I'd shot Phantom when he'd stood in my way, but a woman? A *very pregnant* woman in pain? I didn't think I could.

"Just don't hurt her." I scanned the fence line, stopping at a large gash in the chain links at the corner.

"Hurt her?" Vitold mumbled, and took a step closer. "I just want us to get out alive…how's that?"

I swallowed hard, lifted my gaze to the smashed glass beside the back door, and let out a sigh.

Christ, I hated it when I was right.

Vitold snatched his phone from his pocket and pressed the button. "Yeah, it's me," He whispered. "No, of course she didn't listen to me. Why? Because she's been hanging around with you too much. Wait, save your ass-reaming. I'm sending you directions. I think you better get here…and fast. We might've just found your sister."

26

CARINA

We slipped through the cut fence and slowly made our way closer to the smashed in back door. Greendales was the largest vet clinic in Crown City, and the only one with advanced pregnancy and whelping care. The one I'd go to if I were a pregnant Wolf in trouble. Maybe she was still here, maybe she was gone. I lifted my gaze to the dull security lights, but if it was her, then we had more to go on than we'd had before.

"Stay back," Vitold muttered as he surged forward.

The guy was packing, yet there wasn't a gun or a knife in his hand. A pang of pride moved through me. Vitold was one of the most savage fighters I'd ever seen, yet he didn't want to hurt her anymore than I did. But the woman was known to come out swinging with teeth and claws. The familiar burn of panic followed as he neared the door, glanced inside, then reached through the busted window.

Shards of glass clicked and clattered, the sound would be deafening to a Wolf. I held my breath as he flicked the lock and opened the door. How long would it take Phantom to get from where he was to here? *Where the hell was he, anyway?*

Apprehension filled me as Vitold pushed the door open and stepped inside.

I followed, my heart beating loud enough that I was sure anyone in a ten-mile radius could damn well hear. Instinct kicked in the moment I stepped through the doorway and we entered a small room filled with deep baths and stainless steel tables. There were clippers and brushes lining the wall. A grooming room, not really what we were after.

Vitold veered left as we exited, there was a second when I tried to do what he wanted me to and stay behind him like the good little mortal I was. But that gnawing in my gut pulled me left. I glanced that way, then back to Vitold as he slipped through a doorway and disappeared. *Shit.*

A scrape had me jerking my gaze toward the doorway further at my left. My heart boomed, trembling and aching as I focused on that sound and moved. Seconds ticked like bombs detonating in my chest. Silence came from the other end of the clinic. Vitold was long gone…*and where the fuck was Phantom?*

I swallowed hard and kept moving, reaching out to grasp a handle and tried to peer around the blinds. Something shifted in the darkness, something so far back I could barely see. I held my breath and eased the handle, bearing down inch by inch until the door swung open soundlessly.

Energy shifted, and a low whine followed, leading me to step inside. A growl came from my right, the warning dangerous. I jerked my gaze toward the sound and found a giant Doberman standing in his cage, ears pointed, white teeth bared to me. I curled my lips, baring my own teeth back, and kept moving past the cages to where the plastic divider cut the large room into two.

"Hey," I whispered, barely mouthing the word.

Hey, your own goddamn self, Chaos moaned, sounding like death warmed over. Maybe she was…maybe her dark, treacherous ass was weak enough for me to ward until the end of oblivion. Maybe if I made it out of this, my Unseelie curse would be gone?

Wish in one...and slit your throat in the other, she chuckled, until she moaned. *See which one fills up first.*

I ground my teeth and kept walking, rolling my heels, and reached for the end of the curtain. There was a smear of blood on the floor, not enough to bleed out, but it was there. I lifted my gaze to the curtain, reached out, and grasped the corner. With a shotgun blast of fear, I yanked.

Blood, gauzes, half-empty bottles lying on their sides. The stainless steel table was a mess. I scanned the room, finding nothing.

"I thought I told you to stay behind me?"

I flinched and spun at the sound, finding Vitold in the room behind me. He scanned the items, his gaze lingering on the mess on the table before he shifted his gaze to the Doberman. The hound gave a whimper and sat, ears flattening.

"It was her, wasn't it?" I muttered.

One nod, and he turned. "Come on, she's gone."

Gone. I exhaled but didn't move. Instead, I stared at the mess she'd left behind and moved closer, reaching out for the bits of gauze matted and wet with blood. This was a woman...a pregnant woman. "Do you think she's had the baby?"

Footsteps resounded behind me. "I don't know," his voice deepened with regret. "If she'd only come to us, had only let us help her."

I swallowed the tremble of desperation.

"Phantom should be here by now." He voiced the same words running through my mind.

Worry bloomed like a poisonous flower as I turned and followed Vitold out of the clinic and into the night. Green spilled across the night sky, stopping my steps. Vitold froze midway to the fence line, his gaze fixed on that emerald light covering the horizon like a heavy splash of northern lights.

But as I stared at the luminescence, that spark of beauty turned cold and terrifying.

"Something's wrong," Vitold warned as the screech of brakes sounded.

The bright glare of headlights carved through the fence line as a Camaro careened around the corner, heading toward us. But it wasn't just any Camaro...*it was Phantom.* My heart lunged, and my body followed. It was just instant now. They reacted and I followed.

I charged across the yard and ducked as Vitold slammed through the opening of the fence and lifted the wires.

"Get the fuck across the bridge now!" Phantom roared.

Red and blue lights were swallowed by the green glare, but still the cop cars descended, three cars wide and three cars deep. I was already running, already hauling ass as Phantom shot past.

"Get down!" Vitold roared.

I lunged, head down, body impacting the pavement with a *thud.* I sucked in dirt and grass, waiting until the howl of tires and the gunning engines tore past.

"Let's go." Vitold grabbed my arm and helped me up.

He took the time to give my lip a careful swipe of his thumb, brushing away the grime, before he gently pushed me toward the passenger door and raced for the driver's. We were moving in an instant, pulling out and swinging wide. I held on, pressed against the door as we turned once more and headed for the other side of the city.

"What the fuck is going on?" I stared at the green lights swirling into the darkness.

"I have no idea," he grumbled as we flew past three unmarked cars heading our way.

My gaze went to the side mirrors, watching as the brake lights flared bright.

"Vitold."

"I see it," my Wolf growled, and pushed the Explorer harder.

The four-wheel drive surged even faster, whipping past other cars on the highway until the bridge came into view.

"Hang on."

I'd barely registered the words before we were turning, cutting across the lanes of traffic to shoot onto the off-ramp. "Umm, Vitold, the bridge is that way."

"I know where the damn bridge is, female," my Wolf snapped as we hurtled toward towering buildings. He wasn't taking the direct route. Instead, he turned hard as the red and blue lights glared behind us in the distance. I was in a damn washing machine, thrown side to side as we speared down backstreet after backstreet, trying our best to shake them off our tail.

But no matter where we turned, there were more waiting, clusters of unmarked cop cars parked along the streets. I jerked my gaze to Vitold as we shot past. His brows were furrowed with a look of confusion that quickly turned to fear as we turned the corner and caught sight of the blockade in the distance.

Our headlights splashed across the cars, lighting up the officers' faces. Only one of them stood out to me...only one made my gut clench. *Harlan.* He stood out front from the others, his gaze fixed on us as we came around the corner...until we turned once more.

"Did you see?" He cut me a quick look.

"I saw." I forced the words through clenched teeth. "Get us across the bridge, Vitold...*do it now.*"

The Wolf whipped his gaze to mine again, those silver eyes glinting in the dark. Gears downshifted as we turned hard and raced forward, this time making a line directly for the bridge.

Green splashed across our world as we slipped out from the towering buildings and saw the other side of the river in all its terrifying glory. Unseelie power hummed through me, dragging Chaos closer to the surface.

She let out a moan and the green ward embedded in my chest came to life.

*Something's wrong...*she moaned.

"No fucking shit," I snarled. "Nice of you to join the party."

No, asshole, she cried, her power driving higher and higher, sending shivers along my arms and through my fucking brain like a raw nerve.

"Carina," Vitold growled as he cut across the traffic, heading straight for the on-ramp to the bridge.

Headlights were blinding. Horns blared. I yanked my hand up, shielding my eyes, as she whispered, *Look...really fucking look, Carina.*

Cars were stopped in the middle of the bridge, some sideways as though they'd skidded hard. But it was the lights that drew me, sparkling on the bridge until they...just ended. Darkness consumed the half that led to the other side of the city. It was those shadows that had drawn Chaos's power to the surface. That Dark Fae hunger grew bolder the moment our tires hit the bridge.

My gaze was drawn to the cause of the power...to where the green Unseelie glow pulsed like an electric current into the sky. Shadows clung to him, lashing the air as Shrike, the leader of the Unseelie Fae, held his hands over his head and unleashed his power into the night sky.

"Jesus fucking Christ," I muttered.

He can't help you, she whispered.

I swallowed hard as Vitold tapped the brakes. *Crack!* I jerked my gaze to the side mirror a second before it exploded.

Crack!

Crack!

"They're fucking shooting at us?" I barked, ducking low to peer over my shoulder.

"Keep your head down!" Vitold roared as the night opened up with the deafening *boom!* The rear window shattered the instant. Vitold veered to the right, whipping around a braking car as the hail of gunfire came once more.

Cars were stopping in front of us, red brake lights neon bright against the shimmering deep green.

"They're fucking stopping." I jerked my gaze to the bank of cars.

"Keep down," Vitold barked as he whipped the Explorer around braked cars. But the headlights hurtling toward us drew my gaze. Something was coming at us...*fast.*

Black glinted under the bridge lights. Only one person I knew drove like that. My heart lunged, slamming against my ribs. "That's Phantom."

Bursts of gunfire descended all around him. It was that goddamn night all over again. That night they'd shot at us...that night we'd run. Vitold let out a curse and braked hard, throwing me forward until the snap of the seatbelt cinched tight.

"Get out, Carina!" Vitold ordered, and shoved against his door. *"Run!"*

I was moving before I knew it, my trembling fingers stabbing the seatbelt release before I shoved open the door. The crack of gunfire was swallowed by the hum of Unseelie power. Car doors opened around us and mortals climbed out to stare at the Fae warrior, oblivious to the hail of bullets.

"Get down!" I screamed at them as a window exploded. "Get the fuck down!"

But the cops didn't care there were civilians, they didn't slow, didn't stop. Just chased that black Camaro as it fishtailed and skidded sideways, coming to a stop at the edge of the parked cars.

Boom! The window exploded in front of me. I ducked, skidded, and went down hard. The bridge shuddered, the thick, supporting wires overhead howled with the strain as I felt the shift. I lifted my gaze to the shimmering glow in the distance and the inky black air behind Shrike. Salvation was there, but behind me the howl of tires filled the air. I wasn't going to make it. None of us were.

I punched the asphalt, driving myself upwards as, out of that inky blackness, movement came. Pale skin, armed to the teeth. I caught the flare of red hair as it swirled around her like a damn halo of death. Ruth. My pulse thundered…the Vampires…*they'd come!*

The sight drove me forward as the thunder of footsteps came from behind me.

"Move, Carina!" Phantom roared.

Crack…crack…crack…crack.

I jerked my gaze behind me, to catch my Phantom throw his arms open wide. His body jerked, throwing him sideways. He stumbled, his face contorting. Still he shoved me forward, using himself as a shield.

A savage roar came from in front of me as Church strode forward with the Vampires, his panicked gaze finding his Alpha, then me. His lips curled as he turned to the gunfire, took two steps, and lunged. He was a blur, cutting between cars as he tore past us.

"Carina!" Arran was there, racing toward me, his eyes wide.

"Move," Phantom urged behind me, his words tight with pain.

But the moment Arran reached me, I was shoving him away. "Phantom…get Phantom."

"Here." Elithien was there in a blur, reaching out to take my arm.

But the gunfire was still coming, unleashing in the air. The Unseelie warrior roared as he was hit. The mighty Unseelie power clawed the steel cable as it wavered.

Ping! One powerful cable snapped free. Mortals screamed all around us. But the Vampire were there, tearing those in the cable's path away with blinding speed. I was picked up like I weighed nothing and hauled back toward the safety of my pack once more.

"Stay here," Elithien commanded.

"She will," Ruth urged next to me.

I tried to yank my gun free, but my hands were shaking. She took one look at the terror in my eyes and the fright in my hand and stepped closer. "You got this, Carina." She turned her focus to the cops running toward us in the middle of the bridge. "Draw your weapon, Special Agent. It's about to get ugly."

The determination in her voice was all I needed to hear. Chaos swept through me, her dark, savage hunger stilling the shakes and tearing the weapon from my holster. Mortal against beast. We were back here once more.

"Get back," Shrike growled as he claimed that bestial Fae power.

"Let them take care of this." Ruth reached for my arm and took a step back.

The shattering of car's back window resounded along with the screams as the Vampires, Wolves, and Fae protected the innocents and unleashed their rage against everyone else.

Blood shot high in the air as Church attacked a cop, tearing his throat out with a bloody howl of rage. My stomach clenched at the sight.

"Carina!"

The familiar bellow stilled me instantly. My gaze searching the unmarked cars, finding movement.

"No," I breathed. "No fucking way."

Still, I tracked the movement as my father stumbled around the cars and headed toward us. He was drunk, drunker than normal. His shirt was open, the once-white undershirt now filthy and stained, bared for all to see.

Still, he wasn't drunk enough not to find me across the mess of parked cars.

"You!" He stabbed a pointing finger toward me. "Are my

fucking daughter and you *will* do as I say."

Behind him came the mastermind. Harlan strode forward, lifting his gun as he turned his head and took aim at Church, three cars down from him. "Don't make me shoot, Carina."

The bastard then swung the muzzle, taking aim at the back of my father's head.

"No." I stepped forward, feeling the life drain from me.

"I need to talk to you." My father was fucking oblivious, his face a mixture of torture and pain.

I stepped forward.

"Carina, *no.*" Ruth was the voice of reason behind me…then again, I'd never been any good with reason.

All I saw was that gun aimed at my father's head, and the hostile look of determination in Harlan's eyes.

"Carina." Phantom stepped in front of me as I made my way toward them.

"Get out of her way, *Wolf,*" Harlan ordered. "Or you won't like how this ends."

Wolves. Vampires. Fae…*my father.*

"I need to own it, Car," he slurred as he stumbled forward a step. "This." He waved his hand around at the nightmare. "It's all my fault."

"No, Dad." I worked my way around the first car, and glanced at Phantom. *Please,* I pleaded with my eyes. *He's my father.* "It's not."

"Yes, yes, it is. It's my fault I got caught up in Costello business."

I flinched with the name. Elithien and Hurrow stilled as they carried mortals from danger and met my gaze. I didn't need to turn my head to know Ruth was listening. The mere mention of her family made my pulse race. "It's okay, Dad."

"I didn't love her." He took a step, intent on pulling out all his goddamn secrets right…this…fucking…second. "But I knew he was a bad man. He warned me away, but still I tried to help her, tried to get her away from him. It was my fault she died in that car accident. All my fucking fault."

"Dad...*no.*" Cold slipped in.

"She hated that *Vamp*," he spat, his unfocused eyes suddenly sparkling with rage. "The bastard wouldn't leave her alone. I tried to help her, tried to get her somewhere safe. She was leaving both of them, packed her stuff in the car...but she didn't make it. I couldn't get her away from the monsters, Carina." His voice turned hard as he glanced behind me. "But I can save you."

"The fuck you can," Phantom growled behind me.

I turned enough to see Phantom, Arran...and Vitold behind me, and Church as he dropped the body of the dead officer and neared. It was going to be a bloodbath. Maybe not for my Wolves...not at first. But mortal deaths meant more focus, and I knew there were others watching.

"Get in the car, Carina," Harlan urged as he swung his gun from the back of my father's head to Church. "Get in and this can all be over."

But it'd never be over, not like this. Not while there was hate in his heart. But I needed time, time to think, time to make a plan.

"Don't make me shoot them," Harlan warned.

"Leave them alone," I demanded. "Let them all go. Ruth, the Vampires, everyone."

Harlan's eyes widened, but he gave a nod. "If that's what you want."

"You're doing the right thing, Carina," Dad mumbled as I strode past.

"Shut the fuck up, Dad, and get in the goddamn car."

"Carina," Phantom called my name.

I lowered my head, the thud of my footsteps deep, hollow just like my heart. *Just trust me...please,* I sent the plea through the emptiness of my mind, hoping like hell he'd heard it as I made my way through the parked cars and headed for Harlan.

27

CARINA

I climbed in and slammed the door, lifting my gaze to my Wolves as slowly, one by one the law enforcement retreated. People were hurt...maybe even dying, and it was all because of me...*again.*

Car doors opened and closed. Harlan climbed into the passenger seat while an agent I didn't know slid behind the wheel. Dad took his time, swaying as he gripped the open door and then flopped inside with a groan. We were moving before the door was closed, still there was enough self-preservation left in the old man to slam the door closed at the last second.

I looked behind us to my Wolves, standing amongst the bullet-riddled cars. I wasn't leaving them, not like I had last time. This wasn't good-bye, this was *let me fix this once and for all.* I turned back, narrowing my attention on the one and only cause of my pain. Harlan.

"You know this can't keep happening." I bored my hate-filled gaze into the back of his head.

"Yes, it can, as many times as you choose," he answered.

"Car..." Dad started.

I just turned my head and stared into the inky abyss of the

231

river and imagining sinking into its icy depths. Ruth had been thrown into the water, her feet chained and weighed down. It was her Vampires who'd saved her, just like my Wolves had been the ones who'd saved me.

"Did you shoot Lenny?" I snarled.

"No, but I killed him, just the same. We don't belong in their world, Carina, and they don't belong in ours."

I sucked in a breath at the words. "*Your* world, you mean, not my world. I chose my side to fight for."

"And yet, you're here," Harlan answered from the passenger seat.

Not for long, Chaos whispered. *Tick tock, motherfucker.*

The glow roiled in my chest, the power simmering under the surface. I said nothing, letting the stone-cold silence speak for itself as we drove back across the bridge and turned toward the FBI offices once more.

It was over, just like that. No sister to save, no goddamn Finis to annihilate. One fucking threat of a bullet to the back of my father's head and I'd caved like the weak-ass bitch I was.

Not weak...just calculating.

The ride back to head office couldn't be over quick enough. The agent pulled up alongside the curb out front as dull lights glowed inside the foyer, spilling over the pavement as I shoved open the door and climbed out. "Go home, Dad. Go home and get yourself cleaned up."

"You're coming back with me, Carina."

"Over my dead body." I slammed the door behind me and stepped backwards onto the street.

Harlan climbed out, rounding the back of the car, coming up behind my father. For a second, I thought he had the gun in his hand as shadows moved.

"That's an easy fix, Special Agent."

I froze at the chilling, guttural snarl, then spun. Movement came at me in a blinding blur of fangs, claws, and death. I was hit sideways, slammed against the back of the car with a *thud*, and fell to the ground. Stars collided in my eyes as a roar of agony filled my ears...*my father's agony.* But it was over before it began with a choking gasp, then a groan...before silence.

Hands were at my chest, yanking and tearing the weapons from the holsters.

"Take her." The cold command came.

"And him?"

I blinked and tried to shove upwards. But heavy footsteps came closer, until Finis squatted low enough to stare into my eyes. "Take the both of them."

"You sonofa—" I roared and shoved myself forward, desperate to bite and claw.

Harlan let out a howl of agony as he was dragged across the asphalt by one arm. Another came for me as Finis rose to his feet. I shoved backwards, shaking my head as the male smirked. "No...no...no!"

But the lowly Wolf obeyed his Alpha, yanking me upwards until he grasped me around the waist. I kicked and clawed. *"Phantom!"*

"Save your breath," Finis snarled, and lifted his shirt.

Green jewels sparkled, embedded into his skin low down on his belly. I stared at the Unseelie ward as the bastard smirked. Hands moved over my ass as the Wolf heaved me onto his shoulder. I kicked as his fingers sank between my thighs, pressing into the crack of my ass and against my core.

"I can fucking smell your cunt, mortal. Gonna enjoy watching you squirm," the Wolf growled as Finis just dropped his shirt and turned.

"Fuck you!" I screamed, thrashing and clawing.

But it was my father's still body I stared at before my captor followed. *"No,"* I whimpered. *"Dad, no."*

The pool of blood glistened black, the image staying with me.

Chaos let out a hiss and unleashed a flicker of power into the air. The green glow bounced off the Wolf's shoulder, but it was gone before it barely rose, my chest darkening once more.

"Kill them," I urged.

But the bitch was quiet. Tears threatened to prick my eyes. "I fucking hate you," I growled.

"Not as much as you're about to," the bastard underneath me promised. "I can assure of that."

Harlan let out a moan as the trunk of a car was opened, before a heavy *thud echoed.* He moaned again, the sound bordering on a whimper. I kicked, shoving myself upward as I was dropped, landing on top of him with an *oww!* The trunk was slammed shut, and darkness closed in before the car doors were opened.

"Get...*off*...me," Harlan whimpered.

But there was nowhere to go. I rolled, feeling the softness of his stomach and the hard bones of his thighs. I tried to shove him backwards, my hand cupping his crotch before I wrenched it away.

The engine started, then we were moving, the momentum driving me face forward. Panic rose inside me as Harlan started to hyperventilate. "I need to get out of here...*get me OUT OF HERE!*"

But I was trying to track the movement of the car, and felt around the inside of the trunk.

"I can't fucking breathe!" Harlan howled.

I shoved my hands out in front of me, fingers curled, knuckles spread. "You want to stay alive?" I growled, searching for the latch. "Then shut the fuck up."

Tires howled as I touched the plastic lever. We were thrown sideways, my head smashing against the interior. White sparks danced in my eyes, then darkened.

"Harlan," I slurred as the world sank into darkness. "The latch—"

I came to with the sudden collision, red lights fought the stifling dark before the crimson glow was gone.

"Chase." The moan came from behind me.

Memories flickered, green Unseelie glow, gunshots...*death.* My father's death.

The trunk popped open and I lifted my gaze to the steely stare of the Wolf. It all came back to me in a rush as the sound of footsteps followed.

"There she is." Finis glanced to me, then shifted his stare to Harlan. "Get them out. I want him on his own."

A low whimper tore from the assistant director as our captor reached over me.

"No...*no!*" Harlan roared.

He battered and kicked, his fist driving into my back as he fought for his life. But he could no more change this than he could ease his own hate against them.

"Chase!" he screamed as he was lifted and yanked from the boot. *"CARINA!"*

I pushed up on trembling arms, and glanced at the darkened building behind Finis before I settled my gaze on the Alpha of Alphas.

"Don't kill him." I swallowed the burn of acid in the back of my throat as Harlan kicked and screamed. "He's worth more to you alive."

"Is he?" One brow rose on the smug piece of shit. "I doubt that."

My gut clenched as I gripped the trunk and climbed free. "He *is* valuable, Finis. You want power with the mortals? You want control? It starts with him."

Rage danced in the Alpha's eyes for a second before he took a step forward. I couldn't help but cower a little as he leaned close, his lips curled, teeth bared. "*I* have all the fucking power I need."

My heart hammered as I stared into the abyss. Hate,

control…pure brutal rage. This was no Alpha…this was a fucking psychopath dressed in Wolf's fur. I swallowed hard as he pulled away and, for the first time in my entire life, I realized there was no getting out of this, not for me…not for Harlan.

He fought in the Wolf's hold, wrenching to turn and find me. Blood smeared his cheek, his lip was swollen. His clothes were disheveled. I knew what real fear looked like now…it was pathetic and weak…*it was mortal*. "Chase," he yelled before he was shoved forward, driven toward a small single building off to the side.

I jerked my gaze to the other buildings. *Where the fuck were we?*

The place was dark, and in the middle of nowhere. Two lone light poles out the front cast a pathetic glow.

My stomach kicked. I knew where we were now. The brickworks on the edge of the city, a place closed down over a year ago. Quiet, secluded, no one would come here.

"Get her inside," Finis snarled.

Darkness shifted around me. I stumbled sideways as the rest of Finis's pack strode into the light. There were at least four that I could see. One jerked his head toward the main building. "Move."

My heart hammered as Harlan was shoved forward, heading to a nearby portable building as the door opened. Separated, we were prey…separated, we were dead, and Harlan knew it.

"I'll give you what you want," he cried as he hit the first stair. "I'll call them off…*I'll call them all off! THEY'LL LISTEN TO ME!*"

His screams dulled as he was thrown inside and the door was slammed shut. I clenched my jaw and tried to slow my breaths. But it was useless. We were going to die here, out here in the middle of nowhere…all alone.

One shove against my back sent me careening toward the door. The bastard behind me yanked the handle and shoved me inside. I was alone in a heartbeat, standing in the dark as the door was closed and locked behind me with a *click.*

Weak lights spilled into the dark room between the metal bars and busted window. I tried to think around the savage pulse in my head, tried to remember to streets leading here, and the ones I could use to escape. But the ache was consuming, pounding and throbbing, stealing my panicked thoughts.

I tried to breathe.

Tried to calm the terror.

Until Harlan screamed.

I jerked my gaze high and stumbled to the door, yanking on the handle. *"Stop it!"* I yelled, pounding useless fists against the door, but there was no stopping those beasts...or the screams.

A low moan came from behind me, so weak and soft I barely heard it.

I spun, heart hammering, and stared into the dark.

Howls of agony came from the separate building behind me, but it was the chilling moan I focused on when it came again. A ragged gasp filled with pain...and terror.

"Easy," I murmured, and licked my lips. "I'm not going to hurt you."

Yellow eyes opened and stared at me from the corner of the darkened room.

And as my eyes adjusted, I saw her...a woman...curled in the corner of the room, her arms wrapped around her very swollen belly...and blood all over her skin.

28

CARINA

S he bared her teeth. Those yellow eyes were 'wild with fear as she let out a moan. "Come closer and I'll fucking gut you."

My pulse was deafening. I took a step backward and jerked my gaze to the smashed window as Harlan's screams ended in the night. "I'm not going to hurt you."

"Fuck...*you*," she whimpered, and drew her knees closer as she pressed her body against the filthy wall.

Think...*just fucking think, Chase.*

I sank to my knees, drawing her gaze as she winced and moaned. "I can help you," I whispered. "Please, let me help you."

She gave a hard bark of laughter. But there was nothing funny about the way she bared her teeth or in the way claws curled from the tips of her fingers.

"Are...are you in labor?" I asked, glancing at her belly.

No answer.

"I've had some training, though granted, it's been a while. But I can remember the basics."

"Shove your fucking basics up your fucking ass...*you*

goddamn mortal bitch!" she howled, her body contorting, wracked with pain.

Shadows smothered what little light we had.

"Thought you two might get along," Finis chuckled. "Seems you have plenty to talk about…seeing as how you're fucking the man who left her behind."

I froze at the words, my stomach hardening until it was a rock.

He lies, Chaos warned.

"That's fucking bullshit and you know it," I growled, never once taking my eyes from her. "He'd *never* do that."

But it didn't matter what I said. Her unhinged gaze fixed on mine. It was the same look I'd seen the night Murphy had lured me to the outskirts of the city. Unhinged. *Feral.* Finis's laughter spilled through the holes in the glass as he walked away.

That pain-filled moan turned into a promise of torture. "Left me…" she growled, and shoved forward onto her hands and knees. She winced, jerking with a pang of agony, but still she pushed forward, using that pain for something else now…*fuel for her rage.*

I shoved backwards, pushing my heels against the filthy floor as she crawled two steps toward me and stopped. She sank until her forehead touched the floor. A low, haunting sound came from her as she rocked. That whimper hit me harder than her claws ever could. I stilled, staring at her, until she eased to the ground and rolled on her side.

Her body rocked, the pain unmistakable in her eyes. She stayed like that, rocking and whimpering, until that haunting sound eased. Slowly, achingly slowly, she pushed back toward the corner of the room, and there she stayed. Deep breaths sounded, harsh and slow. Too fucking slow. I sat on the other side of the room and watched her, unable to look away.

How long I sat there, I didn't know. Long enough for the bitter night air to creep in and send goosebumps across her skin. I licked my lips and eased my body forward, sliding off the leather jacket that still smelled like Vitold. My weapons were gone, the damn holster now fucking useless...unless I wanted to hang myself with it.

I lifted my gaze to the broken window. It was quiet out there, too quiet. Was Harlan dead? Maybe...might be a good thing. To be alive, alone, and a target for those fucking monsters was terrifying. I thought of my Wolves as I shrugged the jacket free and gripped it in my hand, easing closer to her.

One eye cracked open with a sickening yellow stare.

"I'm not going to hurt you," I repeated, the jacket in my hand.

Still she watched me as I slowly crept closer and slid the jacket over her body. Her belly moved, a tremble, then a kick. I looked away, sliding the leather higher until it draped over her chest, then crawled back to where I'd been across the room.

She said nothing, not a thank you. Not that I expected one. I leaned my head against the wall and watched the silver glow of the moon sink. *Phantom,* I sent out a call. *Are you there?* A flicker echoed back to me, but it was gone in an instant, and Chaos was quiet once more, too.

Still, I felt her, deeper...wrestling in the darkness of my mind.

Control, she sent the word higher until I snatched it close. *Opposite...*

Whatever the fuck that meant. Minute by minute. I watched the darkened shape across the room until finally shadows drew closer around her, and the wall at her back slowly brightened until I stared at the ugly wood paneling and blinked.

My eyes burned and my lips were dry. It wouldn't be long before the sun would beam through the window and into the small, derelict room. I stared at the closed door to what had to be a bank of offices. One glance toward the sleeping Wolf, and I ease forward.

She opened her eyes at my movement and watched me

without saying a word as I crawled on hands and knees toward it. One twist of the door knob and of course it was fucking locked. I crawled back and went around the counter, to an old water dispenser. The bottle was empty, the plastic faded and white.

"Fuck," I snarled, and punched the damn thing.

A scan of the open drawers of a desk gave me nothing. I lowered my forehead to the floor. *This is fucking bullshit...think, Chase. Think!* I turned my head and caught the metal glint of a pen.

"Wow," I muttered, sliding my fingers under the gap between the drawers and the floor and pulled the pen free. "Maybe I can use it to write my last will and testament."

But the metal glint didn't disappear with the pen, instead it shone from further back in the gloom under the desk. I shifted closer, stretching my fingers under the damn thing as far as I could. Still it wasn't far enough. My knuckles ached, twisting until agony ripped through my fingers. I shoved up on my knees, using my shoulders to force the desk up from the floor.

A grunt and a few choice words followed. I sank back down, pressing my cheek to the filthy fucking grime and tried once more, then stopped, glancing at the pen. "Fucking idiot."

I grabbed the pen, shoved it as far as I could, and by the tip of the full ballpoint dragged the metal ring free...and the key that came with it. My heart hammered at the sight. The key... looked like it just might work. The crunch of boots on asphalt came from outside. I palmed the key in an instant as the door rattled, and scurried back to the far wall a second before the door swung open and the ugly bastard who'd thrown me into the car stepped in.

He took one look at me, then at Marian across the room. "You bitches playing nice?"

"Fuck you, Maverick," she moaned, not moving an inch.

He just grinned before casting a bottle of water her way then one toward me. I caught it in midair and set it down. But Marian was already moving, yanking the top open with a twist of her wrist and sucked down the contents. She finished the bottle, draining the contents with greedy gulps and the piece of shit just watched before he turned.

"Hey, how about some food?" I barked.

"No."

"More water then? You can see she's thirsty."

He stopped for a second, then glanced over his shoulder as she swiped the back of her hand across her lips, catching any drops, and then licked her skin, taking everything she could get. "Won't need it soon anyway."

She just glared at him and clenched the plastic bottle, piercing sharp claws all the way through. The bastard just left, slamming the door shut behind him before locking it and striding away.

Her harsh breaths filled the silence. "It'd be perfect timing to show up," I muttered, hoping like hell Chaos heard my plea. "Right...about...now."

But there was only silence. Figured, right when I needed her the most. I'd waited for the asshole to leave before shifting my gaze toward Marian. She was tipping up the pictured bottle, draining the last drops from inside. She was gaunt, malnourished, weak, and God knows what else.

"Here," I rolled my bottle toward her. "Looks like you could use it more than me."

She grabbed it from the floor faster than I could track. Hungry eyes watched me as she twisted the top free and drank. Only this time, she saved some, screwing the top back on and slipping it under the leather jacket.

I risked a glance, rising up to peer through the filthy window. Empty vials and blood-soaked gaze came back to me as I turned. "You were at the veterinary clinic."

She just stared at me.

"Figured that's where you might go. I must've been too late, maybe an hour, two at the most. Your baby...is he alright?"

"She," she answered with a deadpan stare.

I glanced toward the locked door on the far wall, then back at her. "Is *she* alright?"

She didn't answer, just watched me as I tried to swallow my heart back into my chest, slid across the floor, shoved the key into the lock, and twisted.

The door snapped open, and a gust of stale air that smelled too much like cabbage and sewage spilled out. I gagged, slammed my hand over my mouth, and quickly rose to my feet before I stepped inside. My heart was thundering as I hurried, making my way along the empty hallway. The first and second offices were empty. A desk, toppled chair, and trashcan were all that remained in the third.

But the fourth was packed with empty filing cabinets. I stepped inside and hurried around to the side, searching every inch, but all I could find was a few empty folders and three out of date granola bars. I carried them from the office, closing the door behind me as I went. The desk. It was the only thing I hadn't searched. I hurried back along the hallway, stepped inside the office, and made my way around the desk. Telephone cords hung from the socket on the wall. I yanked them free, and wrapped them around my fist before pulling open the drawers.

I expected nothing, but something inside one slid and smacked against the back of the drawer, something heavy. I peered into the space, shoved my hand in deep, and skimmed steel. The letter opener glinted slightly as I pulled it free. It wasn't a knife...but it was something. And something was more than I'd had before. I tucked it into the waistband of my jeans and pulled my shirt over It, made my way out of the back offices, and eased the connecting door closed once more.

"Here. They're old, but beggars can't be choosers," I murmured, and tossed her the bars.

She grabbed them, ripped open the top, and attacked the bars one after another.

"He's going to kill us, isn't he?" I questioned, sliding back to the floor.

She chewed and swallowed, then after a while, took another swallow of water.

Sure, awesome. Hate my guts. "He wouldn't have left you. No way, no how."

"What the fuck do you know?"

Oh look, she speaks. "I know he's more than a damn Alpha. I know he's a hard ass, a damn pain...and the most honorable man I've ever known."

She flinched at the words.

"You hate me," I said. "I get that. But whatever Finis told you is a lie. Phantom would *never* leave you. He's been searching for you day and night."

She looked away, chewing the last of the bars, and was silent once more. But I couldn't be silent, couldn't wait here any longer. I rose to my feet and stared out the broken window to the portable building. Harlan was in there, probably dead...or if he wasn't, he'd be wishing for it.

"Chaos," I commanded. "Get your fucking ass here now."

She pushed to the surface, screaming with blind rage. Power pulsed around me, shaking the walls and the shattered window. Shards of glass fell free, crashing to the floor. I stumbled, slammed my hand to my chest.

Fucking controlling! she screamed.

"What? What does that even mean?"

What is the opposite of Chaos...you goddamn idiot!

Cold moved through me, spilling through my veins to wrap around my heart. The opposite of chaos was control. That's why she couldn't help me...that's why she wasn't here. With a roar, she sank back down into the darkness, to the place where she battled for control.

Laughter spilled out of Marian's lips, the sound taunting and cruel. I whipped my gaze toward her. "Shut the fuck up."

But the sound just grew louder, only growing quiet as I sank back to the floor. But I wasn't done yet, not anywhere near done. I leaned across, grabbed the biggest shard I could find, and cut the bottom of my t-shirt, ripping the fabric free before I wound it around my fist and palmed the weapon.

I'd stab the next bastard who came through that door, then run.

I'd rather take my chances with my mortality than just wait for fucking death.

I looked over at her, meeting those sickening yellow eyes, and fought a pang of compassion.

"He'll kill me," she said. "That's why he keeps me weak. Any day now…" she lowered her gaze to her belly. "Any day."

This torture wasn't fair. Not fucking fair in the slightest. "He never left you." I stabbed the words home. "Whatever you *think* he is…he isn't *that.*"

As usual, she said nothing, but I knew my words had hit home. We sat in silence until slowly…the pain returned. Beads of sweat glistened across her forehead, her jaw muscles bulged, and her teeth ground together as she fisted the leather.

My bladder was starting to hurt now, as sharp pains stabbed deep. But the moment she let out a groan, my own discomfort faded away. This wave of agony was bad, bleeding the color from her face in an instant as she tried to climb to her hands and knees. She slipped and crashed to the floor, the guttural groan in the back of her throat filling the room.

"Hey!" I jumped up and screamed. *"Hey!* We need some help here! *WE NEED SOME FUCKING HELP!"*

But no one came. Not when I screamed for an hour…not when she started to bleed.

I stumbled toward her and sank to my knees. There was too much blood…far too much blood. It seeped from between her thighs and coated her legs. I cast the shard of glass away and yanked what was left of my shirt free. "I don't know what to do," I cried.

"Help me." She grabbed hold of my hand, desperation filling her eyes. "Please…please, help me."

Phantom! PHANTOM!!! I screamed into the darkness, desperate to find a way to get to him. This was about more than my life now, more than my safety. I clutched her closer, pulled her against me, and held on tight.

29

CARINA

"**D**on't let him take her."

I found those pain-filled yellow eyes.

"My baby," she whispered from bloodless lips. "Don't let him take her."

Her.

The word hit me harder than a fucking bullet to the chest. "No one is taking your baby." I forced the words around the lump in my throat but, even as I said the words, I knew they were a lie.

There was nothing I could do to stop him. Nothing *I could do* to change this course we were on. I glanced at her belly and the blood that dampened her panties and dried on her thighs, then at the shard of glass I'd discarded.

Fucking mortal.

Stupid fucking mortal.

I shouldn't have gone with Harlan, shouldn't have given a shit if he killed my father. He was dead now anyway. No one could've survived that impact. Marian clung to me and rocked her body, and I rocked along with her. But if I hadn't gone with Harlan...then I wouldn't be here right now, with Marian.

I sank into that panicked emptiness of my mind, *was this you?* The bitch was silent, always silent when I needed her. Control. Chaos. Two sides of the same cruel Unseelie coin. A coin that right now was fucking useless. What good were all those connections and powers when, at the moment you needed them most, they weren't there?

Marian gripped me harder, her fingers digging into muscle, feeling like they went all the way to the bone. I wore her blood on me, smeared from her fingers across my arms and across my belly where she'd wrapped her arms around me like a child desperate for her mother.

But I was no mother, I wasn't even a friend, just someone *here.* Someone who was growing colder and more pissed off with the passing hours. Hours filled with pain.

"I've got you," I murmured as she started to rock and moan once more. "I'm right here."

We stayed like that, alone and in agony, frightened of what was about to happen any second. Surely she couldn't take much more. But where would that leave her? Dead…or in labor in this filthy reception area. I gave her water when she could take it and brushed back strands of slick hair drenched with her sweat as she arched her back and howled with agony. Hopelessness moved through me as I watched the harsh sunlight dull through the window.

Her hand slipped from around my arm, taking the sting with it. She'd grown claws at the crest of the pain. Sharp, the cruel tips had punctured my skin. I bit down on the sting, swallowing the panic as I brushed her hair.

My pain was worthless…

When I looked into her eyes, I saw so much more.

I saw all my failures right there. Broken, bleeding, her face a twisted mess of agony. "You're going to be alright," I murmured, the words barely reaching the air. But it didn't matter, she wasn't listening, sliding from my arms to lay her head down onto the filthy floor of the fucking derelict office once more.

There were no words left to say, nothing that would give her comfort.

Nothing that would give *anyone* comfort.

I'd never felt so helpless before in my life.

Not even in that chopper after I'd left my Wolves...not even in those dark days when I was being hunted. Not even when I'd thought I could lose Phantom. No, not even then. But this, this right here? Marian's fingers curled around my wrist as she clung to me, desperate for kindness...as pathetic as that kindness was—this was fucking brutal.

A tremble cut through me as her breaths finally eased, as well as her grip around my wrist. She slept while I stared at that dimming glow...slept while I ached and seethed and tore myself apart from the inside.

I bit my lip, pressing my teeth against the flesh until it split. The empty water bottle lay next to her. The ache in my bladder was a painful burn now, a throbbing that drove across my back and into my kidneys.

It wouldn't be long now until the night came to stake its claim once more. Another night...I closed my eyes.

Carina...

Phantom's voice filtered through and my eyes flew open. Then I closed my eyes and dove down into the darkness, driving harder to find Chaos than ever before. The walls trembled, the air shook. *"I'm here,"* I forced. "Can you hear me? *Please* tell me you can hear me! We're at the old brickworks at the edge of the city."

"Carina..."

"Phantom!" I unleashed the desperation. *"Phantom!"*

That burn flared in my chest, shining that sickening green. Marian cracked her eyes open, staring at the sparkle. "You've been cursed," she murmured, and closed her eyes. "No wonder my brother loves you. We're all cursed."

We're all cursed.

I stared at her as that glow sparked and flared. But it was the thunder in my chest that lingered. The pounding of my heart… *thud…thud…thud* that grew louder, until it not only filled my head but radiated through my chest.

Marian's gaze sharpened, her nostrils flared. She whipped her head toward the doorway a second before it splintered with a *boom!* Finis charged in, his silver eyes wild.

"You?" he growled, and advanced slowly toward me, dangerous and savage. "You drew him here?"

I held my ground. "Even if you knocked me out, he'd find a way to me, nothing short of death."

"Death?" the Alpha of Alphas barked, "*is something I can deliver!*"

He lunged across the darkening room until he was met with a roar. Yellow eyes filled with hate and rage burned as Marian shoved herself upward and slammed into the towering male. "*DON'T!*" she roared. "*Don't you lay a hand on her!*"

"Or what?" he towered over her, using his full height like a battering ram.

She was so small next to him…*we both were.*

A howl tore through the night. The sound of anguish so cruel it slammed into me like a freight train. Finis whipped his gaze toward the sound. "You think he's here to save you?"

Marian said nothing, just bared her teeth and let out a warning growl, her swollen belly moving as she raged.

"He left you," Finis lied. "Left you to me. You slowed him down, and now he has this *bitch*." He swung that maddened gaze my way.

"At least *this bitch* knows you're full of shit." I shot back at him.

He just smiled and stepped toward me. I glanced at the shard of glass as he stepped and crushed it under his boot. Still, he followed my gaze, but it wasn't to the shattered glass…it was to the telephone cords I'd discarded to the side as I comforted Marian.

"No!" I roared, charging and slamming into him as he lunged, his hand extended, and snatched the cords from the floor.

But it was like hitting a brick wall. I bounced off his chest and slumped backwards to the floor, stars sparking bright behind my eyelids.

"You *will not* win, mortal," he snarled, sounding like the beast he was.

My hands were yanked, the cords wound tight around them before I knew it.

"Finis…no," Marian whimpered, then doubled over with a low, terrifying moan.

She shoved her hand outwards as the howl came again through the night, only this time it was closer…*much closer.*

"You want to see someone squirm?" Finis gloated.

His hand was around my throat, fingers clenched around my windpipe as I felt the prick of his claws. He was going to tear me open, going to make a point, and rip my throat out in front of Phantom. I bucked and kicked out, smashing into his shin with a grunt, dislodging his hold for a second.

But a second was all I had.

He was on me in an instant, grasping my ankle as I kicked once more, and yanking me closer. I slid hard along the floor until I met him. His grip was around my throat once more, until my air was stifled and I couldn't draw a breath.

White bursts of light danced before my eyes as he dragged me upwards. I gasped and heaved, his hand clenching as the roar came again in the distance.

Marian cried out as he reached for her, hauling her to her feet even though she buckled with the pain.

"FINIS!" Phantom howled, his voice etched with agony and fury.

Hard breaths came from the Alpha of Alphas.

But the sky outside danced in blinding green rage. I blinked, finding the glow, but the detonating sparks collided in the darkness of my eyes. My body wouldn't work, my movements slow, my thoughts even slower.

I blinked, and through the growing gloom outside, I caught movement as they came from out of nowhere. *Phantom. Vitold... and Arran.* I blinked at the sight, something was off...

Finis shoved me toward the doorway, his grip still clenched around my throat. Fire lashed my face, the heat moving along my throat and through my chest as I tried to suck in air.

"One more fucking step and I'll tear out her goddamn throat," Finis warned, punctuating the threat with a shake.

I was thrown around like a rag doll, shoving my hands out as I wheezed.

"Or if this bitch doesn't make you heel, maybe this one will?"

Marian let out a moan as Finis wrenched her close to him, her pale skin sallow under the faint silver glow of the moon.

"You fucking hurt them," Phantom started, casting an agonized glance my way, before he slowly moved toward his sister.

"Hurt them?" Finis snarled. "No, *you're* about to do that."

I closed my eyes as a wave of agony washed over me. The ward in my chest pulsed and ached, fighting whatever smothered it with control.

"Choose."

My heart lunged at the words. I opened my eyes as the world bled to gray.

"CHOOSE!" Finis barked with fury. "Only one will survive, Phantom. Your choice. Your sister...or the mortal bitch you're *not* fucking?"

"No." I shook my head, my eyes widening, trying to capture his face.

A bark of agony tore through the night, followed by a howl of rage. I caught movement as Phantom stepped closer, shaking with rage. He cut a glance my way, those soulless eyes chilling me to the core. There was nothing inside them, no spark of life...no *soul.* "No" He shook his head. "I won't do that."

I knew he wouldn't.

But the smell of blood was making my stomach roll.

Dark blood...

A woman's blood.

The blood of life, and lately I'd seen far too much death. I couldn't let that happen again. Memories bounced around inside my head. My father. Ruth. The Vampires. Harlan...and them. It always ended with them. *My Wolves.* The tremble eased in my body, and that fire moved deep.

He'd never choose. Because that was who he was...the kind of man...*the kind of Alpha he was born to be.* So I sucked in a wheeze of air and with all I had left, conjured one panicked plea...*now or never, bitch!*

Emptiness welled in me.

Until there was a flicker of life.

A spark that danced in the darkness.

Then in a rush, she roared to the surface, slamming into me. *NOW!* Chaos roared. I lifted my hands and unleashed that blast of raw chaotic power into the air, tearing out of his hand in one second, and shoved him aside, then as gently and as forcefully as I could, drove Marian through the open doorway and out into the night. *"RUN!"*

The silver moon turned green.

Everything turned green...

Until the wall at my side crashed inwards, splintering wood and glass to smack my face.

Church was a blur, slashing and hacking.

Thunder followed.

The pounding of paws.

The howls of Wolves.

They descended in a pack of bloodlust and rage, driving me backwards as all four of them charged. Finis roared and howled. Claws slashed the air as they swarmed him. But he was no match for them…*he never was.*

Church lunged and landed on his back, driving the Alpha of Alphas forward. Vitold slashed out with his sharp claws across the bastard's belly, gutting him in an instant.

Sick, savage sounds filled the room, and acid followed, spilling into the back of my throat.

Something warm and wet splashed my bare chest as Chaos left me in an instant, sinking back down to the darkness once more. My knees buckled and air was all I felt, rushing through my lungs, battering against my face, until strong hands caught me.

"Easy." Church pulled me closer against him.

"We're here." Vitold stepped closer, his mouth dripping, his face glistening black with blood.

Arran lifted his gaze from over the still body and swiped his hand across his mouth. "He can't hurt you again."

"No one will *ever* hurt you again."

I lifted my gaze, catching movement outside as Wry and Walker caught Marian and pulled her closer.

"I got you." Walker lifted her hand and carefully moved forward. "I'm here to help you. I'm a doctor."

He couldn't choose.

So I'd had to choose for him.

And I'd chosen her.

I flinched, catching the deep green glow of lights washing across the black facade as the limousine pulled up alongside the curb. "Green, huh?" I muttered.

"Do you like it?"

I turned to Phantom, catching that possessive gaze raking over every inch of my body, taking in the very expensive tailored pants and plunging fitted jacket...with not even a bra underneath. His gaze lingered on the swell of my breasts, barely contained, and the green jewels that sparkled embedded deep in my flesh, just like Chaos was embedded in my soul.

He was more dominating now, more *protective* in the weeks and months since the attack, hungrier both out of bed...and in it. "I do."

Relief moved deep in those eyes as he gave a slow nod.

"That shit is crazy," Arran mumbled, leaning forward.

He was dressed in Armani...actually, we all were. Perfectly tailored suits that hugged every damn bulge their bodies had to offer...I couldn't stop staring at all of them. As the limo's engine died, I caught the roar of the crowd gathering outside Crown City's brand-new elite night club called Dark City.

Darkness, it seemed, was all the rage now.

So were the Unseelie.

Mortals still talked about the powerful glow the night law enforcement had attacked, but this time it wasn't in hushed tones with an element of fear. It was gushed and squealed about, it was all across social media in a kind of feeding frenzy. In an instant, the Immortals hiding across the river were celebrities, and that shit was terrifying. I thought about that night as the door was opened and Arran climbed out first. He stopped outside the door and buttoned his shirt. The crowd screamed at his presence...*mostly the women.*

I swallowed the burn of jealousy. But the move wasn't for attention, it never was. Arran surveyed the crowd, scanning every face and every set of hands for a weapon. Vitold was next as Arran stepped to the side and waited. I caught the curl of his lip as my protector glared at the crowd. The savage stare only seemed to encourage a new wave of hysteria from the crowding women. Apparently bad Wolves were all the rage.

Phantom wasn't the only one on high alert, not the only one hating every second I was out here...in the real world. But tonight was the grand opening of the revamped club once called Wild and this was one demon we all needed to exorcise from our memories and replace with new ones. There were no traces left of the old place. The remnants of the fire and Murphy's dead body were gone, even the parking area where Wry had almost been killed was transformed into a bank of gardens crammed with lush green foliage against a backdrop of black bamboo.

Gone were the gaudy red pulsing lights and plastic vines that had once covered the front of the club. Now it was slick, shiny, and dark...*very dark.*

"It's all clear," Vitold growled over his shoulder.

"You ready for this?" Church asked, meeting my gaze.

His blue eyes washed over me, endless, unfathomable blue.

His brow creased as he frowned. "You don't have to be here, you know?"

"And leave you to all the attention on your own?" I cocked my head, listening to the screams of the women outside. My Wolves weren't the only ones who'd grown one very large possessive streak. "Not on your goddamn life."

He gave a smirk, and moved, pushing from the plush leather to climb through the open door. The roar from outside grew to a deafening crescendo of desperation and infatuation. "Seems like they love you out there," I teased as screams of *CHURCH! CHURCH, I LOVE YOU. CHURCH, MARRY MEEE!* *were shrieked at him.*

"I don't give a fuck what they love," Phantom growled. "As long as they pay and pay well."

They would. There was no question about that. The lines were already three rows deep and wrapped around the front of the club and all the way down the street. But I did give a fuck. I was worried about this new rise of excitement around the Immortals. Fear wasn't the driving emotion when it came to them anymore, not since that night the mortals had come for the other side of the city...and we'd met them with force.

Church held out his hand to me. My fingers curled around his as I climbed out and was swarmed by my Wolves in an instant. Phantom stepped out and the screams grew impossibly louder. One woman fainted from the effort and the barricade almost broke.

But the security was there to hold the line. Ex-military and very...*very* mortal. God forbid if we'd had the Breeds here, the city would have had a damn meltdown. I breathed in the cold night air and followed my pack as they strode toward the private entrance. Headlights splashed across the crowd as another limousine pulled up as ours sped off. But the doors didn't open...not yet, at least.

A chill swept over me, cold, savage, *unfeeling.* I didn't need lights to illuminate them…I knew who they were. The Fae. There was no amount of glamor that could hide the pure bestial rush of their energy, no wards they could hide their icy exteriors behind.

"Carina?" Church called, but still I couldn't move.

The limo door opened and Mojin stepped out. The crowd turned silent. *Deathly silent,* as he swept that unfathomable gaze across the mortals. Shrike stepped out, buttoning his jacket. Movement came from behind him as two more stepped out, two I'd never had the displeasure of meeting. They wore black on black, which I understood…it matched their souls.

"They're waiting for us," Phantom murmured behind me. "Unless you'd rather keep staring at the Fae?"

I flinched at the warning in his tone, cast him a smile, and stepped forward through the door. The decor was black on black. Subtle. Brushed black chrome and shimmering black leather. The lights were tiny and white at floor level, just like the ones at the Hunting Ground.

I followed my Wolves, cutting through the public area, which was starting to fill quickly. Mortals stared as we walked through. A group of women, blonde and perfect, rushed forward with ravenous eyes.

"Arran." One reached for him.

Until he cut her down with an icy stare. "No."

Confusion clouded her gaze. She didn't understand, none of them did. But cutting anger replaced desire as she aimed that gaze at me.

Vitold just stepped to the side and pushed her away with his body, his hand gently clasping mine in one move. They *all* touched me, their hands at the small of my back and arms wrapped around my waist. Arran grasped my other hand and pulled me forward toward the heavy black curtains strongly defended by a line of security guards.

We were through in an instant, finding ourselves in the emptiness and the peace. Dancers swung around poles on a stage at my right, two clad only in barely there G-strings, breasts bouncing, hands sliding between parted thighs.

Still my Wolves kept walking and never once looked.

But I looked. I looked at everything. At the private lounges that screamed of dark, erotic deeds. Dark City was dangerous… for my heart. Still, Arran kept walking, leading us even further into the back of the club, and opened a door marked *No Entry*.

The door led to a black hallway, with soft white lights to lead the way. We passed a door marked *Vampires*, then one marked *Fae*, as we headed to a room at the far end, the one marked *Wolves*.

"We have our own room?" I asked, glancing at Church.

"Yes." Those blue eyes sparkled with hunger.

"All for you," Arran murmured as he stepped in and motioned me inside.

They dropped my hands as I entered, instead they turned to watch my reaction. A huge sofa sat far back against the wall. To the right was a fully stocked bar with top-shelf alcohol and sparkling crystal tumblers. "This must've cost a fortune," I exclaimed.

"A drop in the bucket," Phantom answered, his tone deep, *hungry.*

Something soft hit the floor as that erotic beat from the club spilled through the speakers. I turned, catching Arran dropping his jacket, followed by Vitold. Church was already working the knot of his tie, that ravenous gaze on me. *Jesus fucking fuck…*

"If you're not aware by now, female, we're *extremely* well off." Phantom worked the buttons of his shirt, his tie and jacket already discarded.

"How well off are we talking?" I had no idea where the words were coming from.

"Eighty million and counting."

I jerked my gaze to his. "Eighty million *dollars?*"

His wicked smile said it all, but still, he never stopped undressing, none of them did.

"You need to sit down, female?" Vitold cast his shirt to the floor and strode toward me, naked from the waist up, hard muscles rippling as he moved.

I couldn't answer, couldn't think.

I didn't understand how it had all come to this.

Marian was at home, nursing her healthy baby girl, protected, surrounded...*loved.* Walker and Wry were somewhere out there, making sure every plan for the club's opening was executed with precision, and I was here...tongue-tied and mesmerized as my Vitold took my hand and led me to the plush sofa.

The beat turned hard and heavy, sinfully erotic.

"You're shitting me," I moaned as Church gave me a wink and dropped to the floor, his muscles tight and bulging. I was riveted by the way he moved...*by the way they all moved.*

Arran sank with him, the hard V at his hips corded and straining as he thrust against the floor. Phantom was next, casting his shirt to the floor as he moved for me.

"You like?" Vitold whispered as he kissed my palm and slid it down his hard stomach.

I could only nod as they thrust and leaped, landing with palms splayed open, and pushed backwards.

They didn't just dance.

They danced for me.

Showing me how much they wanted me.

And how much I was loved...

Love more Vampires? Dive into the seductive world of Chosen by the Vampire…
Grab the *FREE* first book in the series here: books2read.com/chosenbythevampireone
Or keep reading for a sneak peak.

CHOSEN BY THE VAMPIRE

"You understand what you have to do?" the Vampire whispered from the shadows.

I closed my eyes, refusing to answer...*refusing to see.*

Sinful.

Deadly.

The words raced through my mind as his icy breath spilled down the hollow of my neck, making me tremble.

He was close...*too close.*

I couldn't turn my head, couldn't look into the shadows.

I already knew what I'd find.

Cold, stony, moonlight-kissed skin, and intense eyes that seemed to stare into my soul. But it was his mouth that captivated me. White fangs peeking from blood-red lips as he whispered commands like the devil on my shoulder.

But there was no angel on the other side ready to save me. There was just the darkness...just the *need.* I clamped my legs tighter, stilling the flare of heat that bloomed like a deadly rose between my thighs.

"Open your eyes, Asena. Look at him."

I was helpless to defy him, *drowning in a sea of desire.* But hate swirled around me, *and inside me,* like a tornado filled with the terror of my past. I allowed that hate to consume me, battling the flames of unwanted desire that both disgusted me and intrigued me in equal parts.

Still, I obeyed...and opened my eyes.

My victim stepped through the open doors from a marble patio outside and into the ballroom, following three of his friends into the masquerade ball. Shy, quiet, his brown eyes glittered as he scanned the room and our gazes connected. A hint of a smile as he stared at me, and then a slow tilt of his head, an acknowledgement of my presence.

He stilled, and electricity charged through me like a live wire.

"He looks as awkward as you do," Cassian murmured in my ear. "Tell me how you'll seduce him."

Music swirled all around me, soft music, seductive music. The beat mirroring the panicked thudding of my heart.

Seduce him.

That was the game. *Their game.* I swallowed the urge to tremble. I would not let Cassian scare me, not let him win. The mortal male broke my gaze and searched for his companions. He was good looking, with a ramrod-straight spine and relaxed shoulders. Wealthy. That's what he looked like, kind, careful and well to do.

"Tell me how you'll walk toward him. How you'll give him a hint of a smile," the monster in the dark murmured. "How you'll brush past him just enough for him to be ensnared by the scent of your perfume...and how, when he turns toward you, you'll do the same and smile, that sweet, *innocent,* seductive smile. How you'll step backwards, drawing him closer and closer and you'll angle your body so his gaze will be drawn by the swell of your breasts. How you'll lead him into the darkness and press your spine against the wall, pretending he's the one who trapped you, when it'll be the other way around. How you'll lean close and whisper into his ear, just so he can look into the plunging neckline of your gown. How you'll make the poor sap blush with the whisper of your desire, how his body will harden and quake and that look of hunger will consume him."

I swallowed the bitter tang of acid in the back of my throat. "I won't. I won't do it. I *can't.*"

"Oh, you'll do it," the beast growled. "Or I'll puncture his vein in the middle of the dance floor. I'll spray your perfect sky blue dress with the warmth of his life, and I'll make you watch while I drain him dry. You *will* do this, Asena. You will if you want to save him...*and if you want to be chosen.*"

He moved closer, just an inch--but it was enough.

Enough to snatch my attention and trigger my fear.

"You do want to be chosen by us, don't you?" The faint scent of blood wafted in the air.

Blood and death...*and sex.*

The frigid touch of his finger trailed down my arm before he leaned in and pressed those lips to my shoulder. I never flinched, never moved. I was frozen with fear, *and excitement.*

My body betrayed me, trembling, *wanting.* I could almost feel the tips of his fangs on my skin, almost feel the commanding touch of his fingers delving under my skirt.

Almost *feel his body trapping mine.* I wanted him. I *hated* him. *Hated myself* because of it.

I wanted to be used by him. I wanted to be taken by them all, every savage thrust, every brutal bite.

They were beasts...*monsters.* They were cruel and uncaring, and promised eternity in the slide of their tongue and the hardness of their desire.

"I will make you mine, Asena," Cassian whispered. "I will lash those wrists to the headboard of my bed and ride that sweet body until you quake with fever, and beg for release. I will show you all the sins of this mortal world and all the rapture of mine, and you will know what it's like to be *chosen*. You will know what it's like to be *owned by us*."

My breath caught, and my pulse raced. To be owned by all of them. I glanced toward the others, knowing where they were by instinct alone...*or was it need?* Lorcan stood in the shadows near the entrance, watching the men as they stepped inside--like a moth to a flame.

We were that flame.

I skimmed the darkness to the right, where the glow of the fire didn't reach, and felt a flicker of fear. Arkyn was back there, watching everything, deciding which one of us passed the test. He was the one I was truly afraid of. He was savage and calculated. He was the one Lorcan and Cassian obeyed.

Vampire.

They were almost as dangerous as the Wolves.

Cassian would kill this mortal if I didn't seduce him. He'd make good on his promise to this mortal man...*and to me*. He'd make me stand there and watch while the spark ebbed in the man's eyes, he'd tear my dress from my body and bathe me in the man's blood. He didn't care who watched...only about making me bend to his will.

"I'm waiting," he whispered. "The dance is almost over...and his time in this world is almost done."

Ten other women were imprisoned in this castle in the middle of the woods, they moved around me now. Some meek and terrified, casting careful glances my way, and others stalking the mortal men who came here tonight like prey. They never looked at me, or cared.

They were beautiful. Long, stunning dresses and plunging necklines. Lorcan liked them in bold colors, daring midnight blue, shimmering black, and drenched, blood red. But I wasn't dressed like them. No, I was different.

I skimmed my hand along the pale blue chiffon skirt and

lifted my hand. My fingers trembled, dancing in the air as I touched my lips.

"I can't do this," I whispered.

"Can and *will*," he commanded. "You know what happens if you don't. Pass this test, Asena. Pass it *or else*."

I shuddered at the words. I'd been forced here just like all the others, but there was one difference between us. *I knew who these fanged monsters were.*

Please....

Cassian's voice filled my mind. With a surge of desperation and terror, I clenched my fist around the perfect blue chiffon, lifted my gaze to the mortal man standing all alone and took a step. He lifted his head at the movement, and his eyes widened with surprise.

My lips curled on their own, the smile yearning and playful as Cassian had urged.

That's the way, Asena...

I'll make you mine yet.

Grab your *FREE* copy of Chosen by the Vampire here: books2read.com/chosenbythevampireone